If You Cross Me Once

Stay Connected with Us!

Text **LOCKDOWN** to 22828 to stay up-to-date with
new releases, sneak peaks, contests and more…
Thank you.

Submission Guideline.

Submit the first three chapters of your completed manuscript to ldpsubmissions@gmail.com, subject line: Your book's title. The manuscript must be in a .doc file and sent as an attachment. Document should be in Times New Roman, double spaced and in size 12 font. Also, provide your synopsis and full contact information. If sending multiple submissions, they must each be in a separate email.

Have a story but no way to send it electronically? You can still submit to LDP/Ca$h Presents. Send in the first three chapters, written or typed, of your completed manuscript to:

LDP: Submissions Dept
P.O. Box 944
Stockbridge, Ga 30281

DO NOT send original manuscript. Must be a duplicate.

Provide your synopsis and a cover letter containing your full contact information.

Thanks for considering LDP and Ca$h Presents.

Prologue

"Ladies and gentleman of the jury." Greg Gamble said, rising to his feet. "This trial is about retribution and murder. The defendant, Michael Maurice Carter, is the star here. You've heard from two crime scene search officers. You've heard from the medical examiner, who told you exactly how long it took the victim to die. You heard from a ballistics expert who told you about the weapon used to kill the decedent.

"He explained how much damage a Springfield Armory Colt .45 handgun would do to a person at close range. He explained how that weapon, which was recovered from an apartment that Mr. Carter lived in; was loaded with hollow-pointed bullets, and what damage they inflict upon a person's body. You also heard from a civilian technician who detailed how latent fingerprints…Mr. Carter's fingerprints were extracted from those bullets, and the handle of the .45. You heard from witnesses who testified about the shooting and why it took place…"

"Objection! Your honor, it was never established why this crime was committed and to assert that to this jury would do irreparable harm to my client. The government is trying…"

"Sustained, tread lightly, counselor. Either way, I believe the jury's recollection of the evidence will be the ultimate deciding factor in the matter. Carry on Mr. Gamble." Judge Victor Wise proclaimed.

Greg Gamble smiled his killer smile at the jury and continued his closing argument. "There are a lot of things about this case that we don't know. A lot of things are unclear, but what we do know, and what the evidence does show is that the star of this show here, Michael Carter is guilty of murder. *First-degree murder*, he thought about it, planned it, and then carried it out. And contrary to what his attorney says…the motive for his madness is clear. Michael Carter killed the decedent Dontay Samuels, because word on the streets was that Dontay Samuels raped and killed his wife Patricia Mitchell-Carter.

"You heard from the witnesses who gave you unequivocal accounts of how the defendant reacted hearing that the decedent had killed his wife. They told you what he said and how he threatened to kill Dontay Samuels on sight. One of the things we don't know is whether or not Dontay Samuels killed Patricia Carter. There was never any evidence presented against Mr. Samuels. There was never any evidence gathered, there was no grand jury hearing, no indictment, and no trial. Why? Because the defendant took matters into his own hands and became the judge, jury, and executioner.

"The laws that govern our land are in place for a reason. We cannot just circumvent nor ignore the laws whenever we feel like it. That's what Michael Carter did., ladies and gentlemen. He thumbed his nose at our laws and became a vigilante. He decided that those laws in place did not apply to him. And we all know that where there is no law there is no order. We must maintain order, we have too.

"On April seventeenth, Michael Carter went to the twenty-five hundred block of Sheridan Road and looked for Dontay Samuels with the intent to kill him. At 11:38 p.m., he found him, Dontay Samuels never stood a chance. As he sat on his mother's porch, the defendant walked up to him and shot him. Not once, ladies and gentlemen, not twice. Michael Carter shot Dontay Samuels eight times at close range. Then according to one witness, he calmly just walked away.

"He walked away ladies and gentlemen. It is your duty to restore order to Michael Carter's life. It is your duty to go into that deliberating room and think about the evidence overwhelming evidence that you've heard over the last two weeks and do what's right. To do what is just and fair, what the law says you can do. You must find Michael Carter guilty of first-degree murder. It is the right verdict. The only verdict…"

"Objection, your honor!" Abe Shankle, stood and bellowed. "Government counsel is leading and threatening the jury. I move for a mistrial, right this moment. This is absurd."

The judge banged his gavel, "Your move for a mistrial is denied Mr. Shankle. Mr. Gamble, you are skating on very thin ice. I suggest you wrap this up before you end up in contempt."

"The government rest, your honor."

Judge Wise gave the jury their final instructions and released them to deliberate.

***

The next afternoon, the jury sent out a note to the judge that they had unanimously reached a verdict. Five minutes later, the jury filed into the courtroom.

"Ladies and gentlemen of the jury, it is my understanding that you have reached a verdict."

"We have your honor." The jury foreman announced.

"Would you please read the verdict form."

"On the count of first-degree murder, we find the defendant guilty. On the..."

A loud scream resonated throughout the courtroom.

"...count of carrying a pistol during a crime of violence, we find the defendant, guilty."

Michael Carter had anticipated the outcome of the trial. The guilty verdicts were what he had expected. He knew that his life was in the hands of the twelve-people sitting in that box. His mind tried to drown out the screams and cries that he now heard. Without looking back, he knew exactly where they were coming from. Michaels's heart broke at that very moment. He sat transfixed in his chair.

He wanted to look behind him and see her, but he couldn't. he had remained strong in the face of adversity and if he looked into her eyes, Michael knew he would break down. In front of him, the judge was speaking. But he couldn't hear a word of what was being said. Michael could only hear one voice. The voice that called out to him over and over again.

"Daddy! D-D-A-A-D-D-D-D-Y-Y!"

Michael listened to his daughter Zinfandel and allowed himself to tear up. As the Marshals ushered him into the back of the courtroom, he could hear his daughter's pleas and cries. But there was nothing he could do.

"I love you Zin!" he shouted as the doors shut behind him.

Chapter One
Zinfandel Carter

"I love you Zin!" I awoke out of my sleep and sat up in bed. The day that my father was found guilty of murder came rushing back to me, with alarming clarity. Although, the trial had taken place sixteen years earlier, it still reoccurred in my dreams as if it were yesterday. I could still see my father's face. A face that looked just like my own, depicting youth, love, and sorrow. Even as a ten-year-old child, my young mind could decipher how much pain my father was in. That pain was what broke my heart and made me cry and scream until my aunt led me out of the courtroom and into the cab outside. That day, sixteen years ago, wouldn't leave me alone. Even though I went to see my father regularly at USP Canaan, in Scranton, Pennsylvania. I laid in bed and thought about everything that happened before that day.

I could vividly recall the day that my mother never came to get me from my aunt Linda's house on Howard Road. There were frantic phone calls and hushed whispers all around. I ended up spending the night there and I had never done that before ever. My mother told me one day that she couldn't sleep at home without knowing I was nearby. The next day, my father showed up early in the morning and told me that my mother was dead. With tears in his eyes, he explained to me how she had been raped and beaten until she died. The best way he knew how, he comforted his only child, while grieving for the wife that he loved more than anything in this world.

My whole life changed after that and my young heart knew no deeper pain until a few weeks later when my aunt tearfully told me that my father had been arrested for murder. He killed the man that had killed my mother. I was devastated to lose my father, but I was happy to hear that the person responsible for killing my mother was dead. I ended up staying with my aunt. Linda Carter, my father's sister, had no children of her own. Knowing that her maternal clock was ticking and close to being out of time, she put everything in the hands of God. If it was meant for her to get pregnant and have a child without being married, then it would happen. It never did. So, becoming my legal guardian after my father got locked up was to her a sign from God.

We left D.C. and moved to Forest Heights, a suburb of D.C. and tried to pick up the pieces. It was a little rough for me at first because I was so used to having at least one of my parents around all my life. I missed my parents a lot and cried often in those days, but somewhere along the way I adjusted. Then one day while watching the news with my aunt, something...well someone caught my attention.

"...In other news today, D.C.'s top prosecutor Greg Gamble was promoted this morning to the second highest post in the United States Attorney's Office. Mr. Gamble, is the youngest person ever, at twenty-six years old, to hold that post. Mr. Gamble has successfully convicted every person that he has taken to trial..."

Seeing the man's face that had sent my father to prison was like being slapped. All fifty inches of my aunt's big screen T.V. caught that man's profile and his smile. It was the smile that made my blood boil. For it was the same smile he wore the day that my father was found guilty and sent to prison. At eleven-years-old, I made a promise to myself.

I decided that I would no longer feel sorry for myself. Self-pity was a sign of the weak. And a weakling I wasn't. My mother hadn't raised me to be. I thought about all the things my mother instilled in me while growing up...*let no one tell you that you are inferior to them for any reason...always believe in yourself...be real with yourself, if no one else...crying solves nothing...never let a man put his hands on you for any reason...real love should never hurt physically...*

One of the things that my mother often said stayed with her every day, forever etched into her mind and soul... *To whom much is given, much is required.* I promised myself that day, I would succeed for many reasons. I wanted to get even with the man that I held responsible for sending my father to prison. I wanted to wipe that smile that haunted my thoughts off his face and bring him to his knees. I decided right then and there to become a lawyer. As a lawyer, I could help to eventually free my father, help other people like him, and get back at Greg Gamble all at the same time. I promised myself that I'd become the best female lawyer that D.C. had ever seen. Nothing or no one would get in my way.

Beside me I felt my boyfriend Jermaine stir. He opened his eyes, wiped them, and looked at me.

"Are you okay?" he asked.

"I'm good." I replied. "Just had a bad dream. Go back to sleep." I glanced over at the digital clock on the dresser. It read 4:47 a.m. Knowing that I would have to get up in an hour or so anyway. I decided to take a hot bath and then get myself ready for work. The short trek to the bathroom woke me up completely and thoughts of upcoming trials of Sean Branch and David Battle bombarded every side of my consciousness.

I ran water into the tub and dropped lavender scented bath beads into the water. When it was full, I eased into it acclimating my body to the hot temperature of the water. In minutes, I was able to lie back and let my thoughts run wild. A man from my past had just recently returned and the thought of him was driving me crazy. While doing a pretrial investigation for one of my clients, I was steered into the direction of my old stomping grounds Sheridan Terrace.

My client David Battle informed me that a potential witness…Yolanda Stevens could be found there. It was while driving slowly on Sayles Place, that I ran into him. He had grown over the years, matured, and become a very handsome man. But his face remained the same. It was a face that women never forget after a first glimpse. He was beautiful in a masculine kind of way. His eyes were an arresting shade of grey. His skin was the color of roasted pecans and his jet black curly hair was cut to perfection. Just as I had always remembered him. Stopping my car in front of him as he leaned on a champagne colored Cadillac XTS with a cell phone at his ear, I rolled my window down.

"Quran Bashir? How have you been?"

Surprise along with a smile crossed Quran's face as he walked over to my car. I watched his every graceful step and felt my body temperature heat up.

"Little Zinfandel Carter. It's been…what? Ten years?"

"Fifteen and my name is not Little Zinfandel anymore. Trust me, I'm all grown up." I said with a little too much seduction in my voice.

"You all grown up, huh? Let me be the judge of that. Step out the car for a minute." Quran opened the door to my Infinite G35 Coupe.

I undid my seatbelt and stepped out of the car. I heard Quran whistle as he spun me around slowly.

"You wasn't lying, baby girl. You are definitely all grown up."

I knew that I looked great. Three visits a week to the indoor gym in my office building where I worked saw to that. The two hundred dollars I paid yearly for membership was money well spent. My flat stomach was the results of numerous hours of cramming information in my brain while doing crunches and ab exercises. I felt Quran's eyes all over my ass since it was packed into a Dereon denim skirt that hugged every curve.

I was the shit and I knew it, so it felt good to let my child-hood crush see it. My blue denim thigh high Dolce and Gabbana boots gave my five-foot-three inches frame a few inches in height. The seven for all mankind denim jacket did it's best to contain my 36DD breasts, but failed.

"What brings you back to the hood Zinfandel?" Quran asked as he finally let me go.

"Call me Zin. And my job brought me back here. Is that okay with you?"

"Hey, it's a free country. My hood is your hood. Your family was raised around here just like mine. If you don't mind me asking, what is your job? Don't tell me you're the police."

14

"Never that. I'm a lawyer. A defense lawyer and a damn good one at that."

"Is that right?"

"Yeah, that's right. Hard to believe?" I asked.

"Not at all. I always knew that you were too good for these projects. Even when you were a little girl. You were different than the other little girls your age. Your attitude was different. But anyway, what or who are you looking for. A client?"

"Naw, a witness. Or should I say a potential witness. You might know her."

"Witness huh? A her? What's her name?"

"Yolanda Stevens."

"And what case is she a witness in?"

I didn't know how much I should reveal to Quran. "The United States versus David Battle."

"Lil Dave is my man. You looking for Landa. She lives down the block in 2301. Her family moved in a few years after you left. She works at the Safeway on Alabama Avenue. You can catch her up there or just come back this evening. Your choice."

"I'll try her at Safeway. Thanks Quran."

"You can thank me later over a bite to eat. What do you say to that?"

"I can't I have a boyfriend." I stammered, but I really wanted to accept the invite.

"So, the fuck what? Bring him if you want to."

I laughed and headed back to my car. "Three's a crowd, Quran. Take care of yourself.

"Hold on Zin. At least give me a card or something. I might be in need of a good lawyer."

Reaching into my handbag, I grabbed one of my cards and gave it to Quran.

"The law offices of Nikki Locks and Jennifer Wentz huh? You fuckin' with two cracker bitches."

"Haven't you heard Quran, integration is good. Call me if you ever need a lawyer."

That had been over a week ago and yet, I still couldn't get Quran out of my head. I pulled a foot from the soapy water and inspected my pedicure. It was time to get a touch-up. Every time I closed my eyes, I saw Quran. When I was younger and first started to explore my sexuality, I had often thought about Quran. Even as a teenager, he was breathtaking. All my friends had a crush on him as well. It was his eyes. Nobody could get over his eyes. But we all knew that he was older than us. I figured that Quran had to be at least four years older than me, but back then, just like now, it didn't matter.

Before I even realized what, I was doing, my hand underwater found my clit and rubbed it gently. In my mind, Quran was in the room. In the tub with me. His fingers were where mines now massaged. One of my fingers slipped inside my pussy and I gasped. Quran was fingering my spot as his thumb massaged my clit. The feeling was intense. I squeezed my legs around my hands and threw my head back against the wall. With both hands now between my legs acting as if they had minds of their own, I bit down on my bottom lip and envisioned Quran between my legs about to enter me.

"Ooooh, fuck me!" I whispered to myself and put another finger inside my pussy. I opened my eyes suddenly and eyed a shampoo bottle. The bottle of Fruits of Nature shampoo was shaped oddly like a dick and it was exactly what I needed at the moment. Grabbing the bottle off the shelf on the wall, I closed my eyes and imagined that the bottle was Quran's dick. Even though I didn't actually know what his dick looked like, I could imagine. I figured he was probably packing because he walked like he was hung. The girth of the bottle was a little wider than what I was used to.

Jermaine was nowhere near as big or wide. In and out I pushed. I imagined Quran between my legs pushing himself all the way in. My image of him and my hands became one. He was stretching my walls open while going as deep as he possibly could. The feeling was euphoric. I moaned and squirmed around in the water as if I was a fish caught in a fisherman's net. I envision his lips on mine and the words he'd probably say as he fucked me. The sudden wave of tingles and electricity hit me like Hurricane Gustavo and before I knew it, I was coming. I willed myself to calm down, laid back in the steaming hot water, and closed my eyes. In seconds I was asleep.

Chapter Two
Quran Bashir

I fell out of bed and did my customary set of one hundred push-ups five times straight. Then I rose from the floor to answer the call of nature. After relieving myself, I looked at the disheveled bed and the sleeping beauty lying in it. I walked over to the bed and pulled the sheets from around her waist. A few minutes later, the sleeping woman awoke. She felt all around for her covers but found none. Then she turned over and glared at me.

"You play too damn much, Que, no bullshit. Gimme the sheets, boy!" Ki-Ki said.

I loved it when Ki-Ki got mad at me. She was beautiful, with juicy, pouty lips and a killer body. And…she was freakier when she was angry.

"It's time to get up."

"*Time to get up?* Boy, you trippin' like shit. It's only…" she looked at the clock on the wall. "…Fifteen minutes after ten. I don't get up before twelve. Gimme the covers and stop playing."

"Didn't you tell me that you had to do the book signing thing at The Literary Joint Bookstore today?"

Ki-Ki sat straight up in the bed and grabbed her Blackberry Storm cell phone. "Damn, boo, you right. Today is the twenty-fourth. I forgot all about that shit."

"What time do you have to be there? And what book are you promoting this time?" I asked.

"It's two books actually. The new one I did with Eyone Williams called '*To Live and Die in D.C.*' and my new joint called '*A strickly dickly situation.*'"

"A strickly dickly situation, huh? I'm tryna create a strickly dickly situation myself, right now. What's up?"

"I have to be at the TLJ in Forestville mall at one." Ki-Ki said and lifted her bra over her head and then pulled down her thong. "I think we got time for a little something, something." Ki-Ki motioned for me to come to her. "I wanna show you something…"

19

"Fuck that." I said as I made my way to the bed. "I'm tryna get that same head Kira gave that nigga in your other book. Which one was it? Right after the nigga Ricky got locked up, Kira gave one of them niggas some head that had me stroking my dick as I read the book."

"That was Wifey. I know exactly what scene you talking about, boo. I wrote the scene exactly the way I do it. But you already know that my head is fire, right?"

"Yeah, but..."

"No buts, boo, I got you. First, I wanna introduce you to a few things we do in Virginia Beach. Come and lie down on the bed for me."

I did as I was told.

"Relax your arms above your head and enjoy the ride, baby." Ki-Ki straddled me and slid her legs straight forward. Her feet were on both sides of my shoulders. She reached behind her and grabbed my shins. "This right here is called the Joystick Joyride." Pushing up off the bed for leverage, Ki-Ki started swiveling her hips in a figure eight motion. "We call it that...oooohhh...because your dick is moving around in me...this feels good as shit...like a joystick moves for a video game."

I grabbed the bed sheets and gripped them as Ki-Ki rode the shit out of my dick. Her breasts were large and in charge in front of me bouncing around and I loved every minute of watching them. Ki-Ki knew that she had me open when she heard me whimper like a hurt puppy. She stepped her game up and swiveled her hips back and forth, then side to side.

"D-a-a-a-m-m-n, girl! Work that dick...work that dick, Ki-Ki! Got damn! Hold on, boo!" I exclaimed and pushed Ki-Ki off me. "Hold on for a minute. You gon' make me cum too hard and I ain't gon be able to rise to the occasion for the next round. Let me hit it from the back. I wanna slow stroke that pussy and see that ass clap while I hit it."

Ki-Ki crawled over to the edge of the bed and assumed the position. She loved it when I made love to her doggy-style.

"This is what I want you to do while I'm hitting that ass. I want you to answer my questions, a'ight?" I said as I entered Ki-Ki. "You like this dick?"

"Baby I love it."

"You like sucking my dick, don't you?"

"Yes!"

"You a vicious whore, ain't you?"

"Ooooh...yes!"

"You like swallowing cum, don't you?"

"Yes!"

"Do you like it in the ass?"

"I love it in my ass, Que!"

"What's the name of your first book?"

"Oooooh...shit, boy! This dick is like that. It's so deep in me. I love it!"

"The name of your book is I love it?"

"N-o-o-o-o!"

"Name the book!"

"Wifey...W-i-i-f-f-e-y-y!"

I banged into Ki-Ki another five minutes until I was ready to explode. "Turn around and suck the cum out my dick. Hurry up and catch it." Watching Ki-Ki on her knees sucking my dick as I came in her mouth was like nirvana. "This is one nasty bitch!" I thought to myself as she licked me dry.

***

"I'm out here right now. I been here all day waiting for this muthafucka. When he shows his head, I'ma chop it off. I'll holla back in a little while." I hit the button on the Bluetooth device and ended the call. Then I went back to the book I was reading. It was one of the books that Ki-Ki had given me earlier, the ones she had the book signing for. I stopped mid-sentence and looked at the cover of the book again before continuing. I kept wondering when the book was gonna pick up. With one eye on the red brick house across the street and one eye in the book, I got frustrated after a few more pages.

"This joint some cold-blooded bullshit." I said to myself. "This shit shouldn't be called 'Life in the DMV', it should be called 'Robbing the industry'. I threw the book down and picked up the other one. I was reading the acknowledgment pages when my eye caught movement to my right. A dark green Ford F-150 pulled into the driveway of the red brick house. Seconds later, Walter 'Biggums' Fleming exited the truck.

Throwing the book into the passenger's seat, I acted quickly by pulling down the mask on my head. Quickly I exited the rental Kia Optima. I pulled the silenced 9mm from my waistband and jogged up behind Biggums. Hearing footsteps, Biggums turned around quickly, only to discover that death was upon him.

"You thought that you could hide out here at your mother's house, huh? Well you were wrong, fat boy." I shot Biggums in both legs and then his stomach.

Biggums fell to the ground and writhed around in pain. "Please don't kill me!"

"Shut your hot ass up. Rasul and nem sent their regards." I stood over my victim. "Maybe hell got a witness stand and you can rock the mike on that one, too. Send word back when you get there." With that said, I fired numerous rounds into Biggums's face and head.

I ran back to the Optima and got the hell out of dodge. Safely back in D.C. I drove to a small street called Bowen Road. There were several young men gathered on the corner, but I only focused on one of them. The dude was the spitting image of myself, only younger.

"Get rid of the car." I said to the dude as I exited the vehicle and walked up some stairs to an apartment building.

Jihad Bashir, my younger brother never said a word as he jumped into the car and pulled off.

***

Inside the small apartment in Southeast, I stripped out of all my clothes. It was customary to shower after killing. It was as if I could wash away all the demons that took hold of my body when I went into kill mode. I picked up the house phone and dialed a number. A man's voice answered on the second ring.

"It's done. Check the local news tonight. On your cell phone."

Disconnecting the call, I threw the phone onto the couch and went into the bathroom. I ran the hot water and held my hand under it until I was satisfied with the temperature. Satisfied that the water was perfect, I stepped into the shower and let the water spray beat down on my tired body. The marathon sexcapade with Ki-Ki earlier had taken more of a toll on my body than I imagined. I stretched out under the water and took several deeps breaths. The hot water was good for my muscles. Especially, the one between my legs, I had come about four times that morning and my dick was sore. I thought about Ki-Ki, the day we met and the first time we had sex...

Steven Graham had fled the city after testifying against Murder Incorporated an alleged crew of killers that were responsible for over half of D.C.'s murder rate in the 90's. Phone calls were made and eventually I was approached. People close to Steve said he had fled to Atlanta. Equipped with enough information and equipment to stalk my prey, I drove twelve hours to Atlanta. In the ATL, Steve wasn't hard to find. He frequented all the hot spots and clubs with another notorious rat named Gindus. I salivated literally when I saw them together because I could kill two birds with one stone.

I had been paid to track down and kill Steve. Killing Gindus was a freebie I decided to charge that one to the game. While following the duo in a mall on Peachtree Avenue, I thought maybe they had spotted me. So, I ducked into the first store I could, which happened to be a Barnes and Noble bookstore. Ki-Ki was there doing a book signing for one of her books. I believe it was Wifey part 2. Deciding to abandon my position for the day, I stood in line to get a copy of the book and meet the beautiful author sitting at the table.

Once I reached the front of the line, Ki-Ki took one look at me and flirted. I saw her writing in the book, but thought she was just autographing it. When I walked away I discovered that she had given me her cell phone number.

Beside the number she wrote: *I'm only in town for one night, and your grey eyes seduced me mentally. Call me!*

That one night turned out to be my night. We hooked up and had wild sex for hours. I ended up leaving Ki-Ki's hotel room early the next morning. Later that evening I found Steve and Gindus in the same place as before. By midnight that night I had successfully killed them both...

I remembered that night as if it were yesterday. I remembered in vivid detail all the murders that I had committed. Especially the first one when I was thirteen years old!

Chapter Three
Zinfandel

"I just received the Rosser letter in David's case and it looks like we have a problem." I announced, walking into my boss's office.

Jennifer looked up from her computer screen, motioned for me to hold on. A few minutes later, she clicked off and turned facing me. "What were you saying Zin?"

"I said, the Rosser letter from the U.S. Attorney's office just got here and there may be a problem."

"In what case?"

I laid the letter down in front of Jennifer. "David Battle's."

Jen read the letter, "An earlier letter from them said, 'no statements on file.' How can they send us a second letter saying he made a statement?"

"I was at the preliminary hearing a few weeks ago and I don't remember the government saying anything about a statement."

"He supposedly said, "Y'all ain't got nothing on me. Your witness recanted. My lawyer is gonna eat that shit up."

"Yep. The night he got arrested and was being held at the 7th District. They allege that they were asking him about a gun charge and he just blurted that statement out about the murder case."

"Stupid ass. Didn't he know they could use that against him? Next question. Why bring this up now? I mean…they had months before the indictment to bring this up?"

Without answering the question, I left the office, then returned a minute later. I popped a stack of papers down on Jennifer's desk.

"What's that?" Jen asked.

"Grand Jury statements." I replied.

"Whose?" Jen asked, grabbing the papers, reading the name at the top. "Tommy Caldwell, I should've known."

"The crazy part about it is that Caldwell is David's cousin."

Jen flipped through the pages and read what was said in the grand jury hearing. "He now says that David paid him to tell homicide cops that he wasn't at the scene of the crime. He says David tried to coerce him into not testifying. He says that David knew he made an incriminating statement the night of the murder, so he changed his story to keep David from killing him…and the date on this is…three days ago. That's why the government sent the second Rosser letter." I said and sat down in one of the recliner seats in the office. "They now can use the statement at the police station against David because it proves what Caldwell says. It validates the obstruction of justice."

"Shit, when it rains, it pours."

"Tell me about it. And I had absolutely no luck with the possible witness…what's her name? Stevens…Yolanda Stevens. I went to her job and tried to speak…"

"…I forgot to tell you. I been so busy with this case against Sean Branch that I forgot to tell you that she's on their side."

"Who? Stevens?" I asked incredulously.

"Yeah. I got a call from Greg Gamble yesterday. He called…"

I didn't hear anything after the word Gamble. My mind was elsewhere. The first thing that appeared in my head was his smile. The smile he wore the day he sent my father to prison for the rest of his life. I hadn't seen the great Greg Gamble since he came to Howard University's Crampton Auditorium to give the pronouncement speech to my law school graduating class. Even then he was smiling.

"…something on her. I don't know what it is, but she's a hostile now."

"Have you talked to David?" I inquired.

"Not yet. I was going to go to the jail on Monday and see everybody."

"Since I am the leading attorney, I'll go see David today. He needs to know the latest turn of events. As a matter of fact, I'm gonna leave now and beat the rush hour traffic. I'll call you later and fill you in on what he says."

"Make sure you remind him that, it's time to make payment too." Jen said as I left the office.

***

I sat at the small table and waited for David Battle to enter the small visiting room. The room was a little stuffy, cramped, and smelly. It was redolent of cigarettes and sweat.

An overweight female C.O. peeked into the room and said, "He'll be down in a few minutes as soon as the count clears."

"Thank you." I replied and opened the folder in front of me. David Battle was charged with the brazen daylight murder of a man accused of stealing the rims off his car. In the back alley of Sheridan Road, Solomon Robinson was shot twice in the face at close range. So, far the government had three witnesses against my client.

It was going to be tough beating the case, but I knew if there was a way to attack the government's case, I could find it. David walked into the room ten minutes later, dressed in an orange D.C. jail jumpsuit, black Nike boots, and a black kufi. He smiled as he sat down.

"Ms. Carter, what's up? You look better and better every time I see you." David said.

I was used to my clients trying to shoot shots at me, so I knew how to deal with dudes like David. "Thank you, Mr. Battle, but I'm not here to talk about me. We've run into a few snags and Jen thought you should know about them."

David suddenly became deathly serious. "What snags?"

"The statements you made."

"I ain't make no muthafuckin' statements!"

"Getting loud and upset is not going to help us beat your case." I reminded him. "The night you got arrested, did somebody try to talk to you? A detective, maybe?"

"After they put me in the holding cage, a dude did come to the cage and tell me that they had me on a murder. He…"

"Did he give you his name?"

"Yeah, but I don't remember it. I was thinking about the gun charge they had me on and dude pops up out of nowhere asking me did I want to talk to him. When I said '*no*', he said, '*That's cool' it don't matter if you talk or not. We got you on the murder beef anyway.*' That's when I went off on the nigga."

I flipped open the folder. "That's when you said, and they quote '*Y'all ain't got nothing on me. Your witness recanted, my lawyer is gonna eat that shit up.*' Is that about, right?"

"That's what I said…but I didn't make no statements. That muthafucka got mad at me because I didn't wanna talk to him. He tried to shine on me, so I went off on his ass."

"You went off on his ass, huh? He played you like a flute. He probably read you like a book. He figured that if he made you mad, you'd say some stupid shit and he guessed right. Let me explain to you what happened and how your emotional outburst put us in a rut. We just found out that your cousin Tommy Caldwell is cooperating with the government…"

"That's bullshit!" David interjected.

"That's bullshit, huh?" I stood up and walked around the table. I threw a stack of papers in front of David. "My time is too precious to come all the way over here to bullshit you. You pay me one-hundred-seventy-five dollars an hour to defend you. If you want bullshit, trust me I can give you bullshit."

"I…he…he…said…he…bitch ass nigga!" David continued to read the words of his cousin. "And this nigga lying on me. I ain't never try to pay that nigga shit. He…"

"He's gonna testify that you did. And then the prosecutor is gonna put the detective on the stand. The detective is gonna testify that you told him the witness recanted. Do you know what that does? That corroborates what your cousin says. It shows that you knew the witness recanted because you threatened him or attempted to pay him to recant. Then the detective will tell the jury how you arrogantly said that your lawyer will eat that shit up. Do you know what that does?"

David never looked up from the papers.

"That makes the jury look at us funny. They will distrust us and what we say. They'll think we are just trying to, as you put it, *'eat that shit up'*. This shit is for real. A life was taken, and you are the only one that they are gonna say is responsible for it. You cousin is gonna say it and so are the other two witnesses."

"Other two? Where the fuck did another witness come from? I thought it was just witness one and now my cousin."

I really hated to be the bearer of bad news, but it was my job. "The girl that you told me to find. The one that you said would help you…"

"Yolanda, what about her?" David asked.

"She is working with the government. I don't have her grand jury statements, yet, but I will soon. The prosecutor called the office and gave Jen heads up. So that makes three, we are still trying to get them to tell us who the other witness is. So, that's the bad news. What do you want us to do?"

"Your job! That's what I'm paying you to do. Find out who that anonymous witness is, and I will take care of the rest. Are you finished?"

"I believe so." I said, gathering my things. "Sign this form right here for me and Jen told me to tell you it's time to make another payment."

"I'ma have my man stop by the office tomorrow. Tell Jen's fat ass I said, don't sweat me bout that little bit ass money and she needs to find out who that witness is." With that said David got up and left the room.

Chapter Four
Quran

The Safeway parking lot was dark and empty except for about three or four cars. Across the street, parked in front of the discount mart on Alabama Avenue sat a forest green Mercury Marauder. Inside that Marauder sat me and my brother Jihad. Jihad sat behind the wheel of the car and freaked a Black and Mild cigar. Then he filled the empty Black with hydro. Right before he could fire up the cigar, I stopped him.

"Don't fire that up right now, slim. Wait until after I put this work in. I wanna have my head clear when I get up on her."

"I can't believe that Landa is working with them people. She's the one who came home with that Stop Snitching D.V.D. We watched the shit up her house with Lil' Greg and Bug. Lil' Greg gon be fucked up when he hears that bitch turned out to be a rat." Jihad said and sat the hydro filled cigar in the ashtray.

"Don't nothing surprise me nowadays, baby boy. We living in the last days, so anything goes. Think about it, back in eighty-nine, who would have believed that Rayful would snitch? New York niggas know that Alpo snitched on niggas and they still don't wanna believe it. Look at Pappy, Moe, Stink, Moo-Moo, Lee-Lee, Mark Johnson, Fat Sean, Kevin Wise, Kenny Sparrow, Monya, Tech, Ratbo, Swamp, Fat Cat, Sam from down Minnesota Ave, Red Ray from Uptown, C-Dubb, Quincy Walters, Tone-Tone Lemons, and a rack of other muthafuckas. Them niggas was real live street niggas. Majority of them was head busters. Now look at 'em, they hot as fish grease. Like I said, don't nothing surprise me."

"What about Landa's uncle Mann? I thought he was your man." Jihad asked.

"He still my man, it's his niece that's fucked up. He'll understand in time and if he don't, I'll push his shit back, too. You know it don't even matter to me."

"I feel that." Jihad glanced over at the front entrance to the Safeway. He saw two women exiting the store. "Is that her right there, moe?"

I leaned forward in my seat and tried to make out the two women through the tinted windows of the Mercury. "It looks like her, roll the window down a little bit so I can see better…yeah that's her. Start the car up and keep it moving. I'll be right back."

"Aye moe, you know they got a police substation right next to the Radio Shack."

"Fuck the police." I replied, pulling my hammer, checking the clip. Then I screwed the silencer attachment to the barrel of the .40 Caliber Ruger.

Dressed in all black attire, I pulled the half mask down over the lower part of my face, then exited the car.

***

"Girl, that fat ass nigga gets on my nerves. He always tryna put a bitch on blast. Like everybody don't already know I be late for work every day. Shit, you try coming all the way from Brentwood to here and see what time your ass gets here. If a bitch was tryna put out for his fat funky ass, he wouldn't be trippin' like that."

Yolanda Stevens laughed at her girlfriend Tasha. Not because what she said was funny, but because everybody who worked at Safeway knew that Tasha and Mr. Carney, the store manager were involved with each other. Their pretend hate for one another was transparent. It was see-through and everybody knew it but them. They were the joke of the day almost every day.

"You crazy as shit, Tasha. How you getting home?"

"I'ma catch the bus."

Yolanda knew that was a lie, too. Tasha always pretended to walk to the bus stop on Naylor Road. But in all actuality, she'd wait until she thought everybody was gone home, then call Mr. Carney. He'd leave the store, pick her up, and they'd drive off together. Yolanda and a couple of their co-workers had peeped the whole move months ago.

"A'ight then, girl I'ma see you tomorrow."

"I'm sorry, girlfriend, but you ain't gon' make it to tomorrow. You should've kept your mouth closed."

I fired the gun and hit Yolanda in the chest. The force of the .40 bullets knocked her through the plate glass window of the Safeway. Yolanda never saw or heard anything ever again.

***

"Roll out!" I shouted to my brother as I hopped in the car.

Jihad pulled away from the curb and sped off towards Good Hope Road. "Where to now?"

Pulling off my mask, I waited until my heart rate slowed down before I spoke. I laid back in the passenger seat of the Mercury and closed my eyes. Closing my eyes and thinking about something else helped to exorcise the demons that took over my body when I killed.

"Take me back to the spot. Doesn't Lissen Band play down the H2O tonight?"

"Every Thursday night, yeah. Why you wanna go party?"

"Naw, that nigga Tommy is a party animal. He goes to every Rare Essence and Lissen Band show. If my memory serves me correctly, I can catch him at the H2O. I need to change clothes first."

"Why?" Jihad asked as curiosity piqued.

"Because I never kill two people wearing the same clothes. I never deviate from that, the moment I do, I'ma get locked up."

Jihad laughed at his older brother and his ridiculous superstition.

"At the next light, fire that blunt up and let me hit that." I closed my eyes again and allowed myself to rest for a little while. Tomorrow I had to go and take Dave's lawyer some money. The idea alone brought a smile to my face. Even though I had her card and could've called her, I wanted an excuse to go and see Zin and now I had one.

Chapter Five
Zinfandel

I was sitting at my desk reading over the Motion to Suppress evidence that the government obtained legally against one of my clients, when Jennifer buzzed me and told me to come to her office. When I walked in, I noticed that Jen and Nikki were glued to the plasma T.V. hanging on Jen's wall.

"Check this out." Jen said, pointing to the T.V…

"…as we recap today's top stories. Last night was a bloody one in our Nation's Capital. Four people were shot and killed, and three more victims were wounded. The outbreak of violence started around 9:30 last night. Police were called to the scene of a shooting that took place in the 1300 block of Savanna Place, Southeast. Upon arrival at the scene, they discovered a man, now identified as Phonodus Berkeley, suffering from gunshot wounds to the chest and neck. He was transported to Greater Southeast Community Hospital where he died a short time later.

"At approximately 10:15 p.m., a report of a shooting came in to dispatchers. D.C. police went to the 3000 block of Alabama Avenue and found a young woman dead. Authorities believe that the woman, identified as thirty-year-old Yolanda Stevens, was pushed or thrown through a window of the Safeway where she worked, then shot to death. The night manager of the Safeway, Paul Carney told authorities that Ms. Stevens had just gotten off work and he knew of no reason anyone would want to kill her.

"One hour later, in the Petworth section of Northwest, gun-shots erupted after an apparent house party. Authorities were called to the scene, where they found one man dead and several others injured. The man found dead, who authorities will only say is a male Hispanic. His identity is being withheld pending notification of his next of kin. The other victims were all taken to Washington Hospital Center with non-life-threatening injuries.

"A man leaving a popular D.C. nightclub was ambushed be-side his car, robbed, and killed. Authorities say that thirty-six-year-old Thomas Caldwell was last seen leaving the H2O *nightclub right before the club closed its doors. His body was found in between two cars on Water Street in Southwest. Mr. Caldwell's car keys, money, and jewelry were taken either before or after he was shot to death. There has been no arrest made in any of these brutal homicides..."*

Jennifer grabbed the remote and clicked the T.V. off. Everyone in the room was in a state of stunned silence.

Finally, Nikki broke the ice. "Well, we can't be implicated in any crimes. We will continue to do our jobs in a normal fashion. Besides, I guess this helps our client, so we win again."

"That fucking dummy!" Jennifer ranted. "He had to know that getting the witness killed was going to come back on us."

"Jen, we didn't do anything wrong. We violated no rules of ethics. The information we gave the client was part of the record. Any Joe Blow could've gotten the name of those witnesses from the Freedom of Information Office. Besides, the government still has one witness, so they'll think they still have a shot at winning their case and proceed according to plan. What we don't need is the back draft burning our asses. If David is in any way connected to those murders, obviously that fucks up our case."

"Fucks up the case isn't even the right term. Our office will be under scrutiny forever behind that. I know..."

"What if he had nothing to do with it?" I blurted out. Both women looked at me like I was crazy. "Really though, what if it was just a coincidence?"

"Come on Zin, you can't really be that naïve. Yesterday you went to see David, right?" Jen said.

"Yeah, but..."

"But what? What did you tell him yesterday?"

"I...uh...that...uh...that he had two new witnesses against him."

"And you told him who they were, right?" Nikki added.

"Well, yeah..."

"Let me ask you this...how did he react to that news? Especially the fact that his cousin Tommy was one of those witnesses?"

I pressed rewind in my mind and tried to see what had registered on David's face when I gave him the news. "He was in denial, he told me what I said was bullshit. I gave him a copy of Tommy's grand jury statements. He read them and got upset, before he left me, he told me that he'd handle the situation." The look on both of my boss's faces told the rest of the story.

I was being naïve, I realized that. After leaving me, David went back to his housing unit and somehow ordered the deaths of two people. And those orders were carried out by some unknown person or persons. The reality of it all hit me like a ton of bricks. I had indirectly caused the death of two people. But what if David wasn't involved. What if Tommy Caldwell and Yolanda Stevens' deaths were both unrelated? The sound of Nikki's voice snapped me out of my reverie.

"Let's just hope nothing happens to the last remaining witness and that all of us can put our law degrees on display as we beat this case in court. Things happen, I'm not going to beat myself up about this. We did nothing wrong! I'm going back in my office to finish this 2255 motion I'm working on for Antwan Ball. I also have to prepare for a hearing in the morning, so you ladies call me if you need anything."

Once Nikki left the room, Jen looked at me and said, "Zin, don't stress yourself out about this. It's the nature of business. In the 90's, D.C. was famous for its witnesses being killed. There was nothing we could do then and there's nothing we can do now. Focus now on the witness they do have and what he or she could possibly say. Pretty soon they'll have to tip their hand and we'll be waiting. What are you working on now?"

"A motion to suppress for Antone White and Eric Hicks. Then I have the Sean Branch stuff to work on." I replied stoically.

"Go ahead and finish that stuff, I'll worry about the United States versus David Battle." With a wave of the hand, I knew I was being dismissed.

I walked into my office, sat down at my desk, and tried to focus but couldn't. I couldn't get my mind off the news broadcast.

Chapter Six
Quran

I pulled my Caddy into an open parking space behind a silver Porsche truck. The truck had to belong to one of the lawyers. I eyed the address on the row houses until I found the one I was looking for, 321 D Street. All the row houses were painted the same color but 321 had a small sign hanging over the front door that read: *Law Offices of Locks and Wentz*. The house had been remodeled and converted into a bevy of offices and conference rooms. I walked up the stairs and rung the doorbell.

A minute later I was being lead to Jennifer's office. I hated the fat white woman for no reason at all other than the fact that she was white. I pulled out two wads of cash and placed them on her desk.

"This is for my man Lil' Dave. That's the whole thing, ain't no more payments or none of that shit. All that money y'all charging a nigga, just make sure y'all get my man out of jail."

I turned to leave, but stopped when I heard Jennifer say something.

"Mr. Bashir, why are you always so hostile with me? What have I ever done to you?" Jennifer asked.

"I just don't trust crackers, that's all. Oh' let me get a receipt or something for that money, so my man can see that his legal fees have been paid in full."

Jennifer was writing up the receipt when Zin walked in. Zin looked at me and stopped dead in her tracks. Her heart started racing and the color drained from her face.

"Zin, what's up baby girl? I was hoping that I run into you."

Jennifer looked up from her desk with a confused look on her face, "Zin you know Mr. Bashir?"

It took a moment for her to gather her wits, but she rebounded nicely. "Uh...yeah, I grew up with Quran...I mean Mr. Bashir. It's a small world, what can I say?"

"Oh yeah? Well, Ms. Small World, please pass this receipt to Mr. Quran...I mean Mr. Bashir. What were you about to say when you walked in here?"

"I lost my train of thought." Zin admitted.

"Well, please come back when you remember. Show Mr. Bashir the door for me, will you?"

"Sure." Zin blushed, turned, and looked at me. I was already headed out of the office. When Jen's door was shut, Zin grabbed me from behind and pulled me into her office. "What are you doing here?"

"That ain't no way to greet an old friend." I said smiling.

The smile melted her heart. Zin couldn't resist staring into my eyes.

"I'm serious Quran, what are you doing here?"

"Didn't you just hand me a receipt in Jennifer's office?" I asked.

"Yeah..."

"So, that answers your question, right? I dropped off some money for one of my men. Is that a'ight with you?"

"If course...I just...I thought..."

"You thought I came to see you?"

"No. Yeah..."

"I came for two reasons. To drop off the money and to see you. I been thinking about you every day since I last saw you. I wanted to call you, but I didn't want you to think I was some kinda stalker or something."

"You... a stalker? Naw, I wouldn't have thought that."

"Yeah right, I don't wanna cramp your style, baby girl. You might not have considered me a stalker, but it still wouldn't be a good look for you to be associating with thugs."

"Associating with thugs? All I work for is thugs. I been around thugs all my life, you know that."

"*I know what?* All I know is that you left the hood a long time ago and now you show back up a lawyer. A fine ass lawyer at that. You talk like these crackers you work for. I don't know how much of you is still the same."

"I'm still the same, ain't nothing changed about me except my address, my job description, and my outlook on life. I'm still hood. I just know how to turn it down a few notches when I need to. So, miss me with all that *'associating with thugs' bullshit*."

"I feel that, no disrespect intended. You got this little vein that pops up in your forehead when you get mad. I noticed it when you were little, but I forgot about it. Until just now, so now that we've gotten all that out of the way, can a thug get a hug?"

"A hug?" Zin asked vexed.

"You heard that R.Kelly joint, right?" I asked then in an off-key voice sung the words to the song. *"...heaven I need a hug, it is anybody out there willing to embrace a thug..."*

Zin laughed out loud. "You crazy boy, I ain't heaven, but I think I can arrange a hug. After the hug then what?"

"You tell me, first the hug, C'mere." I motioned for Zin to come to me.

Zin crossed the room and embraced me. Her smell was intoxicating. She laid her head briefly on my chest. She felt comfortable in my arms. Her heart beat fluttered, I could feel it.

Zin broke our embrace and asked, "What are you wearing?"

"What am I wearing?" I stared down at myself and said, "Hugo Boss jeans..."

"Not your clothes, boy. I'm talking about your cologne. It smells good as shit."

"Oh that's, that new *Sean John* smell called *'I am King'*. You like that, huh?"

"Definitely, what woman doesn't like a man that smells good. Even if he is a thug." Zin replied, smiling.

"I tell you what, baby girl, if all a thug gotta do is smell good for you. I got that covered, wait until you smell Emporio Armani, Prada Infusion, and that Cartier Roadster. But here's the catch. I got the hook up with some people that supply all the stores and they ain't even got them joints, yet. So, you gotta smell them on me."

"So, what you saying is that I gotta hook up with you just to smell you smell good?"

"Something like that. But smelling good ain't all you get. There's a whole lot more that comes with it. You just gotta decided whether or not you wanna get it."

"Quran, I got a boyfriend."

I adjusted the gun in my waist to keep it from falling. I looked at Zin long and hard, then walked to the door of her office. "It sounds to me like you got a problem then." I opened the door and walked out.

***

"What's good with y'all?" I asked as I stepped out the car on Howard Road. I walked up to my brothers and their partner Bo and gave everybody some dap.

"I'm good, big boy." Jihad replied.

"What's crackin'?" Tabu said.

"Que, how you?" Bo chimed in.

"Aye, Bo, I gotta black hoodie in the backseat of my car, why don't you get that for me, slim?" Jihad said.

As soon as Bo was out of earshot, Jihad said, "M.C. called my phone, he said that he couldn't reach you and he needs to holla at you."

I nodded my head, "What else is new? Anybody talkin' bout Landa?"

Since it was muggy outside, Tabu took off his sweatshirt, and wrapped it around his waist. "You know the usual talk, who might've done it and all that."

"Nothing to be concerned about, big boy. But I did talk to Lonnie..." Jihad was quickly cut off.

"Lonnie?" I replied. "Who the fuck is Lonnie?"

"My bad." Jihad explained. "Lonnie is my man that I'm about to go on a mission for. But I need your help. I wanna put Lonnie...that's my man David Jones, also known as Bit-Bit, on with that lawyer broad you told me about. Doug, Bernie, Mark, or Jonathan won't take his case. They all saying something about a conflict of interest. Slim, killed two muthafuckas over

Northeast last year. There's two main witnesses against him. Andrew 'Drew' Everette and Vernon 'Boo' Dammons. The nigga Boo we can't get to because he's already locked up on a robbery beef. But Drew I can touch through a bitch that he fuckin'. Who happens to be the same bitch that Lonnie was fuckin'. I'm tryna crush him and the bitch…"

"Did the broad tell on Lonnie?" I asked.

"Naw…not that know of, but…"

"You wanna kill her because she crossed your man and now she fuckin' with the rat that's telling on him? Is that what you tellin' me?"

"Naw…" Jihad stated. "…yeah. Yeah, that's pretty much it."

"You know how I feel about killing innocent women. The bitch is guilty of treason and other shit for fuckin' with the rat, but I wouldn't kill her for that. You are a man and you can do what you feel. Is your man paying for the hit on his witness, the dude Drew?"

"Naw…I'm doing it on the strength, but…"

"Baby boy, I kill for money, not friendship. If you wanna kill them people for your man, for free, that's on you. Do you, as far as the lawyer is concerned, I'll talk to Zin. She might get Nikki Locks or Jen Wentz to represent slim. I'll let you know something soon. Anything else before I leave?"

"Are you for or against me killing the bitch? I need to know." Jihad asked.

"Stuck in the middle, baby boy. She crossed him, but she didn't rat and that's my thing. She fucked another dude who is a rat, but she didn't."

"Didn't dad always say that if you cross…"

"…A person once, you'll cross him twice." Tabu finished the sentence.

"Yeah, he said that, and I live by it, but she crossed him, not you. But like I said, it's your choice. Her biggest crime is really because she fuckin' a rat. I don't care, baby boy, do you. Tabu, what's good with you?"

"I'm coolin', Que. You know me, I'ma roll with Jihad."

"A'ight, y'all do y'all. I got a broad coming through, I'ma be in 203. Holla if you need me."

As soon as I opened the door to our chill spot, my cellphone vibrated. The caller was Tosheka. "Hey."

"I'm on my way, are you on Howard Road?"

"Yeah same spot. My car is parked outside of 1351, come in and knock on apartment 203."

"I'll be there in fifteen minutes, bye."

I disconnected the call, then dialed Michael Carter's number.

Chapter Seven
Zinfandel

"Are you ready to order now?" The waiter asked.

Jermaine Mendenhall took it upon himself to order for himself and me. "Yes, give me the roasted porkchops with Cipollini onions and Escarole. And she'll have the Jack Daniels pork chops with wilted greens, crispy pancetta, and chickpeas. Bring us an appetizer of Hazelnut and Turkey sausage stuffed mushrooms."

"What would you like to drink, sir?"

"I'm in the mood for a cognac. Bring me a glass of Louis the thirteenth and a white wine for the lady."

"Will that be all?" the waiter asked, writing down their order.

"We may have dessert later. I'll let you know after we've eaten."

Sitting at a table in the far corner of the popular bistro in upscale Georgetown I struggled to maintain my composure. "I hate when you do that Jermaine and the funny part about it is that you know that."

"Zin, baby I'm sorry, I just thought that maybe you'd had a rough day and I'd surprise you with dinner."

"By not asking me what I felt like eating and ordering what you want me to have? That's the surprise? How do you figure that I've had a rough day?"

"When I talked to you earlier..."

I cut him off, "Stop trying to be perceptive. I was not having a bad day until just now when you ordered me pork chops and I told you months ago that I was laying off pork."

Jermaine laughed, "I thought that you were joking. You..."

"I wasn't, and I'm also not in the mood for any wine."

"But I already ordered it, I can't..."

"You can't what Jermaine? Cancel the order, you can and you will. If you would've bothered to ask me I would've told you everything I just said. Never think you can read my mind. I

45

am not one of your client's Jermaine. As a matter of fact, I'm not even hungry and I'm ready to leave."

I watched in silence as Jermaine signaled for the waiter, apologized profusely about unexpected turn of events, and gave the man a tip for his time. As we waited outside the valet to bring Jermaine's Jaguar X19, the silence between us was deafening. Neither one of us said a word until the Jaguar pulled into its parking space beside my Infiniti at our condo in Adams Morgan.

"You are stubborn as shit." Jermaine said, opening the door to the building. "Whoever made you mad at work, it wasn't me. I don't appreciate you taking your frustrations out on me, Zin. All I tried to do was make your day a little better." Once we got inside the elevator, Jermaine continued his spiel, "That's some ungrateful shit, Zin."

I kept my mouth closed even as we entered the condo. I was not about to get into a shouting match with Jermaine. I just didn't feel like it. I walked into our bedroom and stepped out of my heels. My Michael Kors shoes were killing my toes. Jermaine was in the living room still venting about my selfishness. I paid him no mind as I undressed and headed for the bathroom. I ran water in the bathtub, then decided against a bath.

The way I was feeling required a shower, not a bath. As the water rained down on me, I contemplated my situation. It was a situation that was thrusted upon me in such short time. Two weeks ago, I was happy with Jermaine, and life was great. Then came my past catching up with me and the man that I've lusted after ever since I was a young girl, was back in my life. His grey eyes seemed to be watching me still.

"Quran, I have a boyfriend."

"It sounds to me like you gotta problem then…"

Quran was right, I did have a problem, and there was no way around it. I had never cheated on Jermaine in the five years we'd been together. I remembered the day that I met him. We were both freshman in Law School and ended up in a lot of the same classes. I became attracted to Jermaine's calm demeanor under pressure, his wit, and snappy dress code. He was a little on the short side in my opinion, standing only 5'9 without shoes on, but I overlooked that. Standing only 5'3 myself, he still had me by inches. Jermaine had the skin tone of pure honey, with hazel eyes to match. What was it with me and dudes with pretty eyes? He kept his naturally wavy hair cut low and tapered. His family was middle class and it showed in him. Being from the South gave him an air of Southern aristocracy that made him seem snobbish to a degree. My girlfriends all called him the Country Buppie all throughout Law School.

During our second year of school, we went into different fields of law. I went into Criminal Law as planned and Jermaine went into Corporate, Real Estate, and Tax Law. We both excelled in our desired fields and graduated with honors. That had been over two years ago, and we were still going strong. Well maybe going strong wasn't the right word.

Because what we shared wasn't really strong. I often questioned myself about love and was I really in it with Jermaine, even before Quran. I knew for sure that I liked Jermaine a lot. He was comfortable, he was stability, he was security, but there was something lacking, and I couldn't really put my finger on it. Then again, I could. As I lathered up, I paid special attention to my sex.

I rubbed circles around my clit, the more I became turned on, the more I rubbed, and probed. This was what I was lacking. Intensity, excitement in the bedroom, tenacity, variety, and cataclysmic orgasms. In the bedroom, I wanted the ceilings to shake, my legs to shiver, and my juices to flow out of me in tidal waves. That just wasn't the way Jermaine made me feel. He was a Southern boy and his grandfather had always told him to never *'eat anything that bleeds once a month and doesn't die.'*

So, oral sex was out of the question in our bedroom. The sex we shared was mundane, trite, and regular. There were no sparks, no rumbles, and no shakes. I continued to rub my clit with a renewed frenzy every time Quran's face popped into my head. I didn't know for sure, but my instincts told me that things with Quran would be different. Quran was a bad boy, a thug, a real man. One with swagger, style, and street grace, if there was such a thing. Sex with Quran would bring the noise. I'm willing to bet it, there would be earth shaking, piercing screams of passion, rumbling, and quivering legs. Biting my lips to muffle moans, I came over and over and over again.

***

"Zin, baby I'm sorry! I'm so sorry-y-y!" Jermaine moaned.

With my eyes closed, I rode Jermaine's dick. I knew that I was putting it on him. The Kegel exercises I did everyday while sitting at my desk at work were paying off. I knew that my pussy muscles were gripping Jermaine's dick. I was in total control.

"...I take back everything I said...oh shit! Ride that dick, Zin! Ride me, just like that...a-a-r-r-g-ghh!"

I was in a zone, I gyrated my hips and grinded my pelvis onto Jermaine's dick. The length of his dick wasn't that long, but he made up for that with girth. Every time I made love to him, the thickness of Jermaine's dick satisfied me and caused me to climax. But I never came, I never orgasmed the way that I did when I pleasured myself. Jermaine's dick wasn't long enough to hit the right spots. Any woman that was in touch with herself sexually knew there was a difference. I willed myself to smell the cologne I had smelled earlier. The Sean John cologne that Quran wore.

Quran Bashir, lately everything started, and stopped with him. I tried to focus on pleasing Jermaine and not think about Quran, but no matter how I tried, I couldn't do it. Quran was inside me, he was there, and I was riding him. I threw my head back, then reached behind me, and placed my palms flat on his knees. I gripped them and dug my toes into the bed. I wanted to feel every inch of him inside me. It felt so good, I moved back and forth, then side to side. I listened to his sounds of satisfaction and that turned me on even more.

"I'm about to cum…oooh…shit…I'm about to cum! I'm about to cum…ooohh Quran, I'm cumming! Don't move…I'm shaking…I'm shaking!"

After the roars inside me subsided, I fell off Jermaine and laid beside him. I had never experienced anything like that with him before.

"Zin?"

"Yeah, boo!"

"Did you just call me Quran or something like that?" Jermaine asked.

I cursed under my breath for being so careless. Then the lawyer in me kicked in. "Of course not, you didn't hear what I said? I said, *'On the Qu'ran, I'm cumming.* I have a client that's Muslim. I never know when he's lying or telling the truth. So, now he always swears on the Islamic Holy book when he's telling the truth. He'll say, *'On the Qu'ran…*this and and on the Qu'ran that. You had me feeling so good, I wanted to tell you how much, and tell the truth about it. So, I said, *'On the Qu'ran…I'm cumming.'*

"But Zin, you're not Muslim."

"I know that, baby, but when you make love to me it's spiritual and my orgasms have no specific faith. When the dick is good and I'm about to cum, I'll call out to the Jews, and put that on Torah. It's all the same to me, I'm tired and about to fall asleep. We'll talk some more tomorrow. Good night." I turned over on my side, away from Jermaine, and smiled. I had lied with the alacrity of a Cheetah and kept a straight face while doing so. That's when I knew I was really becoming a great lawyer.

Chapter Eight
Quran

"...who loved to paint pictures as a girl. Yolanda was a person that gave all she had to everybody. She never turned down a soul. I always told her that she gave too much of herself...Lord, why...why did you take my baby girl?"

I sat in the back row of the Antioch Baptist Church and swiped at tears forming in my eyes. I watched Landa's mother Connie as she questioned God and man. I watched her faint several times and the women dressed in white uniforms rush to her side.

"...The Lord, called Yolanda home to be with him. That's a part of his master plan that we can't question..."

A tap on my shoulder caused my head to spin around. It was Yolanda's uncle Mann.

"What's up slim?" I asked.

"I need to holla at you, dawg, outside." He said.

I'm a paranoid nigga, so I reached for my waist and felt the comfort of the brand-new chrome .45 resting there. Then my mind started racing...*did Mann know that I was the one who killed Landa? Had the cops figured out she was killed, because she was about to rat on Dave? Had they told that to Landa's family? Had Mann traced a line back to me? Was Mann trying to bring me a move at the church?*

I silently got up from my seat and followed Mann outside. Glancing over my shoulder after hearing the church's double doors open and close. I saw that my brother Jihad had probably wondered the same things and stepped out of the church to make sure Mann didn't try his hand.

I kept my hand on my gun and my eyes on Mann's hands. "What's up, slim?"

Tears rolled down Mann's face as he said, "Dawg, I gotta find out who killed my peoples. I gotta crush 'em, my heart won't let me mourn. I gotta get some get back on whoever did this."

"You think I don't know that and feel the same way. I been fucked up about this shit since it happened." I paused to wipe a tear from his eye. "I fucks with you and your family, you know that. I already got a few muthafuckas out there tryna feel niggas out. Word will get back and trust me, when it do, we gon' tear some shit up behind this. Just chill out, slim and bury your niece. When I find out who hit her, I'ma let you know ASAP."

"Thanks, dawg I love you, dawg." Mann said and then went back into the church.

"That's my cue to bounce, baby boy." I told my brother as we walked over to Jihad's smoke grey Acura TL.

"What did Mann say, moe?" Jihad asked.

"He said that he tryna find out who killed his niece and all that bullshit." I replied opening the passenger side door of the Acura, getting inside.

Jihad started the car up and pulled out of the church parking lot. "We gonna have to kill that nigga, moe. If the cops talk to his peoples and get to tryna say that Yolanda was killed because she was a witness against Lil' Dave. You know slim gonna put two and two together and come for your head."

"I was thinking the same thing, baby boy. I hate to do it, but I'ma have to put Mann's head to bed."

"When?"

"A wise man once said, *'Never put off for tomorrow, what can be done today.'* That dress his mother had on looked kinda expensive. I'ma help her out, and give her a reason to wear it again soon."

***

Tabu pulled the truck in the parking lot and blew the horn. "This nigga stupid as shit, slim. You just talked to that nigga this morning at the funeral. Now you call him and say that you know who put the work in. And this dumb ass nigga can't figure out it's you. I would've picked up on that."

I laughed and kept rolling the blunt. I knew my younger brother was all talk and no action. Plus, he was a little slow, so I knew he was just talking to be talking. There was no way for any man to know that his demise was coming. Only a clairvoyant muthafucka could do that and Mann was no seer of the future. I didn't even bother responding to Tabu's last comment as we waited for Mann to come outside.

A few minutes later, Mann jogged up to the truck, dressed in black Army fatigues, and Timberland boots and hopped into the backseat.

"I'ma fuck these niggas around, dawg. How the fuck Lil' Jay-Jay and 'nem 'gon think Landa set that shit up that happened to them? She wasn't even fuckin' wit' that nigga no more. How the fuck she 'gon know that he was sitting on all that dope, on that particular day? I know that bitch nigga Lil' Man probably put him up to it. It's cool though, I'ma bake they ass for this mistake."

Tabu pulled out onto Stanton Road and headed for Oak Park.

"My man Lil' Coo-Wop put me down with the get down." I stated.

"I thought shorty was over the jail waiting to get sentenced on that double they found him guilty of." Mann replied.

"He is over the jail. He said a nigga from down 'Third World' put him down with what happened. Some nigga came over the jail on a gun charge and started running his mouth to cut into Wop and 'nem. You know how them niggas be. Coo-Wop called Jihad's cell phone and they called and told me, that's when I called you."

Mann gazed out the window at the town houses that were being built on 15th Place. "Where are you headed to now?"

Me and Mann had put in work together before, so I knew my next lie would be believed. "I got a car parked down by Oak Park in front of one of my bitch's house. I gotta stop past there and get the Kay. I'ma put that chopper on them niggas ass. You know how I do." I said, inhaling the acrid smoke of the hydro I'd just rolled into a funnel leaf.

"True dat. Pass that bud back here, nigga. You tryna hoover that muthafucka. Why the fuck you so quiet, Tab?" Mann said.

Tabu looked at Mann through the rearview mirror. "I'm just thinking, slim. I'm still fucked up about Landa. I can't believe them bitch niggas pulled some shit like this. Like muthafuckas wasn't gonna find out and come for their asses. Stupid ass niggas."

"Stupid ass niggas." Mann repeated, hitting the blunt several times, then passed it back up to the front seat.

When the gold Nissan Armada bent the corner of Ivanhoe Street, I said, "That's it right there, Tab. The black four door Buick, pull up beside it and park." I threw a set of keys into the backseat and said, "Mann, get the Kay, I'ma run in the bitch spot and take a piss."

"A'ight, dawg." Mann agreed and hopped out the truck the same time as I did.

Mann was slipping, had he been paying attention he would've seen that almost all of the buildings on the street were abandoned and vacant. I walked across the street and ducked behind a car as Mann put the key in the trunk of the Buick. I crept around the back of that car just as Mann got the trunk open. While Mann was bent over and rummaging through the Buick's trunk. I snuck up behind him, pulled my .45, and put it at the back of Mann's head. Then I fired repeatedly.

Out of the darkness, Tabu appeared.

"Help me throw him in the trunk." I told him.

Once the body was all the way in the trunk, we closed it. "Slim was my man, but now I'm glad I killed him."

"Why?" Tabu asked as we walked back to the truck.

"Because I just remembered one of the things I hated about that nigga."

"What was that?"

"He always tried to smoke all the weed."

"Slim, you lunchin' like shit." Tabu said, laughing.

He started the truck up and pulled off.

Chapter Nine
Zinfandel

"Ma'am, I need you to remove your shoes for me please."

Having been to the federal prison several times before, I was familiar with the pre-visit drill. I stepped out of my Guiseppe Zannoti heels, picked them up, and handed them to the middle aged, white, female C.O. I watched as the C.O. inspected my shoes and then I lifted my feet so that the bottoms could be seen. I turned, faced a wall, and let the lady pat search me. Every time I left the prison I felt like had been violated. But that violation never deterred me from making the four hour trek from D.C. to Scranton. My father was my heart and I loved him with all of my being. If there was a way for me to do a part of his sentence so that he could be free, I would do it in a heartbeat. After passing through a metal detector, another female C.O. passed some sort of wand over my hands and arms. My father said the fluorescent light was designed to detect drug residue and if any was found on a person they would be denied access to the prison.

"You are clear to go in Ma'am. Just go through the double doors and make a left. Then walk straight down the hall to the visiting room."

I badly wanted to shout, "Bitch, I know where the visiting room is, but I couldn't. They could terminate my father's visit. So, instead I nodded my head and did as I was instructed.

The visiting hall was already crowded with prisoners and their families. I found a seat in the back of the room, sat down, and waited for my father to come out. About fifteen minutes later, he did. At the sight of him, my heart warmed. Goose bumps shot up my arms. It happened every time I saw him. He was dressed in the customary beige Khaki outfit, with navy blue deck shoes. The grey in his hair was starting to show more, but overall Michael Carter still looked handsome. His hair was cut into a low tapered ceaser and his goatee was trimmed to perfection. He smiled when he saw me and that made me stand up. My father walked right into my arms and hugged me tight. He picked me up and spun me around.

"Daddy stop, you're embarrassing me." I said as I giggled with girlish glee.

"My bad baby, I forgot that you a grown woman now. I see you and I see my little girl. I will always see my little baby girl."

At the mention of the words baby and girl, I thought about Quran and the fact that he always called me baby girl.

"I am your baby, I'm just not a little girl. How have you been in here?"

"It's the same old grind, baby." My dad replied as he sat in the seat directly across from me. "I been doing this shit for almost sixteen years now, so I'm used to it. But God knows I wanna get out of this shit. Everything has changed, the worse thing they could've done to us was close Lorton. Lorton was sweet, this Fed shit is overrated. All I used to hear was how sweet the Feds was and about all this money you could make. You got all the so-called drug kingpins and big-time money handlers in here, but this joint is still broke as hell. These niggas in here are hot as shit. They telling about every little thing. A nigga can't get away with shit nowadays. The muthafuckin' faggies got the sack and they dictating to the men and not the other way around. And this gang shit be driving me nuts. A man can't even be a man no more, shit is way more political than it used to be. This is crazy."

I hated to hear my father complain, but what could I do to change his situation? Ever since I was a kid I promised myself that one day I was going to help free my father, but so, far I had failed. That hurt me deeply every time I visited him.

"I talked to Johnathan Zucker yesterday about your case..." I began.

"Fuck Johnathan Zucker." My dad barked.

"Dad, let me finish. He says that he argued the Brady violation in your case and that the trial court violated your 6th amendment right to confront the witnesses against you. That's a good thing, he filed a forty-page motion in the Appeals Court a couple of days ago. He explained the issues to me and I believe that they have merit."

"Zin, I know my case better than anybody and I'm telling you that Zucker is arguing the wrong issues. My last lawyer interviewed a ballistic expert and got an affidavit from him stating that it is impossible for nine-millimeter ammo to be fired from a .45 caliber handgun. That bitch nigga Greg Gamble told the jury that I committed the murder with a .45, that they recovered from my apartment, right? Okay, then his expert and the crime scene search officer both testified that they recovered nine-millimeter shell casing from the scene and out of the deceased. Greg Gamble lead the jury to believe that the .45 they recovered from my spot was the actual murder weapon and that it was possible to fire nine-millimeter bullets out of a .45 and that's what me and the new expert are saying that's impossible. I need to be filing a Rule 33 motion under newly discovered evidence."

"That makes sense in theory, but the way it works is a little odd. The Appeals Court heard your case years ago and ruled that you were procedurally barred from trying to introduce that new evidence. Why? Because your first Appeal attorney had ample opportunity to raise that one issue on your first 23-110 motion to the trial court. William Morris only raised one issue on that motion and that was something about your trial attorney to do an adequate pre-trial investigation, failure to procure, and call any defense witnesses, and ineffective assistance of counsel. The trial court disagreed with those assertions and denied the motion.

"The Appellate Court affirmed your convictions and sided with the trial court. Then a week or two later, your lawyer tried to backdoor the court and file a supplemental to the motion with the issues you now cite. The court didn't have to entertain that motion, but it did in the interest of justice. The trial court dismissed your issues as moot and without merit. To try and reraise those issues under Rule 33 would be suicide. Johnathan said that, and I agree with him. The only thing that the higher court will listen to is Constitutional Violations.

"They don't care about the evidence showing this or that or the fact that the witnesses had conflicting accounts of the crime. They don't care about whose lying and what the government didn't prove. That is all evidentiary issues. They remanded your case back to the trial court for that court to deal with all the evidence issues. The Appellate Court reads from a cold record and go by that.

"All they are concerned about is whether or not your trial was conducted fairly. The issues about the Constitutional Violations that Johnathan wants to raise can possibly show that your trial wasn't conducted fairly. If he litigates properly, which I believe he will, and he argues the issues aggressively, he'll be successful. Trust me, I'm a lawyer, I know these things."

"You know these things, huh?"

"Sure do. Just let Johnathan do his thing and you'll be alright. The minute I gave him that twenty-five thousand dollars for your case, I had to trust him."

"How are your bosses doing?"

"Jen and Nikki are fine, thank you for asking. Did you get the pictures I sent you of the three of us?"

"I got 'em, I been meaning to write you back, but you know I hate writing letters."

"Well why don't you call, either? You hate calling too?" I asked.

"C'mon, baby you know it ain't like that. We only get three hundred minutes a month and..."

"...and what? I don't warrant at least fifteen of them?"

"I'ma start calling you more, I promise. I been talking to this new broad that I just met outta St. Louis and she be having me geeking."

"Geeking how, daddy?"

My father smiled, "You don't wanna know."

I laughed at him, I knew full well what he was trying to imply. "Ugh you, nasty dog. You go that woman giving you phone sex, don't you?"

"You got me." My father said, raising both hands in a sign of surrender. "I been in jail for fifteen years and change, I need that shit. I'm tryna holla at one of them snow bunnies you work for. What's up?"

"Daddy you better stop playing with me" I answered playfully. Although I knew that my father was kidding and laughed it off. I still ached for him and the fact that he couldn't have a real relationship with a woman. To me it was torture and I didn't know how he was able to live without kisses, warm embraces, and love. Whenever I felt the way I was feeling now that brought on thoughts of the woman that my father loved with all his heart and sacrificed his life to avenge. My mother Patricia. "Dad?"

My father was looking around the visiting room at all the pretty young girls when my voice distracted him. "What's up, baby?"

"Do you still think about mommy?"

My father looked into my eyes and tried to hold back the pain he felt. "Of course, baby, all the time. Too much actually, have I ever told you that you remind me a lot of your mother?"

"I don't think so." I replied.

"Well you do, your mannerisms are just like hers. The way you tilt your head to the side and bite your lip when you're mad, that's all her. That far away look that you do when you are deep in thought, that's hers too. The way that you play with your hair when you are listening to people, the way you're doing now, your mother did that all the time. I loved your mother with everything inside of me. I still do, how can I not think about her? She is just as much a part of me as you are."

"I didn't mean to make you sad, daddy. I…I…just wondered if you still think about her. I know that life goes on and all that good stuff, but she should never be forgotten. You what I mean?" I asked, struggling to hold back tears of my own.

"I know what you mean, Zin. Trust me your mother will never be forgotten by any of us that knew her. That loved her, that had the chance to experience her love and compassion. Patricia Carter will forever be immortalized in the hearts and minds of every person's life she touched. Especially mines and yours. Let's change the subject before we get to crying up in here. I can't let these niggas see me cry. What's up with your boyfriend Jerome?"

"It's Jermaine, daddy and he's doing just fine." I wanted to tell my father about Quran and the way I felt about him. Maybe he was the yen to my yang and I just didn't know it. I quickly decided against mentioning Quran although I wondered if my father remembered him from the neighborhood. "Jermaine is doing real estate law and he seems to be enjoying himself."

"Are you happy with him, does he satisfy your every need?"

"Yes, and yes!" I answered, looking into my father's eyes. I wondered if he could see inside of my soul through my eyes? I wondered how well my father really knew me after all these years? I wondered if he knew that I was lying through my teeth?

Chapter Ten
Zinfandel
Two weeks later...

The deputy clerk recalled the case, "The United States versus Sean Branch, case number F-7089-92."

"Susan Rosenthal, your honor, on behalf of the government."

I shuffled the papers I was reading together and stood up, "Zinfandel Carter, your honor, for the defendant, Sean Branch."

Judge Hiram Piug-Lugo, adjusted the wire rim glasses attached to his nose. "May I have the note, please. We have a note that the jury sent out." He opened the piece of paper and read it, "It says, 'May we have a copy of the grand jury testimony of Maurice Payne, in reference to his identification of the assailant at the scene of the shooting? Signed by the foreperson. What's the government's position? How do you wish to proceed, Ms. Rosenthal?"

"Well, that was something that Mr. Payne was questioned about and admitted to testifying to in the grand jury."

"Right, I know." Judge Lugo said. "But what do you want to do? My inclination is to bring the jury into the courtroom and read them portions of the grand jury, and that's it."

"I agree, your honor, that's fine."

"Not send a copy back there, because that might unnecessarily highlight..."

"That's fine." Susan Rosenthal repeated.

"...the evidence, but on the other hand, if they're requesting some clarification, they're entitled to have it clarified. What's your position, Ms. Carter?"

"A couple of things." I said as my confidence in an acquittal built every moment that passed. "Of course, they're not entitled, it's my position that they're not entitled to the actual transcript. I..."

"I'm not doing that." The judge interjected.

"…okay, I would simply instruct them that, it's their recollection that controls and they're not entitled to anything more. That testimony was given over seventeen years ago. If you are going to read them portions, which I vehemently object to. He was only questioned about very specific areas. From my recollection, it was just about…"

"Right, it would only be whatever was read to them during trial."

Obviously, it's not going to be the whole transcript, and it's not going to include anything that was not said to them during the trial."

"Well…" I started. "I mean, I would object to that being reread to them. But if it's going to be reread, it would just be those very specific questions and answers."

"Okay."

"Your honor, that would-be page thirteen, starting at line twenty-two, carrying over to page fourteen, down to line twelve." Susan Rosenthal added.

"Okay." Judge Lugo said again. "What we'll do is just bring them in and you can read that to them, but I will tell them they cannot have the transcript. That they're to listen and that from this point further, it is their recollection that controls. If they still don't understand it, then they're not going to get a second chance."

"Okay." Susan said.

"And of course, this is being done under the objection of defense counsel."

The jury was lead into the courtroom a few minutes later. The judge spoke to them for a minute or two and then the transcript was read to them.

"…and which person did you see? Was it Sean Branch that you saw?" Mr. Payne answered in the negative.

"Both counsel, approach the bench." Judge Lugo waiting until both Lawyers came forward. "Is that the only portion of the transcript that you read?"

"I read other portions about him seeing two men, then him saying he saw one man." Susan Rosenthal explained.

"That's in reference to his identification of the assailant at the scene of the robbery or the murder? You read it as if it just spoke of the hospital."

"That's the only identification there was. He didn't identify the defendant then."

"Identification procedure, they're saying in reference with his identification of an assailant at the scene. I think what they're asking for is..."

"Okay, I see, I'll read the other..."

"No." Judge Lugo said, shaking his head. "Read the..."

I knew that I had to say something now or forever hold my peace. "He never identified him. At the hospital or at the scene of the robbery and murder."

The judge ignored me, "The thing is I think the reason they looked confused is because what they were asking about was not the identification, but about his opportunity to observe at the time of the shooting.

"Okay, I'll read back those two sections right there. If..."

I cut the government attorney off. "Your honor, they might mean that at the time of the shooting, when the officers arrived, he said he some dudes. Then he said he saw a dude."

"What's the other part that you read?"

"About the part that he had a small amount of time to take off..."

"Excuse me, your honor, just so that we are clear. Who had a small amount of time to take off?" I asked.

"The witness." Susan answered curtly. "He looked into the shooter's eyes and was afraid that he was going to be shot. That was this portion here."

"Yeah, that's all she read." I agreed.

"Then that's all we need." Judge Lugo concluded. "But it's clear from the reaction to what you read, that's not what they were asking. They were completely confused and dissatisfied with what you read. So go ahead and read the other portion."

I walked back to the defense table and sat down beside Sean. Susan Rosenthal took the floor and began reading.

"...He was asked, he jumped into what car? Your car or another car..."

***

In the cage behind the courtroom, Sean Branch paced the floor. He was dressed in an Armani suit, shirt and tie, with Armani loafers. To me he looked like a well-dressed foreigner.

"I think everything is going to be alright." I said to my client to relax him. "And I still think you should've cut that beard. You look like a middle Eastern terrorist."

Sean Branch laughed, "That's what my girl said yesterday. I can't cut it, my beard and my faith in Allah is what got me this new trial. If the jury comes back with a guilty verdict, trust me, it won't be because of my beard. I feel like..."

The door to the courtroom opening suddenly caused me and Sean to turn our heads.

"Ms. Carter, the jury has reached a verdict."

The U.S. Marshal said and went back into the courtroom.

"Fix your tie." I told Sean. "And remember, don't make any facial expressions and don't stare at the jury. Come on let's go."

Inside the courtroom, me and Sean stood behind the defense table.

The court's deputy said, "Please stand and state your names for the record."

"Susan Rosenthal, on behalf of the government."

"Zinfandel Carter, on behalf of the defendant, Sean Branch, who is present."

"Madame Foreperson, it is my understanding that you have reached a verdict in this case?" Judge Lugo stated.

"We have your honor."

It was at that point, I felt like a ten-year-old little girl again. Every time one of my clients stood in wait of the verdict, it transported me back over sixteen years ago when my father was in the same position.

"Will you please read the verdict form."

"In the case of the United States versus Sean Branch, we find the defendant, not guilty on the count of Felony Murder. We find the defendant, not guilty on the count of First Degree Murder while armed. We find the defendant, not guilty on the charge of Armed Robbery. We find the defendant, not guilty for the charge of carrying a pistol during a crime of violence."

"Is that the verdict of the whole jury, say ye one, say ye all?" Judge Lugo asked.

"Yes, your honor." The jury replied in unison.

"Thank you for being jurors on this case. You are all dismissed. Mr. Branch, you have been found not guilty by a jury of your peers, so I hereby pronounce you a free man."

I was so elated that I turned and hugged Sean, "We did it!"

"Naw, you did it, Ms. Carter."

"Call me Zin. Ms. Carter makes me sound like an old woman. Besides you are a free man, that makes us equals. I'm so happy for you, Sean. You've been in jail for what seventeen…"

"Eighteen years…eighteen years and four months."

"Well, whatever, but now you're free. Let's get out of here. Your first meal as a free man is going to be on me."

***

"This is City Under Siege Fox News at 11 and I am Aniyah Fields…today's top story is the release of D.C.'s most notorious killer ever. After an Appeals Court in the District ruled that Sean Branch's attorney in his 1992 murder trial was ineffective, they ordered a new trial. Sean Branch was dubbed 'Teflon Sean' by the D.C. Police due to his uncanny ability to go to trial for murder after murder and win every time. Until 1992, when up and coming prosecutor Judge Greg Gamble was able to successfully convict him.

"For the past two weeks, Mr. Branch has been on trial for the 1991 robbery and murder of a local drug dealer named Raymond Watson. Today a jury acquitted him in the retrial. So, after being incarcerated for over eighteen years, 'Teflon Sean' is a free man. City Under Siege Fox News had the chance to catch up with the man that put Sean Branch in prison eighteen years ago…"

"This is Maria Wilson, reporting to you live from the U.S. Attorney's Office. Where we were able to get a word with the new Chief U.S. Attorney, Greg Gamble. Mr. Gamble, how do you feel about the release of Sean Branch today in Superior Court?"

"Good evening, Maria. All I can say is that I am flabbergasted at the verdict handed down today by the jury in the retrial. Being an officer of the court and a strong advocate of it's ability to mete out justice. All I can say is that I am truly dismayed by the release of such a dangerous man. Sean Branch, terrorized the streets of the District in the 80's and early 90's.

"I was able to take him off the streets for good and now due to a technicality, he is a free man. I feel sorry for the families of his victims and I feel sorry for the citizens of the District, period. I don't believe that a man as evil as Sean Branch can reform or rehabilitate, so he will kill again. And I will come down from my top floor office, prosecute him personally, and send him back to prison."

Chapter Eleven
Zinfandel

"Congratulations, Zin, you did a wonderful job. It was a big-time case and you responded in a big-time way." Nikki Locks, complimented as she grabbed me and embraced me. "The publicity, that the local news has been giving the Sean Branch acquittal is already starting to garner new clients for all of us. We had twelve calls this morning alone and seven of them asked for you. You're on your way love."

Jen Wentz stepped in and hugged me next. "Don't be thinking that you're going to be taking my office any time soon, but definitely keep up the good work. And that sign out there will read 'Locks, Wentz, and Carter."

"Thanks, you guys, but how can I take the credit when y'all guided my path every step of the way?" I replied.

"The accolades are yours, Zin, accept them." Nikki added.

I humbly nodded my head, then walked into my office. All over my office were roses of every color. "What the...?"

Laughter behind me caused my neck to whip around.

"The look on your face is priceless." Nikki said. "These flowers came this morning, too, a whole van load."

"But who...?"

"I took the liberty of interrogating the delivery man, he said that their shop received the order online. Read the card over on your desk and see who sent them."

On my desk laid a small card. I picked it up and read it, aloud. "There is not a flower in creation as beautiful as you. But you do have a little competition, so I sent a few. Call me when you get these. Signed QB!" I looked back at Nikki who was now joined by Jen and they both wore smiles.

"Signed by QB...unless Sean Branch changed his first name, they aren't from him. So, who is QB?" Nikki asked.

Jen put her hands on her hips and imitated a black woman's agitated posture. "There are three explanations for who QB could be. One...you helped somebody from N.Y. and they left the initials to represent their hood."

Nikki and I looked at Jen like she had gone nuts.

"Duh, I'm talking about Queensbridge. It's a neighborhood in Queens, New York. Or you contacted Lil' Kim and offered her your services and you haven't told me and Nikki."

"I get that one." I replied laughing. "Lil' Kim's nickname is Queen Bee, right?"

"Right, let me find out y'all don't watch BET. The last and final suggestion is that you've made a helluva impression on one Mr. Quran Bashir. You do remember Mr. Bashir, right Zin?"

"Of course."

"Small world, huh?"

Nikki interrupted the word game. "I'm lost, who is Quran Bashir?"

"Quran is a friend of David Battle, he paid all of David's legal fees." I explained. "I ran into him here at the office and realized that he was the same Quran Bashir that I grew up with. I have no idea why he would send me all those flowers."

"Like I said, you must've made a helluva impression or the flowers are for old time sake. In any event, it's still good for business. Mr. Bashir will bring us all his criminal buddies to defend and we'll all get rich. I have a ten, a.m. prelim in district court. I'll see you ladies in the p.m. smooches." Jen said before departing.

Nikki hugged me again, "Congratulations, again, Zin and keep up the good work. I'll be in my office if you need me." Nikki turned to walk away, but stopped in her tracks. "I remember the days when men sent me surprise flowers. Enjoy it while it lasts."

I stood beside my desk and watched Nikki leave the office, and close the door. I grabbed one long stemmed rose from the bouquet and sniffed it. What would it hurt to just call him? I walked around my desk and sat down. Then I grabbed the phone and dialed the number on the card.

Quran answered on the second ring, "Hello?"

"Thank you for the flowers, they're beautiful."

"But not as beautiful as you, Zin. I'm glad you decided to call, I miss you."

"How could I not call? You've transformed my office into a flower shop." I didn't respond to the latter part of his comment.

"I need to see you, Zin. We have unfinished business between us. Why are you tryna act like you don't feel the connection between us?"

"Quran...I can't do this, right now, I..."

"You have a boyfriend, you told me that before, but that doesn't stop our connection. Your boyfriend is your problem, not mine. See, that's the problem, Zin. You have a boyfriend when you need a man. I know that you feel something for me. I read it in your eyes the last time I saw you. Why are you tryna fight it?"

Everything that Quran said was true, but I couldn't admit that to him. I had to keep my advantage and not give it away. But at the same time, I knew that I didn't want to lose him completely. All of a sudden, I felt like a musical note trapped inside of an Erykah Badu lyric. The feeling inside of me that I felt for Quran was strong, the longing filled with lust. But for some reason, I kept thinking about Jermaine and the fact that he didn't deserve my disloyalty.

"Quran...I...I...I'm in a situation."

"A situation? So, what are you saying to me, Zin?" Quran asked.

The lyrics of Erykah Badu's song came to mind and wouldn't leave my head. "I guess I'll have to see you in the next lifetime..." With that said and a tear forming in the corner of my eyes, I gently hung up the phone.

Chapter Twelve
Jihad Bashir

"Hold on, start over. What happened again?"

"Damn, goofy ass nigga, pay attention." Tabu told me.

"I was thinking about something else, my bad, tell me."

"Me and Que scooped the nigga from his house. He comes out all dressed like a ninja and shit. Like he ready to body a hundred muthafuckas…"

I drove to Riley Street in Northeast with visions of murder on my mind, but I couldn't help but laugh at the way my brother told the story about Mann's death.

"…Que told him that Lil Coo-Wop from around the Park had ran into a nigga over the jail and word got back through you…"

"Through me?"

"Yeah, nigga. Through you, Que is just making shit up as we ride. Mann tells Que that he's gonna fuck Lil' Jay and nem around because that's who Que told him had killed Landa. Something about a set up and all this and that. Anyways, then Mann asks where we were going when he saw the truck headed towards Suitland Parkway. Que tells him that we gotta go and get the big guns out of a car in Oak Park. All the while, we passing the weed back and forth. Que tells me to turn on Ivanhoe Street. Moe, you know that street dark and spooky as shit."

I laughed at the deception and the fact that Ivanhoe Street was the perfect murder spot. I would've never let a muthafucka trick me like that. I envisioned the nearly abandoned tenements on the Southwest street and laughed more.

"…car parked on the street. Ain't but like three cars on the entire street. Que tells me to pull by the black four door Buick. He tosses Mann the keys and I'm thinking that Que is about to hit him right there, but to my surprise as always, big bro covered all his bases. The keys went to the Buick…"

"Buick? Whose Buick was it?" I asked.

"Fuck if I know. All I know is that Que tells Mann to get the guns out of the trunk, while he goes in a bitch house and use the bathroom. I'm thinking to myself, 'this nigga is stupid as shit'. Quran ducks behind another car, while Mann pops the trunk of the Buick. Que creeps up behind him and knocks his shit loose. With that pretty ass four fifth. He fucked slim up, then me and Que lifts the nigga and tosses his ass in the trunk.

"And he's still in the trunk?"

"As far as I know, ain't nothing been on the news about finding no body in the trunk nowhere. But check this out…as we go back to the car, Que tells me that he's glad he killed Mann. Why? Because he said he hated the fact that Mann always smoked up all the weed."

Me and my brother laughed hysterically.

"That was a weed smoking nigga, wasn't he, slim?"

"I ain't hip." Tabu replied. "That nigga wasn't around me like that. He was you and Que's man."

"You shittin' me, that was all big bruh. That nigga was a…then again, fuck that nigga. Are you ready to put this work in?"

Tabu pulled the Orkin hat down over his head and said, "Let's do it, I got the bitch, you got Drew."

"You remember what I said we gon' do if the dude ain't in the house when we get there?"

Tabu turned and faced me with an exasperated look, "Moe, what the fuck, am I retarded to you or something? I got you on everything, we gon' make the bitch call Drew if he's not there. We surprise him coming in and that's that."

I nodded my head and focused on the task ahead. The humidity outside was stifling and the A.C. inside the van wasn't all that great. Perspiration ran down my back and under my arms. That was normal for me though. The more I thought about that bitch nigga Andrew Everette, the more I gripped the steering wheel and my knuckles whitened. Me, him, and Lonnie had all come up in the juvenile joints together and for him to cross Lonnie over a bitch was the softest shit a gangsta could do. I laughed silently, as I thought about how his weak for some pussy ass was about to go and meet Allah and he didn't even know it. I turned off 4th Street onto Riley Street and parked the van. I got out and walked to the back of the Orkin van and opened its back doors. I handed a bag of rodent killing equipment to Tabu, while I picked up the clipboard.

"I thought you said she lived in a house?" Tabu asked eyeing the four-unit brown brick apartment buildings.

"I never said it was, when we say where a person lives, we call apartments houses, you know that. The building is only a four unit and that's better for us. Besides, she's on the first floor anyway. Again, better for us."

"Do you see the dude's car out here?"

"I don't know what the fuck that rat is driving now. It's been a while since I seen him. C'mon!"

The door to the building was unlocked. There were people congregated on both sides of Riley Street, but none around or in the building at 419. The hallway light was flickering as we entered the building, but I could still read the numbers on the doors. I knocked on Drew's door, his woman's name was Thursday, a well-known hood-rat in the city.

"Who is it?" a female voice called out.

"Pest control, ma'am. The owner of the building called us. Says he's been getting too many complaints about rodents by tenants." I announced.

The locks on the door clicked and then it opened. I recognized Thursday instantly from seeing her at clubs.

"Rodents, ain't nobody said nothing to me 'bout no rodents." She said defiantly.

"Just doing my job ma'am, a rat was spotted entering your apartment recently. It says here…hold on…" I looked at the clipboard. "…apartment two, three, and four. We just wanna spray some new stuff."

"New stuff?"

"Yeah, it's harmless to people. Odorless, colorless, but deadly to rats."

"A'ight come in, but damn why did y'all wait so late to come." Thursday asked, then lead the way into her apartment.

"I apologize for the inconvenience, but hell, it's been a long day. We been at work, me, and my partner here since seven a.m. this morning. Are you home alone…?"

Thursday stopped, turned, and was about to speak, but must have decided to keep quiet." She nodded.

"That's too bad, then." I said as I sat down a spray container that resembled a fire extinguisher.

"Why is that?" Thursday asked.

I pulled the gun from the small of my back. "Because I was hoping that Drew was here already. Tab, go and check the rooms back there. You made a terrible mistake, Thursday. It is Thursday, ain't it?"

"Who the hell are you and what…?"

"Shut your rat loving ass up. Sit down on the couch and keep quiet or I'ma down your ass right now."

Seconds later, Tabu returned to the living room.

"Empty, bruh."

That's when I smelled something burning. I sniffed again, "What's that smell?"

"I was cooking when you knocked. The chicken is burning on the stove." Thursday replied. "Listen, whatever Drew did to y'all ain't got nothing to do with me."

"We are just friends…"

"Tab, go and turn the fire off on that chicken before the house gets too smokey." I told my brother. To Thursday I said, "Friends, huh? Gotta be with benefits. I saw the movie, I like that joint, but I disagree with you on one point. You have everything to do with this. You were my man's ride or die bitch, until he got locked up. That was one thing, but you compounded your sins, by fuckin' wit' the rat that put him in jail."

"Bit-Bit…" Thursday said as the color drained from her face.

"I call him Lonnie, I ain't never like that Bit-Bit shit, geekin' ass shit. But yeah that would be him. He loved your ass and you crossed that man like that. Well, I'm here to tell you that you get the chance to redeem yourself right now. Get on your cell phone and say whatever you gotta say, but get Drew ass here in the next thirty minutes, or I'ma get mad and kill you. You hear me?"

Chapter Thirteen
Khitab 'Tabu' Bashir

"I hear you. I hear you. My cellphone is in my purse." The woman said defeated.

"And where is your purse?" Jihad asked.

She pointed over by the T.V. and I saw the black Prada bag laying on the stand beside the flat screen.

"I got it, slim." I offered and went to retrieve the purse. I handed it to the woman. Jihad took three steps, then snatched the purse out of the woman's hands before she could dig her hand inside it. He gave me a look that could melt ice and then opened the purse. He reached inside and pulled out a small caliber handgun. After tucking the gun, he reached in, and pulled out a cellphone. Once again, he looked at me and ice grilled me. I figured he was cursing me out to himself because I hadn't thought that the bitch would possibly pull out a weapon from the purse.

I ice grilled his ass right back as if to say, *'A'ight, nigga, I fucked up, but you caught it, so the fuck what...get over it.'*

"Dial the number and put him on speaker. If you say anything I don't like, it's over. Your head explodes, and we leave. You decide, then make the call." Jihad ordered.

I stood beside the wall near the hall and watched as the bitch made the call. She was a bad muthafucka, and as phat as she was, I couldn't help but want to fuck her. Her flip flops were cheap, but the pedicure on her toes wasn't. A gold toe ring on her left foot sparkled and complimented the gold ankle bracelet around her ankle. Her sweatpants hugged every curve and fit her pussy snug to where the contours of it could be seen. A matching grey t-shirt rounded the outfit and hugged her breasts so tight that I could make out the imprint of her large nipples.

"Hello? Drew...where you at?" the woman said into the phone.

"I'm around R Street, why what's up?" Drew answered.

"Did somebody outside owe you some money?"

"Naw...why?"

"Because the little dude Tonio just gave me three thousand dollars and said it was yours. Maybe he made a mistake, maybe it's mine…"

"Yours? That's my money and I'm on my way to get it before you spend a dime of it. You cook?"

"Yeah, chicken, hurry up because I'm horny too."

"Say no more, I'm getting in the car now."

I watched as the woman ended the call and tossed her cell on the seat cushion next to her on the couch. She dropped her head into her hands.

"You did good boo, real boo. Tab, you watch her while I got into the hall and wait for Drew."

"I got her."

As soon as the door to the apartment closed, the woman looked at me and said, "Are y'all gonna kill me?"

I didn't respond, if only she knew what was about to happen to both of them. Suddenly, I had an idea, but I'd wait until Jihad came back with Drew to act on it. A wicked smile crossed my face as I looked straight into the woman's eyes. She read my eyes perfectly and all she could do was drop her head into her hands again.

Chapter Fourteen
Jihad

I pulled my hat low and stood out in the hallway with one of the spray canisters. Since the hall light was already flickering, it would be hard for Drew to make out my face. I walked outside the building and pretended to spray pesticide all over the bottom of the walls on both sides of the door. Car after car pulled into the block, but none stopped near 419. I checked my watch nine minutes had gone by since Drew told Thursday, he was on his way.

R. Street was only about ten blocks away from Riley Street, so the man had to be nearby. As if my thought was the cue for him to show up, a beige Acura SUV pulled onto the block and parked. I recognized Drew instantly, quickly I sprayed all around the entrance to 419. I wanted Drew to see an exterminator spraying. I stepped into the building and started spraying the stairs.

Seconds later, Drew walked in, with my back turned, I could tell that he was at Thursday's door. I switched the spray canister over to my left hand and gripped my gun in my right. I heard a knock, then the door opened, spinning around quickly, I stepped behind Drew, and put the hammer in his back.

"Go 'head in or I can kill you right here." I walked behind Drew into the apartment, and watched as the scene registered in his head. Thursday, was still on the couch and Tabu's gun was aimed at her head.

"Bitch, I swear to God I'ma kill you for this." Drew hissed through clenched teeth.

"Rat nigga, you ain't gon' do shit but die, when I say you die. As for your rat lovin' bitch, you ain't gon kill her. You know why?"

"Why?" Drew asked dumbly.

"Because I'ma kill her, better yet…he gon' kill her. Tab, shoot that bitch!" I ordered.

"Shoot me for what!" Thursday screamed.

"For fuckin' wit' this rat..." Before I could finish my sentence, my brother moved up on Thursday, and shot her in the face. Her body fell back on the couch.

"What the fuck...!" Drew uttered.

"Jihad...I got an idea, before we kill this nigga, make him strip.?"

"Strip nigga, go head and kill me, I ain't doing no strip..."

I fired two shots into the back of Andrew Everette's head, quickly ending his life. Tabu walked over and turned Drew's body over. Then raced into the kitchen and came with a skillet.

"What the hell are you doing with that?" I asked.

"Watch." Tabu said and sat the skillet down.

I could hear the grease inside the skillet sizzling. "Slim we ain't got time for this geekin' ass shit, let's bounce."

"Chill out nigga." Tabu, pulled Drew's pants and boxers down. Then he grabbed the skillet and poured the hot grease on Drew's dick and balls. "Now that's what you call a real hot nigga."

***

"Did you touch anything in there when I stepped outside?" I asked Tabu.

"Naw, just the skillet and the knob that turned the fire back on under the skillet, but I had my gloves on. You?"

"Nothing, I had my gloves on, too." I looked at the gun as Tabu disconnected his sound suppression device that we called mufflers. "Tab what happened to the Glock .40, you had?"

"I lost it, why?" he replied.

"You lost it?" I repeated and decided to drop the subject because Tabu was gonna make me curse his ass out. "Did you talk to Quran, today?"

"Yeah, about an hour before I came to meet you. He said something about hooking up with the dude Sean Branch."

"The dude that just got out of prison?"

"I guess so, you know another Sean Branch." Tabu snorted.

"You gotta smart ass mouth for a nigga who like looking at dicks." I joked.

"Fuck you nigga. I'm scared of two things and that's a faggie's asshole and dicks. That's why I poured that hot grease on that hot nigga back there. I emasculated that nigga even in death. So hopefully, he can't take a piss in the hellfire."

I laughed at what Tabu said, "Let's go and dump this van."

Anthony Fields

Chapter Fifteen
Quran

I looked at the address that was text messaged into my phone, then at the one on the house where I now sat. They were one and the same. Hitting the send button on my phone, I waited for a connection.

"Slim, I'm outside, come on out."

Five minutes later, the door to the red brick house on Montana Avenue opened. I looked in the face of my old friend and smiled. The man had aged a little and his hair was now peppered with specks of grey, but the face was the same. The eyes were still cold and heartless. The difference about Sean Branch was the beard. The beard gave him a whole new look. As he approached the car, I stepped out and embraced him.

"Slim, it's good to see you. I thought this day would never come."

Sean broke the embrace. "A lot of people thought this day would never come. But it has, and it's been a long time coming. I waited patiently for eighteen years for this day. I appreciate everything you did for me, Ock."

"Don't sweat it, I did what I was supposed to do. So, what are your plans? I figured since you only been home a few days you'd probably be still in some pussy."

"That will come later. Right now, I wanna visit a few people and I need you to help me out."

Without saying another word, Sean looked into my eyes, letting his silence speak. I heard what his silence was saying loud and clear.

"Hop in and tell me where you wanna go." I said, getting back in the car.

After a few minutes of complete silence, Sean said, "I just talked to another old friend. He tells me that a good friend of mine is staying in a house on Longfellow Street and that he just happens to be home right now. I wanna pay him a visit."

There was no need for anything else to be said. I strapped my seatbelt on and pulled away from the curb. In front of 712 Longfellow Street, on a porch, sat two women, and a man. The man was one he knew very well. Sean looked into the man's face through the tinted glass window of the Jaguar and smiled. Maurice 'Reese' Payne was an old friend. One who had once sat at Sean's mother's table and ate food. For years Sean said he wondered why Reese had fingered him for the murder of Raymond Watson and not the person who had actually committed the murder. Sean was sitting in the car when the murder took place, and everybody knew that.

But for some reason Reese had put the beef on him and nobody could figure out why. That was why Sean wanted to visit his old friend. He wanted to find out why he was made the escape goat and then he'd kill Reese.

"I've seen enough, Ock, go ahead and pull off. I'ma come back later and have a talk with my old friend.

***

When it was pitch black outside in the wee hours of the morning, we made our way through the darkness. I followed Sean up a back alley to the 6th house on the block. I knew that as we climbed the ladder of the fire escape that we were in the back of 712 Longfellow, the house that I'd taken Sean to earlier.

"Slim, they might got an alarm on the house." I whispered as I ascended the fire escape.

"All these years you been in the streets and you haven't learned shit. Black people don't get alarms on their houses. Consider what I'm about to say as a lesson. When we were sitting out front of the house earlier, I scanned the doors and windows. When houses have alarm systems they announced that with little stickers in the windows or on the door. 'Protected by Hawkey Alarms' or something like that. The alarm companies believe that those stickers in themselves serve as deterrents for potential burglars." With that said Sean turned around and used a small device to cut a hole in the window of the back door. As he used that same instrument to suction the cut piece of glass out of its place, I expected an alarm to go off. When it didn't I breathed a sigh of relief.

Sean smiled in the darkness and I was able to see his teeth through the hole in his mask. "Messing with me, you gon' learn something, youngin'."

Once the glass was removed, Sean was able to squeeze his arm the short distance through the locking mechanism on the door. In seconds, he disabled it and opened the door. "C'mon, Ock walk softly."

I followed Sean through the house.

"You take the downstairs and I'll take upstairs. If there's anybody down there, meet me in the hall at the top of the stairs.

Before I could respond, Sean took off up the stairs. I tiptoed through the living room and checked the closets, then the kitchen. A door to the left of the refrigerator caught my attention. That must be the basement.

I turned the knob on the door after pressing my ear up against it. I heard nothing, so I opened the door and descended the stairs. The hall light made it possible for me to see everything. After seeing that the basement was empty, I went back upstairs. At the top of the stairs, in the hallway stood Sean.

"There are two bedrooms on this floor." Sean whispered. "The smaller room behind us is empty. The big bedroom over there is occupied. There are two people in the bed and I'm willing to bet one of them is Reese."

I watched as Sean pulled a backpack over his shoulders and opened it. Something inside the bag seemed to be moving. Then I heard a sound, "What the fuck...?"

Sean smiled again behind the mask, but said nothing. Instead, he pulled a silenced 9mm from the bag. Zipping the bag up, he said, "I know this house has to have a basement, right?"

I nodded my head.

"Good, we gon' take them to the basement and I'll handle it from there."

We entered the room and stood at both sides of the bed. Sean stood over the male and pressed the silenced gun to his head. Then he smacked the man with the handgun.

"Wake your bitch ass up!" Sean barked.

The half-asleep man jumped and sat up startled. The woman sleeping beside him, opened her eyes as well.

Before the man could say a word, Sean shushed him. "Shhhh…don't make a sound until I tell you to. If you make any sudden moves, I'ma put your brains and shit all over the wall. Get up out of the bed slow and keep your hands where I can see them."

The man did as he was instructed.

"Bring her and come on." Sean told me. Then to the man he said, "We going to the basement. Lead the way and remember what I said about any sudden moves."

I watched Sean pick up the bag in the hallway and lead the man down the stairs. I motioned for the woman to follow her man. The woman in front of me was a sexy one. She was clad only in black lace lingerie and her shapely thighs and big ass was causing me to lose focus. "Snap out of it, nigga." I scolded myself.

In the basement, I watched the woman lay at my feet as Sean went to work on the man. Sean made the man lie on his back and stretch his legs straight out. Then he pulled duct tape out of his backpack and wrapped it around the man's ankles.

"Put your arms straight up and out above your head." Sean said as he wrapped tape around the man's wrists. When he was satisfied that the man was secured, he said, "You can speak now if you want to."

"Who are you, and why are you doing this to me?" the man asked.

"Do you really wanna know?" Sean asked him.

"Yeah."

"Okay, I'll tell you…" Sean said and removed his mask. "…but you just killed your girlfriend over there. The less she knew the better, but now she's seen my face and I can't let her live."

The girl across the room started crying.

"Shut the fuck up bitch!" Sean shouted. "I don't have any sympathy for you. In the next life you'll learn to pick your men more wisely. Que, if that bitch makes another sound kill her ass."

"Sean please..." the man started.

"*Sean please* what? Go 'head and finish your statement. Sean please what?"

"Don't do this, slim! Don't do this to me, slim!"

"Don't do this to you? Don't do this to you! Que do you hear this nigga? That's some wild shit. This bitch nigga testified against me in trial and said that I committed a murder that I didn't. I been in jail for eighteen years fighting to prove my innocence and I finally did. Now I'm here and this nigga gon' tell me not to do this to him. Bitch nigga, what about what you did to me? Huh? Does that even matter to you? Naw, I guess it don't, huh? It's all good though, I don't even wanna know the answer to that. But what I do wanna know is why? Why did you do that to me? Why did you cross me like that, knowing I didn't kill Ray? You was right there. You saw who did it and still told them people it was me. Why?"

The man on the ground started crying, but never answered.

"No answer, huh?" Sean asked as he reached into the backpack and extracted a portable CD player. "There was a song that came out right before I went back to court. When I was in Colorado waiting to come back to D.C. I used to wait all day for it to come on. The song sums up everything I felt while doing those eighteen years, listen to it."

Sean hit a button on the CD player and seconds later a song could be heard...

'Sometimes, it feels like everything is passing me by
And every now and then, it feels like
My ship has sailed away
But I...I gotta be strong...gotta hold on
Cause it won't be long, now the tides is coming in

I see which way it's flowing out there on the ocean
I know my ship is coming in
Just past the horizon and right where the sky ends
I know my ship is coming in
Don't keep me hangin'
I've been waiting here too long for this moment
My ship has finally come...'

Sean turned the music down a little.

"People say that music calms the savage beast. I can go for that." He went back into the backpack and pulled out a small cage of some kind. "That's why my partner here been chilling. He likes music, too."

'...will travel the seven seas
I will even go wherever the wind blows me
I'll do anything to find my destiny
It's like fighting with gravity
And it's pulling me down
If this world is really round
Then somebody tell me why
It's so hard to come around...'

Sean hit the button on the CD player and silenced it. "That joint a bad muthafucka ain't it? Now let me ask you this again. Why did you put the beef on me when Ray got killed? Had I ever done anything to you?"

Again, the man didn't respond.

"Okay Reese, have it your way. I saw something in a movie once and even read about somebody doing this in one of them street novels. I always wanted to see if the shit was real, let's see."

I watched the condemned man's eyes grow as big as tennis balls when Sean released the rodent from its cage. That rat had to be at least seven inches long and fat. It looked as if it was pregnant. Sean guided the rat along until it sat in the middle of the man's stomach. Sean went back into the backpack and pulled out something wrapped in newspaper. He unwrapped a glass py-rex pot, and put the pot over the rat. Then went back into the backpack again, extracted a small acetylene blowtorch, and made a long blue flame shoot out. Sean put the torch down and taped up the man's mouth. Then picked up the torch and placed the flame at the glass surface. As the glass heated up the rat inside went crazy. The squeal of the rat could be heard clearly as it desperately tried to find a way out of its prison.

Suddenly, the muffled screams of the man on the ground could be heard over all else. The rat was now gnawing at the man's stomach. Sean kept the torch on the glass pot until he saw the first signs of blood, then he pulled it away.

"I guess that shit really does work, huh? If the rat can't get out of the pot. It will burrow through human flesh to escape. I got all night, Reese, tell me why you crossed me, and I'll stop your pain and suffering. Do you wanna talk now?"

The frightened man nodded his head repeatedly.

Sean snatched the tape off the man's mouth, "Talk to me, slim."

Maurice 'Reese' Payne gasped for air and kept his eyes on the rat in the glass pot. "Kenny made me do it...get the rat off me. What the fuck is it doing to me?"

"What is it doing? How should I know, ask the rat, y'all speak the same language? You do speak rat, right?"

"Get the rat off me and I'll talk."

"Not until you tell me everything. You said Kenny made you do it? What Kenny?"

"Kenneth Sparrow, Kenny had a plan. He wanted to run R. Street. He said he was tired of taking orders from Neugie, Black, and Kevin. He wanted to get rid of them and take their spot on the block. He was the one that started the whole investigation on the R. Street Crew. He contacted that detective...the white dude that used to be coming around..."

"Gossip." Sean interjected, reflecting.

"Yeah, him, Gossip put Kenny in touch with the Feds and he helped him build the case on everybody...Mack, Dre, Jeff, Tim, Black, Neugie, Kevin, Greg, Donnell...everybody. He even told them some old shit on Nehemiah. Since Nehemiah was already in they left him alone…"

"But they still went at Bruce, he was already in too."

"Bruce was different, Kenny hated Bruce for other reasons. He didn't hate the others. He just wanted them out of the way so that he could take over."

"So, where do I come into all of this? I ain't from no muthafuckin' R. Street. Why did he target me?"

"Kenny knew that you fucked with Neugie and 'nem real tough. He knew that once he crossed them and it became public, they'd be out for blood. And the only person that Kenny was afraid of was you. It was always Sean Branch this and Sean Branch that. He'd heard all the stories about you killing niggas. He told me one day that you had killed all your friends and that if you'd killed your friends, a muthafucka that you didn't fuck with was up shit creek. He wanted you out of the way, too. He figured that Neugie and 'nem would send you after him and that was his biggest fear. He was still tryna decide how to get rid of you when that night happened."

"What night?"

"The night Mike killed Raymond. We were all out there when it happened. You were sitting in the car when Mike walked over and shot Raymond. Everybody ran but me, I stood there and watched Mike stand over Ray and empty the gun in him. I watched as he walked back to the car you were sitting in, got in, and pulled off. Kenny was the first person to come back to the scene. He got in my ear, back then I was… I was smoking coke in my weed and didn't nobody know it but Kenny. I was buying coke from him and he'd front me some. He offered me a whole key of coke to say it was you that killed Ray. A key of coke…back then was like being a real live Colombian. Sean, I'm sorry! Please forgive me…I…I…I was strung out on that shit, dawg. I didn't know what I was doing. Please, you gotta believe me, dawg!"

"I believe you, slim. That's not the issue. The issue is the fact that I trusted you. I dealt with you fair and we grew up together. And you still managed to throw all that away. You crossed me for a key of coke. I did eighteen years in jail for a punk ass key of cocaine. That's fucked up, slim."

"Sean…I…I…can make it right, dawg!"

"No thanks, dawg. I can make it right on my own." Sean said. "Aye dawg, do you love her?"

Reese followed Sean's gaze that fell on the woman lying on the floor at Quran's feet. "Leave her out of this Sean…please dawg! She's innocent in this, she ain't but twenty years old and shorty is thorough. If you let her go, I swear to you, dawg she ain't gon tell nobody about this. Let her go, dawg, please!"

"Shorty thorough, huh?" Sean said and walked over to where the girl lay. "What's your name, boo?"

"Yoni."

"Are you thorough, Yoni?"

The girl nodded her head.

"It's your lucky day, Yoni. But let me make one thing clear to you. My name is Sean Branch. Ask your family about me, if you breathe one word to anybody about what happened here tonight, I'ma find you. Then I'ma kill your whole family, old people, kids, and all. I'ma wipe out your whole existence. Do you understand that?"

The girl nodded her head as tears fell down her cheeks.

"Say a prayer to God before I kill you, you got one minute." Sean told Reese.

"Our father which art in heaven…"

That's as far as Reese got before Sean shot him in the face repeatedly. "Wrong prayer, dawg. You should've said, In the name of Allah."

***

"Do you really think the girl will keep quiet?" I asked Sean as he drove.

"I think she'll keep quiet, if she knows what's good for her she will. I got one more person to deal with before I can live in peace."

"Who is that?"

"My baby mother, I'ma make sure she dies a slow, terrible death."

Chapter Sixteen
Quran

"This is City Under Siege Fox News at Four. I am your anchor-woman, Maria Wilson, reporting live from our studios in downtown Washington, D.C. Today's top story is the historic speech that President Barack Obama gave in the Middle East today. In a packed capacity University in Cairo Egypt. President Obama called for reconciliation, tolerance, and peace. He implored the world's Muslim leaders to forgive America for the many years of brutality and sanction imposed by the United States...

"In other news today, a Southeast man was sentenced to death by a judge in Beaumont, Texas. Thirty-year-old Joseph Ebron, who was serving time for first degree murder, was sentenced to death row for the 2005 killing of his cellmate, a District native. Also in other news, D.C. police were called to the scene of a gruesome discovery.

"While fishing on the Waterfront, a man discovered what he thought was a large hurt fish floating. He later realized what he found was a body. Authorities have not revealed the identity of the person floating in the river, but they have confirmed that it was a black female and that she was possibly killed before she was stabbed repeatedly in both eyes, her throat was cut, and she was disemboweled. More on that story when news becomes available..."

I clicked the remote and changed the channel. As I spooned cereal into my mouth, I smiled. The D.C. police had no clue who the woman was they pulled out of the river, but I did. She was Raquel Dunn, the mother of Sean Branch's nineteen-year-old daughter. I'd personally witnessed Sean's brand of torture and the sight of what he did to his baby mother would live in my head for the rest of my days. My cell phone vibrating broke my reverie. The caller I.D. said 'private' and I started not to answer, but curiosity got the better of me.

"Hello."

"Que, it's me."

"Tabu?"

"Yeah, I'm in a jam bruh."

"Jam? What kinda jam?" I said rising from the table.

"I'm locked up, Que I..."

"Tab you calling me from where?"

"From the police station. I called Jihad, but he didn't answer. I need a..."

"What are you locked up for Tab?" I asked incredulously.

"A gun charge, they found a gun in my car." Tab replied meekly.

"Who locked you up?"

"Park police."

"Shit!" I exclaimed, shaking my head.

"I need a lawyer, Que. They gone hold me and make me go to court."

"Was that gun...you know?"

"Naw. This one was brand new."

"Why did they stop you?"

"The inspection sticker expired and I..."

"Didn't I tell your stupid ass not to drive that piece of shit?" I exploded. "Huh? Why the hell you don't never listen to...you'll have a lawyer in court tomorrow."

I disconnected the call and ran my hands over my face. My younger brother was always fucking up and I was sick of it. I should kill the stupid ass nigga myself. As bad as I wanted to kill my brother, I knew I couldn't and wouldn't because above all else I love him. I picked the phone back up and dialed a number I hadn't dialed in a while. When I heard her voice on the other end of the phone, all time stopped, and I forgot what I was calling for.

"'Hello?" Zin, said into the phone for the 3rd time. "Quran?"

"Yeah it's me..."

"Quran, I thought..."

"Zin, I need your help. This is a business call, my brother got locked up today and he needs a lawyer. You told me to call you if I ever needed a lawyer. Well here I am, can you represent my brother?"

"What kind of beef is it, Quran?"

"A gun charge."

"That's it?"

"That's it."

"Where is he now?" Zin asked.

"He said it was Park that locked him up, so I guess he's still down Anacostia."

"Okay, they'll process him there and then take him to CCB. I'll enter an appearance in court for him in the morning. What's his name, again? I haven't seen him in years."

"Khitab Bashir. He looks just like me, only younger and a little taller."

"I'm on it, I'll call you after I see him."

"Good, thanks Zin."

"Bye, Quran I'll call you tomorrow."

Chapter Seventeen
Zinfandel

"Appearing on behalf of Khitab Bashir, your honor." I stood and addressed the court when my client's name was called, and he was ushered into the courtroom. "Who is now present."

"Devin York, your honor, on behalf of the government. Your honor the defendant, is on probation for an earlier charge of the same caliber. Attempts to reach his probation officer have failed. We ask that Mr. Bashir be held on a B1A and 1322C."

"Your honor," I said calmly, rising from the defense table. "The government is requesting a dangerous criminal hold..."

"I know what a 1322C is Ms. Carter." The judge stated cutting me off.

"I'm sure you do, your honor, but with all due respect, a 1322C is used to detain a person accused of a violent offense..."

"And you don't consider driving while under the influence and carrying an illegal firearm dangerous?"

"Dangerous yes, but violent, no. Mr. Bashir, didn't hurt anyone..."

"Ms. Carter, I am not going to sit here and play a semantics game with you. This is Mr. Bashir's second offense of the same nature and he's on probation. Obviously, Mr. Bashir doesn't care about that fact and to me that makes him dangerous and potentially violent. I'm going to agree with the government and order the defendant to be held. Maybe when you come in front of me the next time, you can convince me that your client isn't the person I think he is. His next appearance is set..."

***

"What happened in there, where's Tabu?" Quran asked, as soon as I exited the courtroom.

"The judge ordered him held. Why didn't you tell me that your brother was on probation for another gun charge? How can I represent him and don't know all the facts?"

"Probation! I didn't know anything about no probation. Tabu never told me about no other gun charge or no probation."

I looked at Quran with a vexed glare. "So, you're telling me that you didn't know about any of that?"

"On my dead mother, I didn't."

"Well they held him on a 1322C. That's a dangerous criminal hold. Khitab has to be back in court on the 23rd. That's five business days from now. He's probably going to be held at the jail. Go and see him and find out whatever else we don't know. I think..."

Suddenly Quran reached out and grabbed my hand.

"Quran...what are you..." I started.

"Here." Quran replied, putting a wad of bills in my palm. "That should cover everything you might have to do for my brother."

I felt electricity shoot through me as I stared down at Quran's hand still holding mine. The tingles that emanated from my toes and reached upward had me feeling uneasy and uncertain. "Quran..."

Before I could say another word, Quran simply kissed my hand and then let it go. Then he turned and walked away. Staring at the back of his head, I desperately wanted to call his name.

But the voice inside me spoke yet again... "Don't do it, Zin. Let him go!" And that's exactly what I did.

***

I checked my Blackberry Pearl's calendar as I stood in line at the Bank of America. I had two court appearances left for today, but both were scheduled for later.

"Hello, I would like to make a deposit." I said to the teller as I counted out the ten thousand dollars in cash, Quran had just given me.

After leaving the bank, I decided to be a little spontaneous. I dialed a number on my cell phone.

"Bancroft, Sheffler, and Dunmore. How many I direct your call?"

"Could you please connect me to Jermaine Mendenhall."

"And who may I ask is calling?"

"Zinfandel Carter."

"Hold, please."

A few seconds later, Jermaine came on the line. "Zin, what's up."

"Are you really busy?" I asked.

"Kinda, sorta, why, what's up?"

"I wanna treat you to lunch and dessert. Can you get away for about an hour?"

"Let me see...I have a one-o-clock, a two-thirty, and a three-fifteen. I have to prepare for the one-o-clock, but I guess I can get away for a while. How does forty-five minutes sound?"

"Great, we might have to skip lunch and go straight to the dessert. I'll be there to get you in ten minutes. Bye."

***

"Zin, baby you gonna mess up my Brooks Brothers slacks!" Jermaine protested as I straddled him.

It was the wrong thing to say to me at the wrong moment, but I wasn't paying Jermaine any mind. In my mind, he was Quran. I hiked up my skirt and moved my panties to the side. I grabbed Jermaine's dick with my right hand and guided him into me.

"Ummm!"

"Damn, you wet as shit, Zin! You are going to fuck my clothes up. I have an appointment..."

Silencing Jermaine with my lips. I kissed him deeply, imagining myself kissing Quran and riding his dick. I planted my toes into the leather seat of my Infinite and moved my body like a snake. I rose and sank on Jermaine's dick, while tightening the muscles in my pussy. It was something I had been practicing. The smell of Quran's cologne still on my mind had aroused me even further as I raised it to my nose and smelled it. The scent was like an instant aphrodisiac. I threw my head back and went crazy. I stuck one finger in my mouth and used my other hand to reach under my shirt and massage my nipple. With every deep thrust, I squeezed. I wanted to scream and talk dirty, but I couldn't. I didn't trust myself, the way I was feeling, I was more than positive I'd scream Quran's name. And as gullible as Jermaine was, I doubted that I could get away with the 'On the Quran' line a third time. So, I just sucked on my finger and kept quiet as I moved.

"What the fuck are you trying to do to me? I'm about to cum...Zin! Zin...fuck!"

I kept my eyes closed and imagined Quran releasing his seed inside of me. I kept grinding my pelvis into the lap that I was sitting on and finally with a small cry, I came all over Jermaine's pants.

"Look at my pants..."

I zoned Jermaine out, as I rose off him and fixed my clothes. I felt the warm liquid starting to run down my leg, but I didn't care. The Earth had just moved for me.

"...home and change clothes..."

The car smelled like sex mixed with apple air freshener. Beads of sweat ran down my face as I turned the car on and turned up the AC. Jermaine was still talking when I eventually pulled out of the underground parking lot.

"...was good, but I finally get the chance to negotiate a bigger piece of..."

I stared straight ahead as I drove down Wisconsin Avenue. Deep inside, I had hoped that I could find a way to make love to Jermaine and still feel like superwoman. But for some reason, it just didn't work. While I should've been basking in the afterglow of great sex with the man I loved, I was too busy embracing reality. With Jermaine, there was no electricity, no tingles, no uneasiness, there were no feelings of uncertainty. If I was certain of anything, it was the fact that my body belonged to Jermaine at the present, but my heart, mind, and soul was with Quran.

Chapter Eighteen
Quran

I paced the floor of my condo, searching my mind for the answers I so desperately sought. Why hadn't Tabu told me about the gun charge and that he was on probation for it? Why would he purposely withhold that information from me? I immediately turned my attention to my brother, Jihad who sat in front of a laptop at the table.

He must've felt my glare because he looked at me and said, "I got a rack of new bitches getting at me on Facebook…"

"Man, fuck Facebook and all that shit. Did you know that Tabu was on probation for a gun charge he caught?"

"Probation! A gun charge? Get the fuck outta here, Que."

"Sometimes I think I am the only one around here with common sense. Why do you think them peoples held his dumb ass over the jail?"

"I thought…I thought…then again, I didn't really think about it."

"That's your problem, Jay. You don't think enough and neither does Tabu. But what I'm tryna figure out is…why didn't he tell either one of us about him getting arrested for a gun? What gun did he have and was it dirty? And when did all this shit happen, how long ago did he get arrested? That's what the fuck I wanna know. And why hide it? This shit been fucking me up all day."

"Wallahi, bruh. I ain't know nothing about none of that shit. You know I wouldn't keep shit like that from you. Now you got me fucked up…but you know what. Now that we're talkin' 'bout this, I did ask Tabu where was the .40 that he had up until the day we went on that move. I noticed that he had a new hammer. He told me that he lost the .40 Caliber."

"Lost it?" I repeated confused.

Jihad nodded his head, "That was my reaction exactly. It was an answer typical of Tabu, so I let it go. But now that you're telling me all this, that must've been the gun that he got locked up with, the .40 Caliber. I don't think it was hot unless he shot Mann when y'all went on that mission. He didn't shoot Mann, did he?"

Shaking my head, I started pacing again.

"Why would Tabu not tell us about the gun charge and probation?" Jihad asked. "That's what I can't figure out."

"That makes two of us, then. As a matter of fact, you can go over the jail to see him...naw, scratch that. Them phones be monitored..."

"Phones? The visits at D.C. Jail are on the screen now, slim. All that shit is recorded. You gotta go over D.C. General to get on T.V. to visit a muthafucka at the jail. How long did they hold him for?"

"Zin said for..."

"Zin...Zinfandel Carter?"

I stopped pacing and turned to face Jihad, "Yeah Zinfandel Carter. That's who I got to represent Tabu..."

"But I thought you said...never mind. Is she getting paid to..."

"What the fuck difference does that make?" I exploded, knowing exactly what Jihad was implying. "They held Tab for five days. He goes back to court on Monday. Zin said he will probably be released because the courts know that D.C. jail is over-crowded and Tabu's case is basically a probation violation. The new gun charge won't see a trial for months. He'll be home Monday, Insha Allah and he has a lot of explaining to do."

I sat down in my favorite chair, my thoughts consumed with two things...Tabu and Zin. Zin was someone that I wanted more than anything in the world. The feelings I had surprised even me sometimes. Resisting the urge to pick up the phone and call her. I decided that I needed a good night's sleep.

"Jihad, I'ma lay down and rest my nerves. Don't bother me for nobody."

"I got you bruh, I'll catch you in the a.m."

In my bedroom, I laid across my bed, closed my eyes, and suddenly was transported back in time. To the day I found out my father had been killed. It was fifteen days after my eleventh birthday..."

My mother gathered her three sons together and with tears in her eyes, she broke the news to us.

"I...I...I..." she stammered.

"Ma, what's wrong?" I asked, knowing that something was very wrong. I had never seen my mother cry.

"Yeah, what's wrong, ma?" the other two boys said in unison.

"It's...y'all's father...he...uh...he's gone!"

"Gone where?" I asked.

"He's gone to paradise, baby. Your father has gone to be with the Lord."

"But...you said that a person has to die before he can go be with Allah."

Nodding her head and wiping her eyes, Khadijah Bashir, said, "That's right, baby...that's exactly what I said. Your father died early this morning at D.C. General Hospital."

All three of us, me, and my brothers started crying at the same time.

"Noooo, ma, I just saw daddy, he can't be dead!" I protested.

"You saw him last night, baby, he died this morning."

"But how...why?"

Khadijah grabbed her oldest son and hugged me tight. Then she gathered her other two boys together. "Somebody shot him, as he walked up to the front door, somebody shot him. Right there on our porch."

We all stood there in the middle of the small apartment's living room and cried.

"Quran, you are the man of the house now, remember that. You have to take care of us. No matter what happens, I want you to promise me that you will always take care of, and look out for your brothers. Promise me that!" Khadijah Bashir, my mother, said to me once my brothers were put to bed.

"I promise ma, I promise."

"Good, now, c'mon in the kitchen with me and I'ma make you some food. Tonight, we have to make the arrangements for your father's burial. Under Islamic law his body has to be back inside the earth in seventy-two hours. So, we've got a lot of work to do."

Four days later, after my father was buried, a friend of my father's came over and gave my mother a bag of money.

"It belonged to your husband, Khadijah. I hope that it helps out." As the man turned to leave, he said, "Do you mind if I speak to Quran outside? I wanna share some things with him that his father shared with me. Is it okay?"

"Quran, go with Mike outside." My mother said.

I remember walking outside with the man that I had seen with my father on several occasions.

"Quran, right now, you're too young to understand what I'm saying to you, but when you grow up, you'll remember. I know who killed your father. You have to avenge your father's death, Quran. As the oldest son, the responsibility falls on you. I'll be back to see you in two years, you'll be thirteen years old then and more mature. I will tell you what you need to know and give you the things you need to avenge your father. Do you understand everything I just said to you?"

I nodded my head without saying a word. Then the man Mike left, but just as he said two years later he returned...

I was coming home from school one day when the midnight blue BMW 325i pulled up beside me. The window came down and someone called my name. I looked in the direction of the car and saw that it was Mike.

"Get in the car, youngin."

When I hesitated, the man repeated himself, "I said get in the car, youngin. Don't make me say it again, I hate repeating myself."

I walked over to the BMW and got inside.

"Do you remember our conversation two years ago?" Mike asked.

"Yeah."

"Good."

After we had been driving for about ten minutes, the BMW made a stop in a project called Wellington Park. We pulled backwards into a parking space.

"Look straight down the street where all those dudes are standing. You see 'em?" Mike asked.

"Yeah I see 'em."

"There's one dude that stands about a foot taller than everybody else. He's wearing blue jeans, brown boots, and a beige Polo hoody. You see him?"

"Yeah"

"His name is Tony Wells. He's the man that killed your father. Tony used to work for your father, until he got a connect of his own. He decided that your father was in his way. He followed him to your front steps and shot him twelve times from the back. Do you remember what I said to you when you were eleven?"

"Yeah."

"What did I say?"

"You said that one day you'd tell me who the man was that killed my father and that it was my responsibility as the oldest son to kill him."

"Correct and I also told you that I'd give you the things you needed to avenge your father. Remember that?"

"Yeah."

The man named Mike reached into his waist band and pulled out a gun. He handed the gun to me, "It's a Taurus nine-millimeter. It holds twelve bullets in the clip and one in the chamber." The man named Mike pulled out of the parking lot.

"Get used to the feel of it in your hand because it's now yours and that's the gun you're gonna use to avenge your father. I'ma take you out in the woods and show you how to shoot it. In a few weeks, you'll be ready to fulfill your destiny...

And two weeks later I was. It had just gotten dark outside. I walked down Sheridan Road past all the older dudes, I knew from the neighborhood. A lot of them spoke, but I didn't speak back. Feelings of trepidation and fear gripped me and held my tongue captive. All I could do was focus on the mission that I now had to complete.

"I got you daddy, I'ma take care of this for you. His blood is yours."

The weight of the gun in my waist seemed to weigh me down as if I was walking in wet cement. But I kept walking, walking focusing, and waiting. Waiting for my chance to avenge my father's death. Turning on Pomeroy Road, the words that Mike embedded in me came to mind...

"...take the short cut through the brush on Pomeroy and you'll come out at the bottom of the complex. Walk normal and come up the two flights of steps that lead to the top of the complex. Tony has a silver Sterling. He's somewhere near it at all times...

I followed these instructions to the letter and came upon Tony standing with a female in front of one of the buildings. My heartbeat began racing as I approached. Doing just as I was instructed, I walked towards Tony Wells, as if I was going to pass him. I pulled the gun from my waist, and ran up the first two steps. By the time Tony Wells looked in my direction, it was too late. I had the gun up, firing. I stood over Tony's fallen body and emptied the gun. Then I ran back the way that I came, all the way back home.

I never saw Mike again until a few months later. He was walking down the street with a young girl holding onto his hand. A pretty little girl that appeared to be no more than seven or eight years old.

"Quran, I need to holla at you, youngin." Mike said.

"Talk."

"Not right now, not in front of my daughter. Later, though, tonight I'll come back through."

"Daddy, can I have something from the ice cream truck." The young girl asked.

"Not right now, Zin. Your mother would kill me if I gave you sweets before dinner."

"Daddy...please!"

"I said no, Zin. Don't make me repeat myself again."

"Your daughter's name is Zin?" I asked.

"Yeah, what can I say?" Mike replied and shrugged. "We got drunk the night that she was born, so my wife named her Zinfandel."

Six months later, at Mike's behest. I committed the second murder of my young life and after that there was no turning back...

Chapter Nineteen
Zinfandel

"Your Honor, my name is Assante Orakpo, from the United States Probation Office. I was assigned to Khitab Bashir's case back in November of last year. Since then, Mr. Khitab, has visited with me at least once monthly. His regular drug testing revealed that he was not using any drugs. His employer, Henry Tanner of Henry's Soul Food Café, reports that Khitab is a good worker. In short, your honor, USPO has no objection to Mr. Bashir being released in whatever capacity this courts sees fit. Thank you, your honor."

Judge Gardner leaned forward in his seat and adjusted the glasses at the tip of his nose. "Does the government have any opposition to what Ms. Carter and Mr. Oralpo has said here today?"

"No, your honor." The assistant US Attorney rose and said, "My office does not oppose the defendant's release here today."

"Mr. Bashir, you are hereby released into your own personal recognizance. You are to continue with your probation until your next appearance at this court. Is the second week of May...on the eleventh, good for both counselors?"

I checked my Blackberry, "That's good for me, your honor."

"May eleventh is good for me also, your honor."

"Mr. Bashir, you're free to go. Step to the left and sign the papers that the clerk has. Next case..."

***

"I think I remember your brother from school. Did he go to Savoy?" Zin asked Quran outside of the courtroom.

"Yeah, y'all are about the same age, too."

"Is that right and how do you know how old I am?"

"There's a lot about you that I know, little Zinfandel."

"Whatever, Quran. Your brother has to be released from D.C. jail. Once you've been processed into their system, they have to process you out. What time that maybe, I don't know. So, you should be expecting a call from him later. Is there anything else that you need? Or am I excused."

"Can I take you to dinner?"

"Quran…"

"Zin, it's just dinner. I promise to behave myself." Quran said, smiled, and threw up two fingers. "Boy scouts honor."

"I…I…"

"C'mon, Zin, look at it like it's a business meal. I paid you to defend my brother and now I wanna discuss his case further over a meal."

"Okay, okay, when and where?" I relented.

"What time is good for you?"

"I should be finished here now. I'ma run back to the office and take care of a few things. I should be finished by seven."

"That's a bet, you can meet me at the Zanzibar on the Waterfront. I'll be inside waiting for you, take care boo."

I stood there and watched Quran walk away again and thought. *'Why are you always walking out of my life?'* Quran had a swagger that was off the charts and I was feeling it to the twelfth power. I stood riveted to the spot I was standing in, and didn't move until Quran was out of sight. Snapping out of my trance, I tried to shake off the feelings I was feeling, but found it hard to do. That man is gonna drive me crazy.

***

Walking into the lounge, I spotted Quran at a table along the wall to the back. He had changed clothes and was now dressed in a striped button-down shirt and jeans, he was casual, chic, and wearing it well.

"Hello, again." I said as I sat down.

"What's up, little Zin?" Quran said.

"Quran, cut the bullshit, let's talk."

"Talk about what…your boyfriend?"

"That'll come later, first I wanna hear about you and what you've been up to since we last saw each other."

"No food, first." Quran queried.

"Later."

"Okay, the last time I saw you I believe it was in nineteen-ninety-three or four. I remember saying something to you as we passed one another on Sayles Place. Then you disappeared, I was about fourteen then, and wild as shit. My mother passed away a few months later from Cancer and I had to raise my two brothers. Tabu, you've met, the other one is named Jihad. My story is simple.

"I dropped out of school to run the streets and in so many words now I run the streets. I'ma good guy gone bad. My education was a hard lesson learned every turn of the corner. Everything I have, I took. I love the streets, I live by the rules of the game and the game raised a man...end of story."

"No wives, baby mothers, stalker girlfriends...children?"

"None of the above. I mean I do me, but I chose who I do me with."

"I feel you."

"Do you really?"

"Quran, behave yourself, it's my turn, huh?"

"No doubt."

"After my mother was killed, I went to stay with my aunt Linda. She practically raised me. My father ended up killing the man that supposedly killed my mother. After he went to prison, I vowed to myself that I was gonna one day help him get out of jail. I hate the man that sent him away. The prosecutor at the trial was a man named Greg Gamble..."

"The nigga that run the District Attorney's Office?"

"The one and only, he was a regular prosecutor back then with lofty ambitions. The whole time I sat in that trial, every day that I saw him and what he was doing to my father, I hated him. I blamed him for my father losing the trial. I told myself that's what drove me to succeed. My hate and determination pushed me to become a lawyer. For me, for my family, and for my father. I went to college early and graduated at the age of twenty with a degree in Criminal Justice. I enrolled in law school and finished in three years at the head of my class. All of my professors begged me to go into Corporate Law. I had job offers pouring from the biggest firms in the nation. But I decided to keep my word to myself. I came home to D.C. and got a job with Nikki and Jen and the rest is history.

"Aren't you forgetting something or someone?"

"Can we order a drink first?" I asked.

"Sure." Quran called over a waiter. "What would you like, everything is on me."

To the waiter, I said, "I'll have the strawberry Mimosa."

"And you, sir?" the waiter inquired of Quran.

"Bring me a raspberry ice tea."

"Will that be all?"

Quran looked at me for an answer. When I didn't say anything, he responded. "For now."

Once our drinks had been served, I said, "Where were we?"

"You were just about to tell me about your boyfriend."

"His name is Jermaine, he's a lawyer too. We met in law school, fell in love, and we've been together ever since."

"That was fast and efficient. They teach that in law school?"

"What?"

"The way you summed up your whole situation in three sentences. Zin, I think about you every day. I can't get..."

"Quran, don't do this." I interjected. "I can't do anything about..."

"Your situation? Yes, you can. Do you really love him, Zin?"

"I...I..."

"If you did, you wouldn't be here now." Before another word could be said. Quran signaled for the waiter. "I'm ready to eat. Gimme the stuffed breaded shrimp platter with fries. Zin what are you gonna eat?"

I was dumbfounded, Quran's last remark before signaling the waiter had my equanimity off balance and I was still trying to recover.

"I'll have the…" I grabbed the menu and scanned it. "…chicken and broccoli Alfredo and another Mimosa."

After the waiter took our orders and left, I said, "That's what you think, huh?"

"Naw, that's what I know."

"You think you got all the answers, huh?"

"Not all of 'em, just some."

Chapter Twenty
Quran

After the meal, I walked Zin to her car. On the second level of the garage we found her Infiniti.

"Can I see you again?" I asked.

"Quran…"

"I know, I know, you gotta man. Well can I at least get a goodbye hug? This might be my last time seeing you."

Zin stepped into my arms and hugged me. But when she tried to break the embrace, I wouldn't let go, I couldn't let go. Zin was about to speak when her words were cut short by my lips on hers. Our kiss lasted for what seemed like an eternity. When we finally separated, Zin had to gasp for air. Her heart raced a mile a minute, I could feel it. She was visibly flustered.

"Quran, you promised to behave…"

I didn't let her finish her sentence. I threw caution to the wind and kissed her again.

"…on the Boys Scout's hono…"

"I ain't never been no Boy Scout. That shit doesn't apply to me."

"You smell so good, I can…"

I cut Zin off again with another kiss. This time her body responded to my touch, but her mouth protested.

"Quran…stop it!" Zin whispered, but her words fell on deaf ears. Before she knew what was happening, her skirt was up around her waist. My tongue was in her mouth probing, exploring. My body was pressed against hers with only the car to hold us up. I put my right hand in her panties and searched for her essence. It didn't take long for me to find it.

I used two fingers to hit the spot inside her. With my thumb, I forcefully massaged her clit. Zin grinded herself on my hand, my other hand found her butt, and squeezed a cheek. Then my probing fingers brushed against her back door. The nerve ending in her rectum relaxed to allow my uninvited probe. Zin wanted

115

to cry out, but she couldn't. Her moans were muffled by my mouth that was all over hers.

With one finger in her tightest hole and two in her pussy, Zin gave herself over to the moment. There she was in the parking garage of a well known hot spot in D.C. with a dangerous man, whose fingers happened to be deep inside her lower orifices. I can't believe this shit.

Zin, reached down and unzipped my jeans. She reached inside my pants and wrapped her fist around my dick. Oh my God! Her hand felt so small, but so good around my dick. Releasing it from it's prison, Zin rubbed the head against her labia.

"Don't tease me Zin!" I whispered as I pushed my dick into her flesh.

With no more hesitation, Zin, guided me into her. "It's too big Quran!"

Slowly but surely, I eased every inch of my dick into Zin as she held onto me and dug her nails into my back.

"It's too much…it's too long…too thick…"

"What?" I whispered into Zin's ear as I humped into her body. "My ego?"

"Quran, I'm about to cum! Aaahhh…shit!" Zin, said and came.

I quickened my pace and felt myself about to cum as well. "Me, too!"

"Quran, baby, don't cum in me…don't cum in me!"

Pulling my fingers and my dick out of Zin, I backed up and shot my seed onto the concrete. "Got damn Zin, look what you made me do."

"Look what I made you do? You lied on the Boys Scouts and everything just to get some ass. You did that to yourself." Zin said as she reached out and smeared the last remnants of cum all over the head of my dick. "So, Mr. I Promise to Behave, now what?"

I put my dick in my pants and zipped up. "Now you call your boyfriend and tell him that you gotta work late."

"But…Quran…I gotta…"

"Do it, Zin!"

"Okay, okay…where's my purse?"

I looked behind me and found it. I picked it up off the ground and handed it to Zin. "In the throes of passion, you threw that joint down."

Zin laughed, "Stop fishing for compliments." She dialed her home number and reached her man. "Baby, hi, I just wanted to let you know that I'm leaving D.C. jail right now and headed back to the office. I have to prepare a new trial motion by tomorrow, so I'll be there kinda late. When I'm done, I'll be home. No don't wait up for me. My father called? Why didn't he call my cell? He what…okay, I'll talk to you later. I love you too, Bye."

Zin ended the call and said, "Where are we going now?"

"Get in the car, I'll show you."

"What about your car?"

"I'll pick it up later."

We ended up at the Embassy Suites Hotel in Crystal City. On the elevator, Zin asked, "Does somebody live with you?"

"Naw, why?" I responded.

"Because you could've taken me to your house, but instead you chose a hotel."

"I live alone, but my brothers hang out at my crib every day. I told Jihad to tell Tabu… that's what we call Khitab, to stay at my spot until I got there."

"Do you think he obeyed?"

"Without a doubt, that's why we in this elevator right now. I try to keep my personal life separate."

On the 7th floor, we went to suite 724 and entered it. As soon as the door was shut, we were in each other's arms. I lifted Zin off her feet and carried her to the couch. I sat her down and stood over her. Slowly, I undressed down to my Prada boxer briefs. Then I grabbed Zin's ankles one at a time and undid the strap of her Ferragamo heels. I pulled each heel off and then bent to kiss every one of her toes. I took my time and sucked on each toe before kissing Zin's entire foot. In minutes, I was up her leg and paying special attention to the inside of the thigh.

I reached out and hooked both of my thumbs inside of the strings on Zin's tie up bikini panties. I pulled them down her leg and removed them. "Here bite down on these."

"Bite down for wha..." Zin started to say, but stopped when my mouth found her clit and gently nibbled on it. She did just what I told her to do, put the panties in her mouth, and bit down on them.

I stopped what I was doing and looked around the room. Then I walked over to the table and grabbed one of the four chairs that sat around it. I took the chair and positioned it at the edge of the couch where Zin sat. I sat down and grabbed Zin's legs, pulling her into me closely. Then I grabbed one of the pillows off the couch and told Zin to lift up. She complied, and I placed the pillow under her, elevating her a little.

"That's perfect." I said and bent over. I hooked my arms under Zin's thighs and locked them. Then I put my mouth back on her pussy and focused solely on pleasing her orally. After bringing her to three back to back orgasms, Zin begged me to stop. But I didn't, I kept licking her pussy until she came one more time.

"It's my turn." Zin, said and changed positions with me. Zin palmed my dick in her hand, and licked it from the base to the tip.

She made sure to pay special attention to the hole at the tip and the little piece of skin hanging at the base of the head.

Her head skills caused me to grab her hair and force more of my dick in her mouth. Zin opened wide and accepted my dick into her throat.

"Don't gag, big girls don't gag." The act of sucking dick excited Zin so much that she reached between her legs and fingered herself as she sucked.

"Got damn, Zin! Suck that dick, baby! Suck that dick! You gon' make me cum in your mouth."

Zin sucked me like she wanted to feel my cum on her tongue, rushing down her throat, and I wanted to give her exactly what her head game called for. Zin eagerly sucked me now. She stroked my dick long and hard with her fist as I slid deeper into her throat. Just when I thought she'd gag and throw up all over my dick, I came.

"I'm cumming…Zin, I'm cumming!"

Zin caught all the warm thick liquid that erupted from my dick. She continued to suck me and swallow all at the same time. As if moving on auto, she kept me in her mouth, and continued to suck my dick.

Then the real freak in her came out. Zin released my flaccid dick from her mouth and lowered her head to my nuts. She licked and sucked on my nuts until she decided to go lower. Zin lowered her head further and lifted my nuts. She ran her tongue down the crack of my ass. Reaching up to grab my dick, Zin massaged it as she flicked her tongue around my ass. *'Gangstas get their asses licked all the time'*. I had to remind myself.

By the time she finished tossing my salad. My dick was as hard as granite stone. Zin licked her way back up and put me back in her mouth. I knew that she wanted to taste my seed again. She craved it, Zin gave me another sloppy blowjob until I came for the second time. Again, I came in her mouth, and again she swallowed every drop of my cum.

I lifted Zin's head with my hands and then stood up. I grabbed her hands and pulled her to her feet. "C'mon."

Our next destination was the bathroom. I ran water in the Jacuzzi, when it was full we both got in. Zin, laid her head back for a while. I pulled her to me which brought her back to reality. I lifted her body and positioned her on top of me. Inch by inch, Zin sat down on me until she was fully impaled. Hugging my neck, Zin kissed my lips feverishly and authority. She was zoning out again. My hands on her waist guided her up and down on my dick.

"Quran, your dick is in my stomach!" she said over and over again. "It's too deep in me!"

"They don't teach this shit right here in school." I replied and gripped Zin's shoulders, pulling her all the way down onto me, as I thrusted up into her.

"Aarrrgghhh…don't do that!"

"Be quiet and take this dick like a grown woman. Or should I call you Little Zin?"

"Fu…ck…you…Q…Qu…Quran!"

"That's right, baby. Talk dirty to me, I love that shit!"

Zin kept talking dirty and we kept on sexing until we both orgasmed again. Tired and feeling a little drained, I led Zin into the bedroom. We laid in the bed and talked about everything from sports to local events in D.C.

"Zin, I feel like I'm dreaming. I've fantasized about you everyday since the first time I saw you again."

"To be honest, I've been doing the same thing. I was making love to Jermaine one day and called out your name."

"For real!"

"Believe it, it happened."

"What did slim say?"

"He asked me what did I say and I told him that I said, 'On the Quran' meaning the the dick was good and I was putting that on something."

I busted out laughing, "You bullshittin'."

"I laugh and joke, but I never bullshit, it happened twice."

"What were you doing when you said my name?"

"What do you mean? I just told you I was making love to Jermaine."

"I know that, I mean what position was you in when you said it?"

"Um…let me see…I was riding him the first time and he was hitting it from the back the second time. The whole time I was imaging that he was you. That's crazy, huh?"

"Naw, that's not crazy, let me ask you something."

"Shoot."

"What have you never done with Jermaine or any other man?"

"I never let any man cum in my mouth before. Not until tonight when I let you do it and I even swallowed. I'd never done that before."

120

"What else have you never done?"

"The only other thing is anal sex. I've never done that, Jermaine be pressing me out, but I tell him no every time."

"I can't speak for Jermaine, but one day you gonna give me that ass."

"You think so?"

"I know so."

Zin opened her eyes and stared at me. "This isn't me, Quran. This is uncharacteristic of me. I have never done something so spontaneous and wild. But it felt right, it felt so good being with you. I know I feel something for you, Quran, but I'm not sure what it is. Is that crazy?"

"That's a question for Dr. Phil."

"What have you done to me, Quran? Why did you do this and who are you really?"

"Who am I?" I repeated.

"Yeah, who are you?"

"You don't wanna know, Zin. Trust me you don't wanna know."

Chapter Twenty-One
Zinfandel

As soon as I walked into my front door the phone rang incessantly. I checked the caller I.D. and saw that the caller was Jermaine.

"Hello?"

"Zin, where the hell have you been all night?"

"Don't start with me Jermaine, I'm not in the mood for it..."

"You not in the mood? Zin, who do you think you're talking to? You been out all night and your cell phone's off and you got the audacity to tell me you not in the mood. Where were you?"

"Where did I tell you, I was Jermaine? I told you that I had a new trial motion to do that was due to be filed as of one hour ago. I turned my cell phone off so that I wouldn't be interrupted. You have my work number. Why didn't you use it?"

"I did use it, what the hell are you talking about? You didn't answer that phone either."

"I told you I was busy. I worked on the motion half of the night, then fell asleep on the couch in my office. I got up about two hours ago and finished it. I drove to Appeals Court and filed it. Then I came home. Now what else do you wanna know?"

"You could've called me and..."

"Jermaine, I just told you everything you need to know. Now if you will excuse me, I'm tired, hungry, and I need a shower. I will call you later today."

"Zin, I'm sorry, baby. I was...I was worried, and I thought..."

"You thought what Jermaine, that I was out fucking?"

"I didn't say..."

"Bye Jermaine." I said and hung up the phone.

When it rung again I ignored it. When did I become such a skilled liar? It had to be the day I became a skilled lawyer."

I took off my heels and slowly disrobed. I couldn't get Quran out of my head. I can't do that again. Last night was great, well more than great, but that's it. I have a boyfriend and a life. I can't just throw that all away over one night of mind blowing, toe curling sex. Or can I? Is Quran Bashir, worth giving up my security? Is electricity and tingles worth all that much in the real world?

"Hell yeah." I said aloud, laughing.

I thought about the moments when Quran came in my mouth and the way I tasted his cum and loved it. Damn, he tasted good! But too much of a good thing could be dangerous, right? I walked towards my bathroom with a long hot shower in mind. That's it, I can't be running around like a young girl sprung off some good dick. I'm a grown woman with a career and responsibilities. I can't throw that all away for a big dick thug that smells great. Last night, was my first and last night with Quran Bashir.

***

By the time I realized that I'd lied to myself, it was too late. Two months had passed, and I had fallen in love with Quran. He had taken my mind and body to places I never knew existed. Quran Bashir, was everything that my life had been missing. Lying to Jermaine about my whereabouts had become an everyday occurrence. I was always working hard, long, and late. I had done over ninety different motions for clients that didn't even exist. At least that is what I had Jermaine thinking. The crazy part about my clandestine activities was the fact that I didn't feel bad about any of it. At first, I did, but eventually that changed. To me, I was living an adventurous life that satisfied me to the fullest. Why don't you just get rid of Jermaine and be with Quran exclusively then?

The voice in my head asked me that question almost daily, but I didn't have an answer. It may have been the fact that I didn't want to hurt Jermaine. But won't he be hurt when he finds out you've been fucking Quran for the past two months?

"Zin!" a voice called out, piercing the silence in my office. It was Jen.

"Yeah, Jen?"

"Come into my office for a minute."

'What does her fat ass want now?' I thought. "I'm coming."

I walked into Jen's office, saw the look on her face, and knew something was wrong. "What happened now?"

"We got a big problem." Was all Jen said as she threw a stack of papers and files down on her desk. "Conflict of interest is an understatement."

"What are you talking about?" I asked vexed.

"I hired a friend of mine to get inside the District Attorney's Office and try to find out who our third and final witness is against David. Apparently, my friend did his job too good and it doesn't look good for the home team." Jen said as she slid the pile of papers and files across her desk to me.

I sat down in the chair in front of Jen's desk and read the stack of papers, then leafed through the files. When I finished all I could say was, "Oh my God!"

"*Oh my God*, is right. But what are we going to do with this information. Our licenses to practice law are on the line here?"

I stared at one of the debriefings in my hand and read over and over what was asked and answered. The witness against David Battle, was clear and concise about who, when, why, where, and how the murder was committed. This one witness alone would secure the government a certain victory. Deflated, I continued flipping the pages and stared at the name typed and signed on each page. A confidential informant was what the government called the witness. A rat was what the streets called him. But to me and Jen, he was called a client, and to the man I now loved with all my heart, he was called brother.

Khitab Bashir's name stared back at me and stabbed me in the heart repeatedly. Why would he cross his very own brother? Why would he sell his soul to the devil and become a prostitute for an unjust system? Didn't he know that David Battle, was one of Quran's closest friends? And to think, it all started over a simple gun charge.

"We have to do damage control. This situation can play out a few different ways, so we got a few options. One…act like we never saw any of this stuff and we keep it strictly between us. Since we know exactly what Khitab is going to say, we can prepare a defense for it now. We can systematically take his whole testimony apart and use it against him. We hit the streets again and find two or three people willing to say something totally different about the crime, the setting, the weather, the lightning, etc…you follow me?"

I nodded my head.

"We can push for a resolution in Khitab's case earlier so that he technically wouldn't be our client any longer or we take David to trial with Khitab as our client, then make it an issue in court to preserve an appeal issue. Two…we reimburse Khitab some of his money and you withdraw as his attorney. That way we eliminate the whole conflict of interest aspect that's going to come up. But we proceed as I said earlier with the building of the defense. Or…are you still with me, Zin?"

My head was still spinning from what I had just read. My thoughts were still racing, and I was starting to feel nauseous. "Yeah, I'm with you. Go ahead."

"Or three…we give this information to David and let him handle it in the streets. Are you still in contact with Quran Bashir?"

"I can get in touch with him."

"Or four…you talk to Quran and get him to deal with his brother. It's your decision, you make the call."

"Let me talk to Quran and then I'll get back to you."

"Do it today, Zin."

I stood up and nodded my head. "I'm on it, I'ma need to make a copy of this stuff to show Quran. He might not believe me when I tell him who the witness is."

"Quran, and *Quran* only Zin. Don't even say a word about this to Nikki. Do you hear me, Zin?"

"Loud and clear, Jen…loud and clear."

***

I sat in the living room of Quran's condo and patiently waited for him to finish reading the file. The pain that was etched in his face broke my heart. Finally, after several minutes, Quran dropped the file, stood up, and paced the floor. He gripped his face and stopped momentarily. When he turned around and removed his hands from his face, they were saturated with tears.

I didn't know what to do. I was afraid to speak and afraid to move. I had never witnessed such a display of emotion from Quran or any of the men I knew. Music had become so much a part of my life that a song by Tony Terry instantly played in my head…

'When a man cries
He's giving you his love and his emotions
When a man cries
And he's reaching out his hand
There's nothing more tender
Than the warm and loving tears of a man…'

"Ever since my father died and my mother passed away, I tried to be the best influence on my brothers. I know that I ain't much of a role model, but I tried. I believed that they needed to know the streets because the streets were all we had. There was no sense in tryna teach them about the suburbs, computers, maintaining a steady job, and all that because that wasn't what they saw every day. Their lives have always been marred with violence, drugs, sex, crime, and fast money.

"It's hard to say to two little guys, *'Do as I say, not as I do'*. I led by example and that example was not always a good example. But I tried my hardest to get them to live a different life. They wanted the life they saw, the life they knew. I was taught a lot of things by my father and the various people who raised me. I was taught to respect the code of the streets. *The death before dishonor*. I live that code everyday and wear it as a badge of honor. If there is a thing as an honorable thug, I'm it.

"I never cross a man that doesn't deserve it. I never involve innocent women and children in my wars. I spare the elderly, I give back to the hood. I respect those who are honorable and worthy to my respect. And these are all the things I taught my brothers. So, for Tabu to do this is like a kick to the sternum. Thank you for bringing this to me, Zin. Let the people in your office know that everything will be taken care of.

"Quran I'm sorr…"

"There's nothing to be sorry about." Quran said, wiping his eyes. "I need to be alone now, Zin. I'll call you in a coupla days, okay."

I felt hurt by Quran's abrupt dismissal, but I tried not to show it. Silently, I rose from my seat and walked across the living room. Before opening the door and leaving, I said, "I love you Quran, remember that."

Chapter Twenty-Two
Zinfandel

The last couple days without Quran were pure torture for me. All attempts to reach him had failed.

"I told you not to get involved with that thug." I reminded myself, I sipped on my soda and nibbled lightly on the slice of cheese pizza on my plate. Where was he? After talking to Quran that day I broke the news to him about his brother. I inundated myself with work. It was all I could do to take my mind off the situation. I told Jen that Quran would handle the situation and not to worry. But the truth was I was worried. I was worried about what Quran was going to do and what would happen to Khitab.

I had met with Khitab several times over the last few months in preparation for his upcoming trial for the gun charge. Quran's younger brother was a younger version of him, but not as bright and minus the swagger. But he was funny and engaging and I liked him. I wanted so badly to tell him that I loved his brother, but I couldn't. I couldn't tell anyone. Quran and I both had decided that it was better that way. Quran Bashir, made me feel so good that I wanted to climb to the top of every building in D.C. and shout my love for him.

"Ms. Carter?"

I looked up from my food and saw a Marshal standing over me. "Yes?"

"Judge Kramer wanted me to let you know that she is ready to start the second half."

"Thank you, I'm coming now."

***

"Mrs. Woods, good afternoon. Would you please state your name for the court!"

"Janice Woods." The witness on the stand stated.

"Mrs. Woods, would you please tell the court your relationship to the complainant?"

"I'm his mother."

"Okay, Mrs. Woods, let me direct...no, I'm sorry, your honor. Mrs. Woods, do you anybody in this court that you identify besides me?"

"No ma'am."

"The two men sitting at the table over there, do you know either one of those men?"

"No."

"Okay, let me direct your attention to the evening of April 21st of last year. Do you have a fairly good recollection of that day?"

"Yes."

"Would you please tell the ladies and gentlemen of the jury what you were doing on that day?"

"That was the day I was taking my son to the hospital to have several bullets removed from his arms and legs."

"And what happened on the way to the hospital?" Ann Sloan, asked her witness.

"We were on Suitland Park stuck at the light. I saw a green Cadillac pull behind us. When the light changed the Cadillac pulled alongside my car."

"Then, what happened?"

"I saw my son, motioning with his hands as if he was surrendering. Then I heard him say, *'No, man, don't do it. My mother is in the car.'*"

"Your Honor." I called out as I stood, "...At this time I'd like to renew my objection to this testimony. We heard from the complainant about this incident. I'm not sure as to what the government is trying to bring out here. There is nothing new in this testimony that Quincy hasn't said already."

"Ms. Sloan." The judge said.

"Your Honor, in the interest of justice it is my opinion that Mrs. Wood's testimony is relevant and probative of the facts in this case and it leads to identi..."

"Your Honor, this testimony is moot. The witness can't identify anyone."

Judge Noel Kramer, scooted her glasses higher on her nose and locked her hands behind her head. "Your objection has been recorded for the record, Ms. Carter. Overruled, continue Ms. Sloan."

"Mrs. Woods, you say that your son said, 'Don't do it, my mother is in the car?'"

"Yes."

"And then what happened?"

"I leaned up in my seat and looked over his shoulder."

"Just to be clear, you looked over your son's shoulder?"

"Yeah."

"And what did you see when you looked over your son's shoulder?"

"I saw an arm hanging out the window pointing a gun at my car."

"And again, for the record, you didn't see who that arm belonged to did you?"

"Do you know what kind of gun it was?"

"No."

"'No further questions, your honor."

"Your cross, Ms. Carter." Judge Kramer said.

I took my time gathering papers into my attaché case. I read over my notes and then stood. "Mrs. Woods, how many sons do you have?"

"Two. Quincy and Martin."

"Two, huh? And what are their ages?"

"Twenty and Twenty-two."

"Okay, Mrs. Woods, you told this court that you saw…well first you heard your son say, *'No, man, don't do it. My mother is in the car.'* Is that right?"

"Yes."

"Then you leaned forward, and wanted to see who…"

"Objection, your honor. Counsel is leading and misrepresenting the witness. Mrs. Woods never stipulated as to why she leaned forward."

"Sustained, you can't ask the question like that, Ms. Carter. You can ask her why she leaned forward."

"Mrs. Woods, why did you lean forward?"

"To see who my son was talking to."

"And did you?"

"No."

"Mrs. Woods, you love your son, right?"

"Yes, I love my son!"

"And you'd lie to protect your son, wouldn't you?"

The witness became visibly flustered, "Yes...no I wouldn't lie to protect him."

"If he was wrong, you'd do something to help your son, wouldn't you?"

"Yes...no...yes, I would."

"And if helping him meant lying for him, surely you'd do that..."

"No, I wouldn't...no!"

"Mrs. Woods, you have to let me finish m..."

"Not when you tryna make me look like a liar. Since you wanna act like that, yes I saw who was driving the car!"

"Mrs. Woods..."

"I saw who was driving the car that day! It was the man right there."

Janice Woods said pointing at my client at the defense table. "It was the bald headed one, with the white shirt one, and multicolored tie. He was the one holding the gun!"

The court erupted into pandemonium.

"Settle down in my courtroom or I will order the Marshalls to clear it."

"Your honor, I move for a mistrial!" I declared. "The witness just made an in court identification of my client after swearing under oath that she did not see the person driving the Cadillac. There is no way that we can cure this. I vehemently objected to this testimony and now this witness has prejudiced my client in front of the jury. I move for an immediate mistrial."

"Both counsel approach the bench." The judge said obviously upset.

I walked up to the bench and huddled together with Ann Sloan.

"Ms. Sloan, I am disappointed at you and at this witness. I have no other choice, but to grant the mistrial. I will be on the phone with Greg Gamble this evening and I hope that your office never let's you lead another case ever. Ms. Carter, let me make myself clear. I allowed the testimony of Janice Woods because I felt that she could corroborate the testimony of her son. Your mistrial is granted with prejudice."

Aloud to the court, the judge said, "I have no other choice but to grant the motion for a mistrial asked for by the defense attorney. This court is adjourned."

***

I was pulling my Infiniti into a parking space at my office when my cell phone rung. The caller was Quran, "Hello, Quran?"

"It's me, Zin."

"I know who it is. Why haven't you called me? Where have you been? Where are you now? Quran, I love you, baby, so much..."

"Zin, I need you, baby. I need to see you, right now! Come to me." Quran said.

"Where are you, Quran? I'm on my way."

"I'm on Douglas Road, in a building right across from the school."

"Across from the school? Quran, those buildings are being renovated. Why are...?"

"Look, Zin, don't question me now. You will know everything when you get here. Come to Douglas Road and drive to the dead end. I'm in building 2830. My Lexus is parked outside, you can't miss it. Hurry up, Zin, come now!"

I wanted to say something else and ask other questions, but the line went dead. Quran, had hung up on me, throwing the car back in gear, I pulled out of the parking space and drove to Southeast.

Chapter Twenty-Three
Tabu

Opening my eyes, I tried to focus, but I couldn't. There was something in my left eye and for some reason, my right eye's vision was blurry. "Where am I?" Then suddenly like a punch to the sternum, the pain came. Lightning bolts shot through my whole body and it was enough to make me cry out. "Where am I?"

My brain sent a signal to my arm to move, but nothing happened. I became very afraid as I wondered why my body was paralyzed. The first thought that came to mind was that I'd been in a car accident and somehow, I was pinned inside the wreckage. But then I realized that I was actually hanging by the arms from something I couldn't see. My wrists were bound with something strong.

"What the fuck is going on? Why can't I see?" my mind asked my body questions that it could not answer. Did not answer. Then I heard a sound. It sounded like a small animal scurrying nearby. I shook my head and wondered if I was suspended in time by a bad dream. If it was a dream, my pain felt real. After shaking my head, a headache formed above my eyes and stayed there. I tried desperately to figure out what had happened, where I was, and why I was suspended, and bound in the dark.

The last thing I remembered was riding in the car with Quran. Having called me and then picked me up from one of my girl's houses, he said that he'd decided to show me the place where he had a lot of money buried. He said that in the event of his demise, God forbid, it would be my responsibility to retrieve the money, take care of everything, and then break bread with Jihad. I remembered asking Quran, what had brought on the thought of his death all of sudden.

He had laughed and simply said, *'Death appears like a thief in the night and steals the soul. We can only prepare to face that irrefutable fact head on.'*

The car then stopped in front of an abandoned building on Douglas Road. I was familiar with the complex called Washington View before the city moved all of it's tenants out.

"The money is buried here?" I had asked.

Quran had only nodded his head and said, "Come on."

We walked into the building, down some steps, and then the lights went out…that's the last thing I remembered. I tried again to move, but all my body did was swing sort of. Side to side, to and fro. Then as if someone had turned on a light switch, it came to me. Somehow, someway, my brother had found out what I did, what I said.

Despite all my efforts to take back what I had done, I couldn't and now my secret was known. I was knee deep in shit and I knew it…felt it. That had to be it, it was the only reasonable explanation for my current predicament. Then in a weird, strange sort of way, I smiled at that thought. I thought about the day Quran and I tricked Mann out of his life.

It had seemed oh so simple then and I wondered why Mann didn't see it coming. When I verbally expressed that to Quran that day, what had he said? Nothing! He didn't even respond at all. I remember thinking that I couldn't be tricked like that and here I was alone, in the dark, and suspended from something. I had definitely been tricked, and I never saw it coming.

Chapter Twenty-Four
Quran

Sitting inside my car, I tried my best to get the blood off my hands. I used wipes that I kept in the glove box and even liquid tire cleaner. But nothing seemed to rid me of all the blood. My brother's blood. I saw the headlights of a car approaching and knew that it's driver was Zin. I flashed my headlights once to signal to her where I was. I watched as Zin parked her Infiniti and got out. She walked sexily down the block towards me and I wanted to hold her and love her and smother her with kisses, but I couldn't. Not at the moment, her charcoal business suit and matching heels did something to me inside, but I shrugged it off.

"Quran, what the hell is going on with you?" Zin asked as soon as she was in striking distance of me. "Is that blood on your clothes...your hands?"

I nodded my head.

"What did you do, Quran? And why did you call me here..." Zin motioned to the abandoned building. "...to these spooky ass projects?"

I knew exactly what I wanted to say to her. I had rehearsed my lines beforehand in my head. "Do you remember the day that we ate at the Zanzibar that first time?"

"Of course I do, Quran, but..."

"Do you remember how we made love for hours after that at the Embassy Suites?"

"I remember that, but again..."

"That night, right before we laid down to go to sleep, you asked me a question. Do you remember what it was?"

"We talked a lot that night. I asked a lot of questions, which one are you referring to?"

I smiled a big smile to lighten the tension I saw in Zin's face. "A good lawyer never forgets her questions, Zin."

"Well, maybe I'm not a good lawyer then."

"You are a great lawyer and you'll get even better. That night you asked me who I was. You asked me who I really was, and I told you, you didn't wanna know. Remember now?"

"I remember." Zin replied.

Out of the darkness came a guttural cry and then, Q-u-u-r-r-r-a-a-a-n-n-n!"

Tabu screamed my name causing Zin to jump and stare in the direction of the voice. She turned back to me and said, "Quran, please tell me that, that's not your brother's voice I just heard."

"Follow me." I said to Zin. "And please watch your step."

I lead the way inside building 2380, all the way to my brother. I had to use a flashlight to get there, but we made it there. When I shined the light in the bathroom of one of the abandoned apartments, Zin screamed. Her breath became ragged and she sounded like she might hyperventilate at any moment. I hated seeing the look on Zin's face, but I felt it was necessary. She had to witness it, she had to know how real it was in the field. She had to understand who and what she was dealing with. She had to see the animal that lived inside my caramel skin. She had to recognize that my grey eyes represented the eyes of a predator, an animal, a real beast.

My brother was suspended from a low hanging from a pipe that protruded out of the wrecking ceiling. His wrists were bound together with duct tape and he was cuffed and taped to the pipe. His face was a bloody mess and one of his eyes was out of it's socket and resting on his cheek.

"Quran, is that you bruh?" Tabu asked.

"It's me, Tab." I replied.

"What are you doing to me, Que? Why am I tied up like this?"

"You know why you're here Tabu, let's not play dumb, okay. You violated the code and that's an unforgivable sin."

"Bruh...you gotta let me explain..."

"Explain what Tab? I read the paperwork where you explained everything to the cops. That's what got you in this situation now. Explaining!"

"There a lot of shit that you don't know, Que. Dave is jeal-
ous of you and he's gonna cross…"

"He's gonna cross me and you were the only one who could
see it. So to protect me you ratted on him to the cops? Is that
what you're tryna say, Tab?"

"Yes…no…Que, there's a lot more to it. You have to let me
down and hear me out."

"Let you down, huh? Dave was gonna cross me? Did the
cops tell you that?"

"I knew about it before I ever came across the cops. I
tried…"

"You knew that Dave was gonna cross me and you kept that
a secret!"

"I told you bruh…there's a lot that you don't know."

"And how exactly was he gonna cross me, Tab? How was
Dave gonna cross me?"

"Let me down, Que. Don't leave me up here. I'm in pain
bruh, my whole face hurts and I can't see a thing. I need…"

"You need to make dua to Allah and pray that you are not
tortured I the grave. Whatever it was, you could've told me, Tab.
You bartered Dave's freedom for your own. You cross that man
to make your gun charge go away. You are now a certified government witness. A whore for the government. A witness, a
snitch, a rat. I can't forgive you for that. But Allah can, so make
your duas, Tab. Make 'em now.

Tabu started crying then and it broke my heart. "He was
gonna cross you…"

"So you crossed him to keep him from crossing me. I know,
Tab. I understand, but that doesn't get you off the hook. The bi-
ble has a verse in it that says, if your eyes causes you to sin,
pluck it out, and enter heaven without an eye. I plucked your out,
Tab. That's why you can't see and your other eye is swollen shut.
You saw things that you were never supposed to speak on. It was

your eyes that caused you to repeat what you saw. You took a gamble, brother. You thought that you could violate death before dishonor and you'd be exempt from death because your last name is Bashir. You gambled and crapped out, Tab. Do you have any idea how hurt I am right now? If you could see, you'd see my tears, Tab. My eyes are full of tears. But I cannot turn away from what I know is right, and what I must do.

"Please...please...Quran...you gotta hear me out..."

"There's nothing left that I wanna hear. You just killed a woman because she was sleeping with a rat. She had never told on anyone. But she made the mistake of fuckin' wit' the rat buddy of her boyfriend, and for that you killed her. Did you hear her out and let her explain? No, you didn't, she was a better person than you to me, Tab. I don't need to hear nothing else." My voice faltered a little. I turned to face Zin. "You asked me that night who I was and I told you that you didn't want to know..." Tears ran freely down my cheeks. I wiped them away, but new ones replaced the old ones.

"I never wanted you to know the type of man I was...I am, but fate and destiny has forced my hand. Now you must know, I kill people for a living, Zin. That is what I do, I been doing it since I was thirteen-years-old. I get paid to clean up behind sloppy muthafuckas. I kill people who dishonor themselves and become rats.

"I killed Yolanda Stevens, Tommy Caldwell, and countless others like them. That's who I am. That's the person that you are in love with. I called you here to witness my brand of justice. I am the judge and jury, and I now find my brother guilty for treason, perjury, and conduct unbecoming of a street nigga." To my brother I said, "What did daddy always say about crossing a man that doesn't deserve it?"

"Quran, no! Don't kill me! We brothers, I'm your mother's son! This is me, your lil' brother, you can't kill me!"

"Answer me, what did he say?"

"Never cross a man that doesn't deserve it because everything comes full circle. When you do dirty shit, dirty shit get done to you."

"And what have I always told you?"

"To respect the code that we live by and never forget the death before dishonor. Live the Omerta."

I made no move to wipe away the tears that flowed down my face unabated. I turned back and looked at Zin. "You can leave now or stay. The choice is yours."

Zin didn't move or leave.

"I guess you've made your decision." I told her an turned to face my brother. "I love you all my life and that will never change when you're gone."

"Quran...don't do it...N-o-o-o-o-o!" Tabu screamed.

Zin's mouth gasped open when I pulled a large chrome handgun from my waist. I pointed the gun at Tabu and squeezed the trigger twice, hitting him in the left side of his chest. Then I raised the gun and fired a single shot into my brother's face killing him instantly. That's when Zin, fainted.

Chapter Twenty-Five
Zinfandel

I dropped my purse and my attaché case on the floor by the door and pulled off my blazer. Then I bent down to undo the clasp on my Jimmy Choos. When I stood up, I was startled to see Jermaine standing there. He was leaning on the wall by the hallway with a drink in his hand. I knew that Jermaine almost never drunk hard liquor because he couldn't handle it. So, to see him standing there with a shot glass sipping a brown liquid, threw me for a loop.

"Working late at the office, again?" Jermaine asked.

"Yeah."

"That's where you're coming from now, huh?"

"Jermaine, why all the questions?" I asked perturbed.

"Have things got that bad between us where I can't ask you a question?"

"What did you ask me, Jermaine? Got damn, I can't even come home...what was your question? Oh, yes, I am coming from the office. Anything else you wanna know?"

"I feel like I'm stuck in an R&B video." Jermaine said as he downed his drink and exhaled deeply. "My woman comes home late from work like she's been doing for the last two or three months and I ask her where she's been. She blows up at me like I'm the one cheating..."

"I'm not in the mood for this Jermaine. I swear to God, I'm not." I said, trying to walk past him.

Jermaine stuck his arm out and blocked the way to our bedroom and the bathroom.

Trying to remain calm, I breathed in and out deeply. "Jermaine, I have to use the bathroom. I'm tired and I wanna go to sleep. Please move outta the way."

"Not until we talk, Zin. I'm sick of this shit. You just said that you were at the office. Well, you're lying. You haven't been at the office all day or all evening. How do I know? I came to your office to take you to lunch only to be told that you were in court. I left and came back in an attempt to take you to dinner. You never came back to your office, Zin. I was there all evening up until about an hour ago. You don't believe me, call, and ask Jen. And speaking of Jen, we talked about you and all that work that you've been doing.

"I even mentioned some of the clients that you told me about. The ones that you've been spending so much time on their cases and guess what? She's never heard of any of them. I even thought that maybe I was tripping. Maybe I had the names and cases mixed up. I still refused to see the writing on the wall. Then you came up in here a few minutes ago, smelling like a scent that I smelled recently at the mall.

"The new Usher fragrance. And you stand here in my face wearing the necklace that I bought you and the twelve-hundred-dollar Jimmy Choo's that I paid for and tell me a bold face lie. I'ma ask you one more question, Zin and I want an honest answer. Not from Zin the lawyer, but from Zin the woman that I fell in love with almost six years ago. One, question, one answer, are you cheating on me?"

The moment that I had dreaded for months was here and it was time to embrace it, confront it. No more lies, no more pretending, and no more hiding. I felt the tears well up in my eyes as I choked back tears.

I looked Jermaine straight in his eyes and simply said, "Yes, I am." Then I walked back across the living room, stepped into my heels, and grabbed my purse. Without so much as another word, I left the condo.

***

"…I'm sorry and I know it ain't right
For what I did to you, baby
I can't explain why it's him and not you
And at the end of the day, I just don't want to
And we always seem to fight

He got the perfect body and sometimes he don't even treat me right

But when I'm with him, I said, but when I'm with him

It ain't nobody like him… I can't go on pretending, because I love him…he ain't always right, but he's just right for me.

I'm in love with another man…" I drove my car around town with the Jasmine Sullivan, CD on repeat. I sung the words to her song as if I had morphed into one of the lyrics and become Jasmine.

I imagined myself alone in a room with several empty tables. Jermaine was my only audience, as tears streamed down my face and his I sung. The words crushing him like a two-ton boulder. But it was a boulder that I had carried around for months until I threatened to crumble from it's weight. As I sung I suddenly felt free. Because there was no way to remedy what was now known and that in itself was freedom. Freedom from all the lies and freedom from the guilty. I wiped tears from my eyes and navigated my Infiniti through downtown D.C…

"You should go and find someone else, someone who can treat you right, give you the world, someone who can understand the man you are, cause baby you shine so bright and I would only dim your star…"

I was in love with another man and that scared me, yet excited me. I thought about the way that man had ate my pussy the first night we spent together and it sent chills down my spine. My pussy throbbed and tingled in response to my mental stimuli. I was in love with Quran Bashir, and it seemed right. But deep down inside, I knew it was wrong.

I had just witnessed the man I love take a life. Hours ago, he had killed his own brother. His mother's youngest son, and that scared me. But it also aroused me, in a weird sort of way. I was completely turned on by the power Quran exuded. The principles he stood on and the strength he wielded. Most women would be completely turned off by a man like Quran and his lifestyle, his ambience, his murderous swagger…

"I killed Yolanda Stevens, Tommy Caldwell, and countless others like them. That's who I am, that's the person that you are in love with..."'

But not me, I love the thug in that man. The conviction, the God like qualities of deciding who lives and who dies. It was not only arousing, it was intoxicating. And after almost six years of being completely sober with Jermaine, I deserved to be drunk with lust, love, and great sex. The heart loves who it loves and the body calls out for what it wants and right now, my body calls for Quran Bashir. The same Quran Bashir, who had just executed his brother while I watched.

While I watched and then fainted, I was repelled, and outraged by his actions, but attracted to the danger all at the same time. It was an attraction that I didn't feel for the corporate lawyer, with lots of money, benefits, IRA's, prestige and a degree. Jermaine represented security and stability. Quran represented the exact opposite. The scales of justice are sometimes unbalanced was the saying and it was true. Because I choose instability, insecurity, a gorgeous thug with street cred, swagger, harmful intentions, and dick for days. Am I crazy for that?

"...you treat me so much better than him, and if I was sane, there'd be no competition, but I'm in love with someone else...and I'm so sorry baby, but I'm in love with another man." I picked up my cellphone and called my aunt Linda. I was gonna be living in my old bedroom for a while.

Chapter Twenty-Six
Michael Carter

I closed my flip phone after disconnecting the call from Quran. What he had just told me was heartbreaking. His brother turned out to be a government witness against one of his men and he killed him. He killed his baby brother, his heart, his friend. I quickly dismantled the makeshift charger and put all it's pieces in a different place. Then I emptied the box of spaghetti on my bed. It's noodles had been cut to fit around the cell phone.

After placing the phone back in the spaghetti box, I stuffed the noodles back in the box, and then glued the box shut. I inspected my handy work all the while thinking about what Quran had done. My locked had a section that held over thirty boxes of spaghetti. If there was one thing that I was certain of, that was the fact that correctional officers never opened a convict's food during a shakedown. So the cellphone would be safe inside my locker. As long as I was the only person that continued to know it was there.

I uncovered the window of my cell door and undid the homemade rope that once tied around my bunk and connected to the handle of my cell door stopped it from opening. But if someone wanted to get in bad enough, the rope would only delay them a minute or two and that was all the time I would need to get rid of whatever contraband I was holding.

I laid back on my bunk and digested Quran's news with an ounce of salt and a couple grams of sugar. I hadn't really known his brother Tabu, except through Quran, but I remembered him as a kid. I remembered him as a baby. I remembered the night he was born, third son to a man who already had two sons. I remembered how happy that man was because of the birth of his third son. Quran knew that I knew his father, but he didn't know the extent of our relationships.

He didn't know that his father was the closest person to me beside my wife Patricia. He didn't know that his father had crossed me, just as his brother had crossed him. And what Quran didn't know, could never know is the fact that, just as he had killed his own brother. I was the person who had killed his father. No person had ever crossed me and hurt me more than Ameen Bashir.

***

Ameen drove his candy apple red BMW 325i up Georgia Avenue in route to a restaurant on Colombia Road. I reclined in the passenger seat thinking about my meeting with the notorious crime Lord Carlos Trinidad. He was one of the most powerful men in D.C. and every criminal in the streets knew what type of control he wielded. But why does the Hispanic crime boss want to see me? That thought had wracked my brain ever since the day before when two Hispanic thugs had come to Southeast and demanded that I come to a restaurant called 'Dela Rosa' on Columbia Road to have a sit down with Carlos Trinidad.

After telling my right-hand man, Ameen about the summons by Carlos Trinidad, my most trusted friend, replied, "You've finally reached the big leagues, slim. If Carlos Trinidad wants to talk to you, either we're about to be rich or gonna end up dead."

I couldn't recall any incidents that would have stoked the Hispanic drug Lords ire, so I figured that I was being summoned about something else. But what? In front of the small restaurant sat several large SUV's and exotic sports cars.

"Park over there, behind that Acura Legend. I want you to go in with me, but leave the gun in the car. Ain't no sense in inviting trouble if it ain't gone be none. I don't wanna offend this dude on his turf."

"I feel you." Ameen said. "But slim, if we leave our hammers in the car, we also invite ourselves to be defenseless sitting ducks if this nigga wants to pluck you off. But if you say leave the guns, I'll leave the guns."

"Leave 'em, here." I repeated with my eyes on the entrance to Dela Rosa's. "Put mines with yours."

We were patted down by a large Hispanic man that introduced himself as Benito. The man named Benito then let us into a gallery where several empty tables and chairs sat. At one of the tables in the back of the restaurant sat a man.

"You." Benito said pointing at Ameen. "Stay here with me, amigo. Let your boss speak with Carlos alone."

"Boss!" Ameen started, but then stopped mid-sentence when he saw the look on my face. "A'ight big man, I'm with you."

I walked to the table where the Hispanic man sat, upon approach, the man stood and offered an outstretched hand.

"Thank you for coming, Mike. I'm glad that you accepted my invitation to talk. My name is Carlos Trinidad."

"Invitation, huh? It was more like a court summons, Mr. Trinidad." I replied as we shook hands.

"Please, sit down, Mike. In this business, you'll find that invitations and summons are not unlike one another. And please call me, Carlos."

After I was seated, I said, "Nice to meet you, Carlos, but I'm a little befuddled as to why such an important man would request a meeting with me."

Carlos Trinidad, picked up a cup and sipped a liquid that looked to be coffee. He took his time setting the cup back down before speaking, "We both have a mutual friend, Mike. More like an associate, I should say. You know him as Victor Martin. I know him as Victoriano Martinez. The streets call him 'Vic', am I correct so far?" I nodded my head. "You buy keys of cocaine...about six keys a month if I'm not mistaking...from Vic correct?"

Again, I nodded. "You're probably wondering how I know this? Well Mike, there is not a lot going on in D.C. that I don't know about. Up until about a week ago, I provided Vic with those keys of cocaine that he sold you. Vic mentioned your name to me a few times and I heard good things about you in the streets. You are probably wondering why I called you here and what does Vic have to do with this discussion?

Anthony Fields

"I am well connected in this town, I have friends in high places. And those friends have informed me that our friend Victoriano was arrested by the DEA coming out of the Sheraton Hotel on Wisconsin Avenue about nine days ago. It appears that Victoriano broke under questioning and decided to give up to the DEA. He made a deal that includes setting me and several of my associates up. Your name was also mentioned." Carlos stopped to let that piece of information sink in.

"Me, my name was mentioned?" I asked disbelievingly.

Carlos nodded his head, "Michael Maurice Carter, you have a wife named Patricia, and a five-year-old daughter named Zinfandel. You live at..."

"Okay I get the picture, so now what...what do we do?"

"Forgive me for my lack of manners. Would you like something to eat, Mike? A drink maybe?"

"An orange juice would be nice."

Carlos called out something in spanish and minutes later another Hispanic man came out of the front of the restaurant and placed a bottle of Veryfine orange juice and a glass in front of me. I decided to drink straight from the bottle.

"What do we do, you asked a minute ago?" Carlos Trinidad said after the man who brought the orange juice had left. "I'm offering you an opportunity. If you choose to accept my offer things will be okay for you. For me...things will be okay regardless. Let's just say that I am a card carrying member of the NAACP and I believe in the advancement of black people. I wanna put you in the position to cop your keys directly from my people at a better price than Vic gave you. In essence, you'll be taking over the spot that Victoriano is about to vacate. How would you like to be the person who supplies keys to everybody in Southeast, D.C.?"

"And what would I have to do to become such a person?"

"Kill Victoriano Martinez, with his death, your name becomes removed from a DEA file in downtown, D.C. and you take Victoriano's place. How does that sound to you?"

150

I pretended to think over Carlos's proposition. "I accept, when does Vic's death need to take place?"

"Let's just say that one should never put off for tomorrow, what can be done today."

"I feel you, I feel you."

"I hope you do, Mike. After our mutual friend has been confirmed dead, you and I will meet back here to discuss business. You can leave now." Carlos said dismissively.

I stood up to leave, as I turned my back to Carlos Trinidad, and took two steps, Carlos's booming voice stopped me in my tracks.

"And Mike, the next time you come here, please don't bring guns with you. The two handguns that you and your companion left stashed in the BMW are in my possession. I'll give them back when we meet again."

I turned around and was about to speak, but was silenced by Carlos.

"And please, Mike never ever try to cross me. The first time I will have you killed. Why? Because if you cross me once, you'll cross me twice."

***

"If you cross me once, you'll cross me twice, huh?" Ameen repeated. "I like it, it definitely makes sense. And that's the last thing he said to you?"

"Yeah...after he threatened to kill me."

Ameen laughed, "Don't worry about it, if anything happens to you, I'll slump a rack of them migo, niggas."

"That really makes me feel better, thank you." I replied facetiously.

"On the real though, I still can't believe Vic, did that shit."

"Believe it, if Carlos Trinidad said it, that's like God's mouth to my ear. It's a shame too, because I actually liked Vic."

"You, too? Why the hell would Vic do that to himself?"

"To save himself from the wolves in prison. Vic's pretty ass wouldn't last a day in the penitentiary and he know's it. That bitch nigga gave them peoples my name, too. I'ma barbecue his ass for that."

"How do you plan to get at him?"

I smiled a mischievious grin. "How else do you trap a rat...with cheese."

***

Victoriano Martinez, pulled his Benz behind a red four door Forerunner. I leaned on a wall in the parking lot of Sheridan Road. Leaned on the wall and watched Vic approach me. In the Benz was one other person, a woman. From where I stood, I could make out her skin complexion and features. She resembled Appelonia.

"Pretty lady." I said to myself as I got off the wall and walked towards Vic, we shook hands.

"Mike, what's up, joe?"

"Ain't shit, Vic. I'm tryna cop them thangs, did you bring 'em?"

"The bitch in the car got 'em. Give me the money and then she'll go with you wherever you want to drop 'em off."

"That's a bet, C'mon in the house with me."

Once we were inside the house on Sheridan Road, Vic looked around and noticed that the house was empty except for plastic that covered the whole floor. Apprehension and fear crossed his face.

"You remodeling or something Mike?"

"Something like that." I responded, and headed for the brown shopping bag sitting in the corner of the living room. I reached into the bag and pulled out a handgun. I pointed the gun at Vic.

"What the fuck you doing, Mike? You fucking crazy or something?"

"Naw, Vic, I ain't crazy. You are, if you thought that you could rat on the Trinidad Organization and me, you're crazy as fuck. You asked me if I was remodeling, well I am because I'm about to paint the walls with your blood."

Victoriano Martinez, made a feeble attempt to beg for his life, but I wasn't trying to hear it. I shot the man in the face and watched him fall. Then I emptied the whole clip into the rat's face "I hate rats Vic."

A few minutes later, gunshots rang out in the parking lot. And I knew that the beautiful lady in the car was dead. I rolled Vic's body up until it was covered in plastic. Then me and Ameen disposed of the body. After cutting off his head for Carlos Trinidad to see.

***

"How long will you be gone?" Patricia Carter asked.

"Just until tomorrow. I'ma leave in a few hours and I'll be back tomorrow around this same time. Why? You gon' miss me baby?" I said playfully as I packed an overnight bag.

"Me and Zin, will miss you terribly, baby. I don't know a lot about this Carlos Trinidad character, but if you trust him, so do I. You just make sure you come home safe."

I looked up at my wife with adoration and my heartbeat fluttered. Patricia Carter was the epitome of beauty. At five-five inches and one hundred and thirty-four pounds, she was everything that I had ever asked for in a woman. Her golden-brown complexion and jet black hair accented her almond shaped eyes and thick eyebrows. Patricia was hairy in a sexy way and she turned me on in every way.

I zipped my bag and then walked over to my wife. "You know I love you to death, right?"

"I know baby, and I love you more than you'll ever know."

"You and Zin, mean more to me than anything in this world. I'd rather die than be without you. That's why I made this deal with Carlos. He's putting me in position to make some serious *money. In a year or so, I should have enough money to get out of the game. I wanna be able to give you and Zin the life you both deserve."*

Patricia reached up and hugged me, then she kissed me. "All I need is you, that's the only life I need. You and Zin are my life and that's all I need. No amount of money or no other man can change that."

With that said Patricia Carter undressed me and then herself. For the next, hour we made love to one another, as if we had no a care in the world.

***

"Stinky Dink get rickety raw...Stinky Dink get rickety raw. I'm coming...Stinky Dink get rickety raw...Stinky Dink get rickety raw. Hurry, hurry, step right up, it's the bomb. And old McDonald got some new stuff on the farm. It's the E-I-E-E-EIO! It's the rickety, rickety, rickety, raw rapper solo..."

Ameen turned the Rare Essence tape over to the B side. "This new R.E. be crankin' like shit. Stinky Dink, be fuckin' that joint up but I miss Fat Rodney. Them niggas couldn't fuck with Rodney."

I heard Ameen, but my mind was elsewhere. My life as I knew it was about to change and I wondered if I was truly ready for it. By accepting Carlos Trinidad's offer and killing Victoriano Martinez. I had signed a pact with the devil...in blood. Business relationships with men like Carlos Trinidad ended one of two ways. Life in the pen or death. There were rarely any happy ending and I knew that better than anyone. But all in all, I believed that I could get the job done. After all, I was a superb business man, hustler, and gunslinger. I knew that I possessed all the necessary skills to become one of the big boys in the city. It was my time and just as George Jackson had said in a California prison cell almost twenty years earlier, "It's time to seize the time."

My dominance in the streets would take patience, control, cunning, and strategy, and a little bit of good luck. I thought about the organization that Carlos Trinidad ran and how vast it had to be. Then I thought about my organization which consisted of just two men. Me and the man sitting to my left. I glanced over at Ameen and smiled. Ameen Bashir was the most realest and loyal dude I'd ever met. He was evident and understood. While we both grew up in Sheridan Terrace, we never became close friends until I was eleven and Ameen was fourteen. An act of bloodshed had bonded us together forever.

Over the years, I focused on the getting money aspect of our union, while Ameen killed everybody that got in our way. I remembered all the things that me and Ameen had done together in the past and then pondered all that we could do in the future. Everything would be lovely. I told myself that when I got back from my business trip with Carlos Trinidad that it was time for a family outing. I would tell Ameen to get his three sons and his wife Khadijah ready for a vacation out of town. I knew that Patricia and Zin would love to leave D.C. for a little while.

"How long you gon' be gone, slim?" Ameen asked me, breaking our silence.

"I'll be back tomorrow, have some fun until I return. When I get back it's time to grind. Feel me?"

"I feel you, slim... I feel you."

Chapter Twenty-Seven
Michael Carter

The gulfstream three private jet landed at a small airfield some-where and I had no idea where we were. On the jet with me were Carlos Trinidad and three of his ever-present henchmen. One of these henchmen was the man who I knew as Benito. The after-noon sun shined hotly on my skin as we got off the jet. Two black Range Rovers sat idle a few feet off the tarmac. At the sight of the entourage of people, the Range Rovers came to meet us.

"Mike, you ride in this one with me." Carlos said while put-ting a hand on my shoulder. "Benito, you ride with Serge and Luiz."

Carlos Trinidad stared impassively out the window as the dense woods turned to open countryside. The Rovers sped to-wards an unknown destination. Having been told absolutely nothing about our trip, I wanted desperately to question Carlos.

As if he could read my mind, Carlos said, "You are probably wondering where I am taking you?"

"Yeah, something like that." I replied.

"You are a trusting man, Mike. Not many people would take a trip outside of his comfort zone without any information as to where he's headed. I respect that, I did tell you that this trip was business, right?"

"Yeah, you said that."

"This trip is business, Mike and I want you to always re-member that. You are twenty-four years old and you still have a lot to learn. Today, you learn one of the greatest lessons in this business. I'll explain more when we get to our destination."

Twenty minutes later, the Range Rovers pulled into a circu-lar brick driveway that had several expensive cars adorning it. The driveway's walkway led to a beautiful two story grey brick house that looked like a mansion.

"Nice house, huh?" Carlos, asked once we stepped out of the truck.

"It's huge, yeah it's a beauty." I answered.

157

"Too bad the person who owns it will never see it again."

The front door to the house opened and I wasn't surprised to see another Hispanic dude step to the side allowing us entrance into the house.

"Where are they?" Carlos asked the man.

"In the living room, follow me." The man replied, then led everybody down a hallway.

The hallway let out into a spacious living room with a stone and brick fireplace that climbed the wall to the ceiling. Beautiful brown leather furniture adorned the room with a mixture of lacquer and wood furnishings. It was a scene straight out of the Architectural Digest magazine. In the middle of the room sat three chairs. In those chairs sat three people with black hoods over their heads to hide their faces.

"Remove their hoods." Carlos demanded.

One by one, the hoods were removed to reveal the faces of an elderly woman with long grey hair, pulled into a ponytail. Next to her sat another woman, her beautiful green eyes were pleading for understanding that I was unable to give her. I didn't understand what was happening myself. In the last chair sat a teenage boy. His boyish good looks resembled someone that I had seen before. Over their mouths was a strip of duct tape. Then I realized that all three people were taped to their chairs.

Carlos, turned facing me. "In the car, I told you that this was a business trip and it is. This house belonged to Victoriano, and these people here..." he swept his hand past the three people taped to the chairs. "...are his family. The octogenarian is his grandmother, Esla. The beautiful lady here is his wife Natalia, and the boy is Victoriano's son, Victoriano Jr. In this business, Mike, examples must be set and lessons must be learned. There is no trial and error. The most important thing that you must know is that everything and I emphasize everything, is about business. Nothing..."

Carlos pulled a handgun out of his waist. Then he walked up to the old woman and shot her in the forehead. "...is ever personal. Victoriano made a decision with the DEA and then signed his name on a typed document. When he signed that document..." Carlos turned and shot the beautiful woman next. One shot to the forehead at point blank range. "...for the Feds, he unknowingly signed the death certificate for himself and his family. His actions directly showed that he didn't give a fuck about them. So, if he didn't care about his mother, his wife, and son, that he so elaborately tried to hide out here in the hills of Upscale New York, then why should I give a fuck about them?

With that said, Carlos stepped in front of the teenage boy. "Let this be a lesson to you, Mike. If you cross me, you cross yourself and you cross your family, because they all will pay the ultimate price. That means that you will die, your wife Patricia will die, and your only child, Zinfandel will die as well." Then he shot the boy twice in the head. "So you enter this business deal at your own risk and at your own peril. If you are a stand up man who honors the death before dishonor, then you will have no problems, and you will get rich.

But if you are an inherent, degenerant piece of shit like Victoriano, it will come out one day. And that day, like God says in Genesis of the Bible...you shall surely die. Don't answer me now, Mike. In a few days, give me a call and we'll talk again then." Then to one of his men he said, "Jorge, take Mike back to the plane. Instruct the pilot to take him back to D.C. Benito, find somewhere to bury these bodies and somebody find me something to eat in here."

On the plane ride back to D.C. I sat and thought about what I had just witnessed. Carlos Trinidad, had just executed Victoriano Martinez's whole family without compunction. He killed an old woman, a wife, and her teenage son as easily as if he was throwing a frisbee. The Hispanic drug Lord was as ruthless as the streets proclaimed and he had an uncanny ability to know exactly what people was thinking. I thought about the fact that Carlos knew my wife's full name and my daughter's name and that scared me a little. How did he know so much! Deciding right then that Carlos Trinidad was the perfect ally in my quest to get to the top. I planned to accept his offer of being the main supplier of cocaine in Southeast. And I also decided at that moment that I would never cross a man like Carlos Trinidad.

* * *

By the time the Gulfstream touched down at Reagan Nation Airport, the sun had set and evening was upon me. I glanced at my watch. It read 7:38 p.m. and put my special code in. After waiting about ten minutes, I called my house. There was no answer there, either. "Tricia must've went to pick up, Zin from my sister's house." I said to myself. I walked around the airport until I spotted a cab. I paid the cab driver to take me home, then laid back in the air-conditioned back seat, and closed my eyes. The first thing that I noticed at I stepped out of the cab was Ameen's BMW 325i parked in front of my house. Why would his car be there?

My imagination started to run wild and an instant scowl crossed my face. Slowly, I made my way to my front door. Being as quiet as I possibly could, I put my key in the lock and opened the door. The lights in the living room were out as well as the other lights in the house. Slipping out of my shoes, I crept softly to the hall closet. In the closet, I kept a spare nine-millimeter Baretta. Feeling around in the dark, I finally felt the butt of the pistol. I pulled it out, chambering a round, I walked softly up the carpeted stairs. Two steps from the top, the sounds of soft moans could be heard. Heartbroken and now furious, I made my way to my bedroom.

My wife's unmistakable sounds of passion filled my ears. The bedsprings croaked and squeaked from the beating it was taking. I gently pushed the bedroom door open. Standing in the shadows of darkness, I watched the greatest act of betrayal that had ever been perpetrated against me. My wife, the woman that I loved more than anything on Earth was on the bed on her elbows and knees in doggy style position. And my best friend, comrade, and partner was on his knees behind her pounding himself into Patricia with beastial ferocity.

160

The sounds of their skin slapping pushed my invisible knife deeper and deeper into my heart. With each thrust, I felt my resolve crumble. My first instinct was to kill them both in the bed, but somehow, that thought quickly left me. I turned around and crept back out of the house. For a second, I actually thought about sparing them both, but something that Carlos Trinidad said to me came quickly to mind.

"If you cross me once, you'll cross me twice."

And I knew the dangers first hand of letting a person cross you twice. My mind was made up, both Patricia and Ameen would die when I decided it was time. And Ameen would be the first to go...

***

Knock...knock...knock!

I opened my eyes and sat up on the bunk.

"It's me, Duck, Mike. I'm just letting you know that the compound police is up in the block. They going in cells shaking down."

"Thanks for the heads up, homie." I answered as I got up and grabbed my knife and stamps off my desk. I put them both down by the toilet closet to the door. I pulled my pants down and sat on the toilet as if I was taking a shit. Not long after that, someone knocked on my cell door.

"Who is it?"

"Compound, we need to shake your cell down." an officer called out.

"I'm taking a shit, come back."

"We'll be back."

I had been in Canaan long enough to know that the lazy C.O.s would wait, but not for long. Eventually, they would leave. I would just have to wait them out. If they persisted, I was prepared to bend the knife and flush it down the toilet. The stamps they could have. After about ten minutes, a knock on the cell door got my attention.

"I'm still on the shitter, I got real bad diarrhea."

"It's me again, moe, they gone. They just left out the block." Duck said.

"Good looking, homes." I stood up and pulled my Khakis back up. I picked up the knife and stamps and placed them on my top bunk. Laying back down on my bunk, I went back into time again...

My wife and partner never knew that they'd been caught with their pants down literally and that's the way I wanted to keep it. After leaving my house that night, I drove to a motel in Maryland and rented a room. The visual images of Patricia being fucked savagely by my right hand man permeated me to the core. Inside the four walls of the motel room, I allowed myself to get emotional. As painful tears fell down my face, the love that I had for both of my betrayers evaporated. I never knew a pain so great could exist. Love and pain were two of the greatest extremes that I had ever faced.

Having known Patricia all my life and loving her for over half of it. I remembered the day I decided I needed her in my life forever. I remembered the day that we got married. I remembered our honeymoon. I remembered the day that Patricia gave birth to my daughter. I had been the happiest man alive, and then, in one night, twelve years of love had turned into two hours of intense pain. I laid on my motel bed and plotted and planned, never again would I be fooled or tricked by love and loyalty. At some point, in my pain, I fell asleep.

The next day, acting as if nothing had ever happened. I went home to my wife and fucked her. More like raped her, our sex was violent. I would never make love to her again. To me she was a whore and whores got fucked, not made love to. I had decided to delay her punishment. Not for the benefit of myself but for my daughter. But Ameen was a different case all together. He would be dealt with swiftly. For the briefest of moments, I thought about Ameen's wife Khadijah and his sons Quran, Jihad, and Khitab. Khadijah would mourn her husband, her sons would mourn their father. His betrayal had become theirs.

Three days later, I took Ameen with me to pick up a shipment of cocaine from Carlos Trinidad's people. Once the coke was dropped off at the spot that we agreed upon. It was time to call it a day. I asked Ameen to drop me off at home, but instead of going inside my house, I ran around to the back alley, to a waiting hoopty I purchased at an auction. I caught up to Ameen's BMW in no time and followed him to his house. Careful, to stay in the shadows, I allowed Ameen to get to his front door before I pulled down my mask and ran up onto his front porch.

Startled by the sudden presence, Ameen turned around, facing me. "What the fu..." Was all that Ameen got out of his mouth.

"If you cross me once, you'll cross me twice, remember!" I said and fired the gun. I shot Ameen in the head and face. Then I ran back to the hoopty and sped off into the night.

I paid for Ameen's funeral and gave his wife all of the money I had that belonged to her husband. I wanted his life, not his wealth. While at their house one day, I saw Ameen's oldest son Quran. There was something about the kid that stood out. He had to be eleven at the time. Quran was a man child and the son who resembled his father the most. He had those eyes, the grey eyes that made so many fear Ameen and his gun. The same thing that lived inside of the father resided in the son. I could see that easily. In the young boy's eyes lived a callousness. A hunger that couldn't be described. I decided to harness the youngsta's unbridled emotion. I wanted to control that energy. So, I pulled Quran aside and told him my first lie. One that would change his life forever!

Chapter Twenty-Eight
Zinfandel

I sat at the kitchen table in my aunt Linda's house and prepared the motion to dismiss all charges against David Battle. His trial started in eight days and I knew all the witnesses against him were now deceased. The judge in that case would have no other choice but to release David and dismiss all charges with prejudice. Deeply ensconced in the legalese of the drafted document, I never heard the footsteps, behind me. When familiar hands caressed my shoulders, I jumped.

I turned around and stared into the face of my aunt. My shero "Hey auntie, you startled me."

"Sorry baby, you hungry?"

"Naw, I stopped at Ms. Debbie's on the way home, I'm good."

"Ms. Debbie's? That's that new soulfood place on Marlboro Pike."

"Yeah, you mean to tell me you never been there?"

"Haven't had the chance yet. But I heard some good things about it. I really try to stay away from them greasy, spoon places." Linda said as she opened the refrigerator and rummaged around inside.

"Aunti, Ms. Debbie, ain't no greasy spoon joint. T and T was greasy spoon. Henry's is a greasy spoon. Horace Dickies is a greasy spoon. Mama Cole's is a greasy…"

"Okay, already, I get the picture. I'll make it there one day, you sound like you own some shares in the company."

I laughed, "I wish I did, besides, speaking of food, I thought that you and Barry were going out to dinner."

"I cancelled at the last minute." Linda replied pulling a half gallon carton of Hagen Daaz ice cream out the freezer. "That nigga ain't tryna do nothing, but get some of this snapper.

Getting up I walked over to the fridge and pulled out a bottle of spring water. "He wants you to fry him some fish."

Linda gave me a look of bemusement, "Ain't talkin' about frying no fish, baby. I'm talking about these goodies between my legs."

Spitting out water, I laughed hysterically.

"Zin, you spitting water all over me, girl." Linda added as she wiped at the water now staining her shirt. "You goofy as shit, girl."

"I'm sorry auntie, your ass is crazy as hell."

"I'm serious." Linda said still laughing. "That nigga dick too big any goddamn way. I need me one of them handsome white-boys with an average sized package.

I leaned on the kitchen counter to hold myself up. I had tears in my eyes and my stomach was starting to hurt. "Auntie stop it. You gon make me pee on myself."

"Chile, I ain't playing. I'm getting older now, I can't be lay-ing down with them big dick ass nigga's. Barry's bald headed ass is all dick. One hundred percent grade A beef. The last time I gave him some, he had me walking funny for a whole week. Fuck that shit. Shit always start out with dinner. Then drinks, and that nigga know how I get off some of that Grey Goose shit."

"Auntie stop it." I said while struggling to catch my breath.

"I ain't lying. That nigga always order me Grey Goose or Patron. And my stupid ass always drink that shit. The next thing you know I'm ass up and face down with a yard of dick in me. Uh huh, not tonight, I'm tired of being sore messing with that nigga and all he ever tell me is…blame it on the alcohol. Can you believe that shit?"

Again I wiped tears from my eyes as I imagined my aunt getting laid.

"So, I ducked his ass chile. That nigga was mad as shit, too. I told his ass to go home to his wife and give her some attention."

"Barry's married?" I asked skeptically.

"Of course, all my men have to be married for me to mess with them. When I get tired of their asses I send 'em home."

"Auntie you are crazy."

"Naw, baby I'm real. I know how dirty men can be. Why should I be the one at home crying over their asses? No thank you. I'm good on all that. I'd rather borrow someone else's man and then give them back."

Suddenly, I thought about the two men in my life and wondered was either of them now with other women. At that exact moment. It had been two days since I walked out on Jermaine and he hadn't called me not one time. Neither had I heard from Quran. The thoughts of what I witnessed in that bathroom on Douglas Road scared me to the core. But I was still around, the last words that Quran said to me continued to chill me to the bone...

"You asked me that night who I really am and I told you that you don't wanna know. Zin, I never wanted you to know what type of man I was...I am. But fate and destiny has forced my hand. Now you must know, I kill people for a living. That's what I do, I killed Yolanda Stevens...Tommy Caldwell...and countless others like them. That's who I am, Zin. That's the person that you are in love with."

"Are you listening to me, chile?"

I snapped out of my reverie. "Huh?"

"Which one should I get?" Linda asked.

"Which one what, auntie?" I replied puzzled.

"The dildos, chile. I told you I'm about to get me one of them B.O.B.'s that fine ass man Raheem Devaughn keep singing about."

"B.O.B.?"

"Damn, child, where you head at? B.O.B. battery operated boyfriend. They got these little fingers ones, but I need something bigger than that. I went online and saw this one they call the rabbit...it has an insertable shaft that can do different shit like vibrate or rotate. It has internal beads and thrusting action. Attached to the shaft is a vibrating clitoral stimulator. Gurl, they got acrylic dildos, glass pyrex ones. Dildos with cyberskin, they advertise it as silicone and plastic. They U shaped ones for double penetration, they got strap ons, suction cup dildos...all kinds of shit. I'm about to swear off of men for a while, so I'ma need me a toy. What do you think?"

"Aunt Linda, I think this T.M.I., too much information for my naïve ears. I'm about to go take a bath and then go to sleep. I have to get up early tomorrow." I walked over to my aunt and hugged her. "I'm sure your crazy butt will think of something, goodnight." I gathered up my things and prepared to go upstairs.

"Zin." Linda called out.

I stopped in my tracks and turned to face my aunt, "Yeah auntie?"

"How long are you going to stay here and hide from your life?"

I thought long and hard about the question my aunt had just asked.

"Zin, baby you are the daughter that I never had, but always wanted. This house is yours as well as it's mine. You know that, you can stay here until you're old and grey, but will you be happy? You told me months ago about this guy Quran and I understand Jermaine's pain and the reasons why you walked away. But the fact remains that you're in love with two men and you're only one woman.

"Nobody can serve two masters. You know that, so you have a decision to make. Do you repair your life with the man that you made one with for the last six years or do you give that up for the life that you can now have? No matter what you decided you have to face life head on. You can't run away from it. Well you can run for a while, but you can't hide forever. Think about that, goodnight!"

Drying myself off after getting out of the tub, I laughed to myself at what my aunt had said in the kitchen about her friend Barry and the dildos. Then my mind settled on the last words that she had said...

"Nobody can serve two masters..."

"Nobody can serve two masters..." I repeated to myself as I rubbed lotion on my body. Despite how the situation looked, I knew that I had no intentions of serving two masters. That wasn't my dilemma. My decision was made, it didn't take long after being with Quran, to realize that I was living a lie with Jermaine. Compared to Quran, Jermaine didn't measure up. No matter what metric system I used, Jermaine didn't balance out on no scale. I remembered the hurt look on Jermaine's face as I admitted infidelity and left the apartment. Did he deserve what I'd done to him? Probably no, but what's done is done. I knew deep in my heart that my chapter with Jermaine was over whether I stayed with Quran or not. Crawling into my old bed, my last conscious thoughts were of Quran…the man I love.

Chapter Twenty-Nine
Quran

I couldn't bring myself to mourn or grieve for a brother who had turned rat. After drying my eyes the night, I killed him, I vowed to never cry for him again. My love ended at the end of the barrel that pushed out the bullets that stopped his life. My morals and principles refused to let me harbor any feelings for Tabu, and apparently, I was the only one that felt that way. I laid across my bed and thought about the scene when I told Jihad that Tabu was dead. Hours after coming to grips with what I had done, I called my brother to my condo and told him everything.

"Zin called and told me that she needed to see me. She said that it was important." I explained. "She came here and sat right there where you are sitting right now, and she gave me the paperwork."

Jihad sat on the love seat across from me, reading the papers that Zin had given me. The grand jury statements and the affidavits that Tabu had signed. I could see the confusion and hurt on his face as he read.

"What you're feeling right now is the exact same way that I felt when I read that shit. I was devastated, destroyed, I couldn't believe that Tabu would do that…"

"I don't under…I don't…why would he…?"

"Believe me baby boy, I asked myself those same questions a thousand times before I made my decision. I keep drawing blanks."

"Why didn't you tell me? When you first heard…well read the papers…I mean?"

"Baby boy, I made the decision on the…"

"Just answer the question, Que! Why didn't you tell me when you first got the papers? Why wasn't I included in the decision-making process? Didn't my input mean something?"

"Jihad, I made the decision…"

"But it wasn't your decision to make! Not on your own, he was my brother too!"

"You really wanna know why I didn't tell you, baby boy? I didn't tell you because I knew how emotional you'd be. I knew that you'd want to spare him. I knew how close you two were. I knew you'd be hurt, but you'd find a reason to try and get him off the hook. And most importantly I didn't want to be influenced by the pain that I see in your eyes right now. Beside...telling you wouldn't have changed the fact that Tabu snitched. He snitched on a friend of ours. He had..."

Jihad stood and threw the papers across the room. I watched the papers rain all over my living room and then landed on the carpet.

"You had no right!" Jihad bellowed. "You had no right to kill my brother..."

I remained calm, and spoke softly, but with authority, "Why? Why didn't I have the right, Jihad? Because Tabu was born a Muslim? Because only Allah has the right to take life? How many lives have you taken, Jihad? Huh? How many lives have we taken together? We been crushing these rats since we was teenagers. It's what we do, and I never heard you say shit about us not having the right to do it.

"You never said a word. You took your money and did what you had to do. Tabu knew the rules, he hung with you almost every day. He knew what we did, what he did. He knew and he purposely disregarded everything he knew to save his ass. He thought that his blood was sacred enough to get him a reprieve after committing the most egregious sin ever.

"He became a snitch and that broke my heart into pieces. I loved him more than you will ever know, but when he decided to become a government whore that sealed his fate. And I killed him because I had to. I had to let him know that he was wrong and that he had to pay the ultimate price. The same price that all the other rats paid."

Jihad dropped to his knees and put his face in his hands. He broke down in a fit of deep wracking sobs. I wanted to reach out to him and comfort him, but I couldn't. I had to appear to be made of iron.

"I know you're hurting, baby boy. I am, too, but I had to do it and right before I did it, all I could think about was our parents. I thought our mother and what she told me on her death bed. As cervical cancer ravished our mother's frame she told me to take care of you and Tabu. And I did, the best way that I knew how. But somewhere we went wrong.

"I say we because you and I raised him. We failed him along the way because we gave him a false sense of bravado. He became brave enough to become a rat and think that we wouldn't hurt him. I thought about that before I pulled the trigger. I thought about everything that our father told us, Jihad. The three of us, before he died. I remember it by heart, I was ten years old when our father said…

"As you grow up, be wary of the type of men that you associate with. Watch for signs of discord, dislike, ambition, pride, greed, and betrayal. To be hurt or killed because you never saw what was coming, makes you a fool. And no one wants to appear to be a fool. However, you are my sons and that means a lot in the streets, but that may not always be so. So, you must surround yourself with people you can trust and forge your own path. Leave behind you a trail, so that those behind you may follow. Push yourselves harder, longer, and faster than anyone else ever could. When you get scared, hide it. No one will know, whatever frightened you will pass in time. How you react in the scariest of moments will be remembered by all. When you tired, never show it, and never speak of it. Those around you will think you are made of iron…"

Jihad looked up at me with tears in his eyes and said with me… "Never let those around you mock you, even in jest. It is something that men do to test you and later that man will oppose you. Show people at all times that you will not be cowered. And that you will kill if you have too. If you have to fight, fight. But as you grow older, fight no more. Fighting has no place in a world filled with guns. If you forget that and go fight your enemy, he will shoot you.

"No man can stand to be bested in a fist fight. That man will grow resentful and seek revenge. Boys fight to win or lose. Men fight to live or die. So, always strike first in war. As teenagers or men, no matter who it is, friend, brother or foe, crush those who seek to harm you. Never waiver and never show mercy. Anyone who crosses you must know that they are gambling with their life and that they will lose. That they will die. Dudes in the streets only respect strength that is greater than theirs and men who go harder than themselves. But above all else…they respect a killer.

"A killer with success defeating his enemies. If you are betrayed or crossed by anyone, and I do mean anyone, let that slight be their last. Because those that will cross you once, will surely cross you twice. Never give anyone that chance. I remember when pop told us that. I took it to heart then and I still do." Jihad paused to wipe tears from his eyes. "But I also remember something else, I remember the day that our mother died. As we gathered around her bed. She said…,

"The streets talk, Quran. And I'm a good listener. I have two ears to hear and one mouth, so I talk less and hear more. I know all about what you do. I know why Mike Carter calls you and what you do for him. I have always known, I just never said anything. I also know that you and Dontay have been taking Jihad with you when you do it. You kill people, Quran. And now you've taught my second born son to do the same thing. I never objected because I believe that it's the will of Allah.

"I tried to raise a man, Allah made you Muslim, but Michael Carter made you a killer. Your father was a killer, too, Quran. I knew that then and like now never said a word. You were too young to know that and I don't know if Mike told you, but he was. Ameen Bashir, was feared killer. But eventually, someone killed him.

"Why? Because he killed so that that the streets would bow to him, worship him, and do what he wanted. But he forgot one thing and that was that his will was nothing and all that matter was the will of Allah. The apple doesn't fall far from the tree and in this case it didn't. You and Jihad are just like your father. But your brother…Khitab is not. He's more like me, that's why you must promise me that you will always take care of him. Do you remember that, Que?"

"Like it was yesterday." I replied.

"Our mother knew that Tabu was weak. He wasn't like us she said, she knew it and we knew it, you knew it…"

"Where are you going with this, Jihad? Are you justifying what Tabu did? I hope not because when Tab became a rat, he became my enemy. He crossed Dave, he crossed you, and he crossed me. He gambled with his life and lost."

"He lost?" Jihad spat. "He was our brother…"

"Brother? Did you hear a word I just said? Tabu was a rat, baby boy and a vicious one. He stopped being my brother the day he told on Dave. The man I killed wasn't my brother. He was my enemy. What part of that don't you understand? Didn't you listen to our father? When a person crosses you once, they will cross you twice. Never give them that chance.

"How long do you think it would've been before Tabu told on one of us? A rat cannot be trusted. Just because he was weak, doesn't mean that he should've been spared. You trippin' right now, baby boy. Clouded by emotion, you ain't thinking straight. All the muthafuckas that we killed, we didn't give a fuck why they told.

"We killed them because they told. What makes Tabu any different? As a matter of fact, I'm through entertaining this conversation about my rat ass brother. I crushed his ass and can't nothing or nobody bring him back. What's done is done! If you wanna beef with me because I killed Tab, tell me right now and I'm…"

My brother rose to his full height, stared at me defiantely, and said, "You gon' what, big brother? Kill me too!"

"Get out of my house, slim. Get your soft ass out my house. You trippin' fuck I wanna kill you for? I love you, nigga and you are all I have left. You kill niggas that ain't close to you, but you gotta problem with me killing one who was. In the killing game, you can only be one way. Either you hate rats or you don't. Ain't no such thing as a halfway rat killer. Get the fuck out and don't say shit to me until you realize that." When Jihad didn't move, I repeated myself. "Get the fuck out nigga! You think I'm bull-shittin' with you? Bounce!"

Without a backwards glance, Jihad turned and left the condo. That was almost two days ago and I haven't left the condo since. I hadn't heard anything from my brother or Zin. Deep down I felt that I might've been too caught up in the mo-ment to really see how much I messed up in regard to Zin. I never should have made her come to Douglas Road and witness what she did. I didn't even know if mentally she was okay.

I thought about the moment when she fainted. Right after I shot Tabu. Quick reflexes had stopped a bad situation from get-ting worse because I saw her eyes glaze over. I immediately dropped the gun and caught her in my arms just before she could hit the floor. I held her in my arms and breathed in her scent. My tears fell down my cheek and moistened her hair. I lifted her completely and found my way in the dark until I reached her car. Once Zin was tucked into her driver's seat, she started to come around.

When she was able to decipher where she was and what had just happened, the first thing she said to me was, "You killed your brother."

My reply came out simple and concise, "What I told you in that bathroom back there is true. I kill people who break the rules. You witnessed it, now you know who I am. This is me, I had to do it. One day, you'll understand why. I am in love with you, Zin and I wanna be with you, but this is who I am. Either you take it or leave it. Think about it and contact me in a few days. If I hear from you, I'll know your decision, if I don't…well I know either way." Then I kissed her and closed the car door.

I stood there in the middle of Douglas Road and watched Zin's Infinite disappear.

My cellphone vibrating caught my attention. I reached down onto the floor and picked it up. The caller I.D. display said that the caller was Ki-Ki, I picked up, "Hello?"

"Quran, what's good baby?"

"Ain't shit, Ki-Ki what's up with you?"

"I'm missing you, that's what's up."

"Is that right?"

"Yeah, that's right, so when can I see you. I just off tour and I need a little bit of that thug D.C. shit in my life."

Ki-Ki would be the perfect distraction for me, "How about tomorrow I can come to you."

"You wanna come to Virginia Beach?" Ki-Ki asked.

"Yeah, why not, I ain't never been and I need a vacation."

"That sounds good to me. I would love to show you around down here. I can't wait to see you and do unspeakable freaky shit to you."

"I need it, God knows I do. Listen, I'ma take care of some business first and then I'm on my way, Okay."

"Kay, call me when you hit the road."

"I will, I'm out." I ended the call, then I hit the shower.

By the time I got myself together after my shower, the text message that I'd been waiting for popped up on my phone. I read the text, reread it, and then erased it from my phone. I stored all the info in my head, grabbed two hammers out of my drawer, and went to work.

Chapter Thirty
Quran

I dialed the phone number given to me on the text message and asked for Junie. We talked and I agreed to meet him on North Capitol Street, by the Golden Rule high rise apartment building. I pulled into the parking lot and saw a short, brown-skinned dude with braids and a hairy face standing there. Pulling alongside the dude dressed in dark jeans and a hood with a Helly Hanson ski vest on and hit my window to roll it down. I called out to the dude.

"Junie."

"That's me." The dude said and walked over to the car. "All I do is point out Diddy, right?"

"That's it, slim, then I pay you."

Junie got into the passenger seat of my car and as soon as he sat back, he said, "This nigga Diddy is a gangsta rat, dawg. He hitting heads, strong arm robbing niggas, carrying guns, and making niggas hustle for him for free. This nigga is on his real live Deebo shit. But at the same time, he real cool with all the police in the area and them people down five-five-five. He do shit, get locked up, tell on muthafuckas, and then get out. He got a sho nuff get outta jail free car, hot ass nigga."

"Do dudes around the Cordas know he hot?" I asked as I pulled off and headed to Sursum Cordas, a project nearby.

"Yeah they know, but slim family big as shit and his people's are head busters. Plus, if they bullshit with Diddy, he gon' kill a nigga, then tell on another nigga and get out. You can't beat him, dawg."

"And you know he's outside right now?"

"Positive. I just talked to my man Lil' Jaha and he said that Diddy's out there hustling. He's right in front of Temple Courts."

"A'ight, this is how we do this. You go and make sure that he's out there and then come back and tell me. Plus, I need to know how many other dudes is out there and who might bust their gun back when I go to hit him."

"That's a bet, let me out right here and I'll be back in ten minutes."

I parked by the old Market on North Capitol and let Junie out. I let the Scarface CD take me to another place while I waited for the dude to return. Seventeen minutes later, he did.

"He out's there, he's wearing an Ed Hardy skull and bones sweat hoody, black jeans and Nike boots. He got shoulder length dreads and he's lighter than me and you. He got a couple of youngins out there with him, but I don't think they strapped. Besides, them youngins wanna see him get slumped anyway. Trust me, I know, you gon' recognize him when you see him. You go through the cut right there and just walk down the walk. They the only ones out there, just act like you coming to buy weed. That's all you need me for, right?"

"Yeah." I responded, getting out the car.

"Well, pay me then." Junie said.

"Not until I get back, sit in the car and wait on me. I got you."

I did as I was instructed and found the crowd in front of Temple Courts. I pulled out my cellphone and faked like I was talking to someone as I stared up at the numbers on the building. I headed directly for the crowd, all the while talking on the phone. I acted like I was receiving instructions on how to get to a specific place. Nobody in the crowd paid me any mind as I closed the distance between me and them, I spotted Diddy and locked on to him. They were completely caught by surprise when I stopped suddenly, whipped out, and hit Diddy in his head. I watched him fall as the crowd scattered. Stepping on him, I fired two bullets into his head for good measure. Then I turned and ran back to my car. I reached the car, got in, and started it up.

"Did you get him?" Junie asked.

"I nodded my head as I pulled off onto North Capitol and hit K Street. I pulled over by Dominoes pizza, reached in my pocket, and handed Junie an envelope. "This is yours."

"What's this?" Junie asked. "My money?"

I gave the dude a chance to read the documents that was in the envelope. "Naw, dawg, that's a copy of the affidavit where you gave sworn statements on Khalid Abdul Latif and Andy Daniels."

Junie looked up from the documents, right into the barrel of my gun. He never got a chance to speak because I put two bullets into his cranium. I got out the car and wiped down the stolen Toyota Camry. Then I calmly walked up K Street to the subway. Two hours later, I was on I-95 headed to Virginia Beach. I still hadn't heard from either Zin or Jihad, and that was okay with me. Who really needed love anyway? And since Jihad cared so much about me killing, Tabu, he could deal with the trouble of burying him.

Chapter Thirty-One
Zinfandel

"I caught the local news the other night, I take it you showed the papers to Quran Bashir." Jen said as she stepped into my office and closed the door.

"I did talk to Quran and what was on the local news? Did I miss something?" I asked feigning ignorance.

"You mean to tell me you don't know?"

"Know what, Jen? What don't I know?"

"I can't believe you don't...Khitab Bashir is dead. He was killed Wednesday night. The police found his body hanging from a pipe in a dilapidated tenement on Douglas Road. I thought you..."

"You thought I what, Jen? Orchestrated his death?" I snapped.

"Don't put words into my mouth, Zin. I just assumed that you knew about Khitab's death. I never implied that you had a hand in it. You couldn't have known what Quran Bashir would do, if in fact it was Quran who did anything. But we have to keep the fact that we revealed sensitive information to an outside party. We have..."

"Jen, I know the drill. I knew the potential ramifications behind my actions. I talked to Quran the same day that you gave me the paperwork and he read it. I left his condo and that's all I know. I try to stay away from the news nowadays because it's too depressing. I...I...don't know what..."

"Zin, like I told you before, it's the nature of the beast. Things like this happen in the streets. We are one less client, but on a better note, we are one less witness against David Battle. And with Khitab Bashir dead, that means that... oh my gawd!" Jen said and rushed out of the office. She returned five minutes later with a manila envelope.

I sat there confused as Jen tore into the envelope.

"This was just delivered a few minutes before I came to see you…" Jen started, then paused to read a motion or brief of some kind. "Shit, I knew it."

"Knew what…what happened?"

"I saw the return address on the envelope, but I paid it no mind until we just discussed David Battle. I remembered the envelope and had a sudden premonition that the certified package was something to do with that case and I was right."

"What is it, Jen?"

"Here, read it for yourself. We've officially been blindsided."

The brief had to be at least fifty to sixty pages. I flipped to the last page and saw that the brief had been prepared by the U.S. Attorney himself. Greg Gamble, seeing his name made my skin crawl. I flipped back to the brief heading…

Governments motion for admission of statements and Grand Jury testimony of deceased witnesses, Thomas R. Caldwell, Yolanda Stevens, and Khitab A. Bashir. An individual named Thomas Caldwell stated on several occasions that he met with the defendant, David L. Battle in March, August and September of two-thousand eleven. At one of these meetings he provided the defendant with a black and grey Ruger P.89 handgun, and a clip that held seventeen copper jacketed ammunition. Said gun was found to be used in murder of Sloman S. Robinson. Caldwell also stated that he feared for his life as a government informant/witness. Mr. Caldwell intimated that the defendant had dangerous friends, namely a man whom he called Q.B. that would kill him if he testified. Mr. Caldwell is now dead. The government asks the court to admit Mr. Caldwell's prior statements and all testimony given to the Grand Jury, through hearsay, into evidence.

Since I already knew everything that Khitab had told the government, I skipped his statement and read Yolanda Stevens…

"Her statement would've nailed David's coffin shut." I said to myself. "But can he do this? These statutes he oited are from the third and fifth circuit courts and have no precedence here in the District of Columbia."

"The Battle case belongs to Anne Sloan, right? Okay, she couldn't have gotten away with a brief like this, but he can. He's the Attorney General and the courts will give anything with his John Hancock on it a lot of consideration and due diligence. And the better question is…why would the Wizard of Oz come to Dorothy instead of waiting for her to travel down the yellow brick road?"

"I understand you and ask one of my own. Why this particular case?"

Jen crossed the room and stood by the window in my office, "It's gotta be the deaths, and judging by that motion, he's pissed."

"At us?"

"Yep. Our office just helped free Sean Branch. Greg Gamble made his prosecutorial bones off of the Sean Branch murder trial. He proved to the city that Sean Branch wasn't made of Teflon after all, that was eighteen years ago. Now Sean is free and he blames us. All the witnesses against our other high profile client, David Battle have been killed. Yeah I'd venture to say that the Wizard is pissed at us. Otherwise, he wouldn't have come down from up high to smack our ass because we been bad. How many times have he actually left Olympus in the…"

"Olympus? That would be Zeus, I believe…"

"Same difference, Zin. That motion wreaks of megalomaniacal personality disorder."

"Also known as Greg Gamble." I skimmed through the motion again. It was well put together and the case law cited was on point. "You really think the judge in that case will go for this?"

Jen shrugged her shoulders, "Who knows, but I'd wager and say that he will. Well, you know what you have to do. Research everything you can find to rebut that brief. I have to go and meet Nikki at the office of the Bar Counsel…"

"The Bar Counsel?"

"Yes, you know the drill. Another ex-client, in the Bureau of Prisons has filed suit against us, claiming that we robbed him, and took his money without effectively pursuing his freedom. The usual 'sour grapes' bullshit."

"Who is it this time?"

"Williams Sweeney, they call him Draper. He got locked up on that K Street conspiracy back in nineteen ninety-eight."

"I'm familiar with him and the case."

"Are you going to be okay in here alone?"

"Why do you ask that?" I asked.

"Because I know you'll sit and brood over the Khitab Bashir case. And speaking of which, Khitab was Muslim. So, according to Islamic law, his body has to be buried within seventy-two hours after the cops release it. They did, and his funeral is in two days. At a Masjid on Islamic Way called Masjid Muhammad or something like that. That info is online at the Washington Post website if you want to check it out. How's Jermaine doing, Zin?"

"Jermaine?"

"Yeah, your fiancé, at least that's what he told he was when he came here the other day. Is everything okay between y'all? I mean, I'm not trying to pry, I know it's a personal question, but he mentioned a lot of clients that I didn't know and said…"

"I know all about what was said, Jen, and you were right, that whole topic is personal, but since you asked. No everything is not okay, but if you're worried about my work and whether or not it will suffer as a result of my personal problems. The answer is no. Anything else?" It was my turn to dismiss Jen's nosy, fat ass, and it felt good.

"Uh…no, well I'll see you later, bye."

As soon as I heard the door to our office, shut, and lock. I pulled out my laptop and logged onto the Washington Post website. I scrolled down the obituaries until I found Bashir.

Khitab Amman Bashir…
Suddenly, on September 3rd, Khitab Bashir entered into eternal life. He was preceeded in death by his parents, Khadijah,

and Ameen Bashir. He leaves to mourn his passing, two broth-
ers, Quran Tariq and Jihad Abu Bakr Bashir, one special friend,
Adirah Mujahid. And several other relatives and friends. A view-
ing will be held at Masjid Muhammad on Islamic Way in North-
east, D.C. immediately following the Jinazah prayer...

I stopped reading and stared into the of Khitab Bashir. The
picture used on the site had to be an old one. Khitab Bashir, had
a full grown beard and his braids were gone, replaced by a low
cut taper with waves. He resembled the rapper Stalley from Ohio
that was down with Maybach Music. Khitab's smile was beautiful. Similar to Quran's, but not as electric. He was a handsome
man that resembled his brother, without the eyes.

I thought about the Khitab Bashir, that I'd seen in court that
last time and then the one hanging form the pipe, bloodied, and
mutilated. I decided right then to go to the funeral. It would give
me the opportunity to see Quran. I needed to observe him in that
environment and see if his actions gave away what he'd done.
Over the last few days, I'd thought long and hard about calling
Quran and going to him, but I suppressed those feelings because
I needed time to be sure that with him is where I wanna be. One
day I feel like I can't live with him in my life and then then next
I feel like I couldn't live without him in it. I clicked on the obi-
tuary and highlighted the entire section, then printed it out.

"You can leave now or stay. It's your choice..."

"I guess you've made your decision..."

"I loved you all my life and that won't change when you're
gone."

"Quran...no...don't do it! No-o-o-o!"

"That's who I am...I kill people...that's who I am..."

The voices in head wouldn't be silenced. I could hear Quran
and Khitab's voice as clearly as I could hear the voices that came
through on my Blackberry. Again I glanced at the monitor on
my laptop. Khitab Bashir's smiling face now filled the screen.
Quickly, I exited the website, I couldn't bear to see his face anymore. Shaking my head in an attempt to clear my mind, I rose
from my desk, went down the hall to the water cooler, and got

some water. Hoping that it would douse the fire burning inside me. Quran Bashir, was a fire that raged in my chest and I knew that whenever a person played with fire, they were bound to get burned.

Chapter Thirty-Two
Zinfandel

By the time I finished researching case law to refute Greg Gamble's motion to the court to allow dead witnesses statements, stand in a murder trial. It was late afternoon, early evening. I had let the whole day get away from me. My stomach rumbling reminded me that I hadn't eaten since breakfast with aunt Linda. I fished my phone out of my purse and checked my missed calls. Something inside me silently hope that Quran had called, he hadn't. But to my surprise there was two missed calls from Jermaine. I checked my text, emails, and voice mail, but he hadn't left a message. I wasn't ready to deal with Jermaine just yet, but yet I needed to stop pass the condo and get somethings of mine that I needed.

I closed up and locked up everything at the office and decided to eat first. Ending up at Ms. Debbie's Soul and Seafood Café. I ordered the fried whiting fish dinner, with steamed rice, and gravy, and macaroni and cheese. I sat inside the restaurant and listened to soulful music while enjoying my meal. Trying desperately not to think of Quran, his dead brother, Jermaine, Greg Gamble, his motion to admit deceased people's testimonies or any other law or clients. Having never really been religious, it was times like these that I contemplated yoga and pilates. Which reminded me that I hadn't been to the gym to workout or had my nails and toes done. The recent events in my life had caused me to neglect the most important person in my life...me. I made a mental note to self to get back on track and then finished enjoying my meal.

***

I made it to Adams Morgan in record time with a clear head, a full stomach, and a desire to be peaceful. My plan was to just get my things I needed and leave. No arguing with Jermaine, no fighting. When I pulled into the underground garage, I recognized two vehicles nearby, but assumed I was trippin' and kept it moving. A foreboding feeling bottomed out in the pit of my stomach and I started to ask myself why didn't I call Jermaine back. I rode the elevator up to the 5th floor and walked down the hall to the condo.

Inside, I could hear music playing, opening the door, I eased into the condo and noticed that the lights in the living room were dim. The dining room table had two plates set up with half eaten food still on them. From the dining room to the bed, a trail of hastily discarded clothes littered the floor. I could see panty hose and women's underwear amongst them. My heartrate quickened as my anger rose.

"How dare he?" I grumbled under my breath.

I couldn't believe that Jermaine had the audacity to have another bitch in my our…in our condo. My footsteps seemed like they were weighed down with lead. I never imagined that Jermaine…my Jermaine would get over my betrayal so fast and move on in only a few days.

"This muthafucka…" I muttered, grabbed the door knob on the door of our bedroom, and slowly turned it. *'Don't go in there!'* My conscience screamed, but I've always been a little hardheaded. Something inside me wanted to know who it was that he was fucking, something inside me wanted to see her. Slowly, I pushed opened the bedroom door. It never made a sound due to the thick carpet on the floor. I couldn't believe my eyes, bile rose in my throat as I heard her moans. They were in the sixty-nine position, her on her back with his dick in her mouth and him on top with his face between her legs, eating her pussy.

Two things instantly crushed me. One, after all the years, I'd been with Jermaine, he never ate my pussy. He claimed he didn't like doing it. And two, it was the person receiving oral pleasure. I stared into the face of my boss, Jennifer Wentz, and felt fucked up. Jermaine nor Jen ever looked up to see me standing there in the doorway. They were both too caught up in their carnal act to see me. I couldn't believe it…Jen and Jermaine. 'But how?' As

I stood there and watched Jermaine pleasure Jen. I remembered what he had said the night I walked into the condo after leaving Quran the night he killed his brother...

"...said that you were at the office. Well you're lying. You haven't been at the office all day or all evening. How do I know? I came to your office to take you to lunch, only to be told that you were in court. I left and came back in an attempt to take you to dinner. You never came back to your office, Zin. I was there all evening up until about an hour ago. You don't believe me, call and ask Jen. And speaking of Jen, we talked about you and all the work that you've been doing. I even mentioned some of the clients that you told me about. The ones that you've been spending so much time on their cases and guess what? She's never heard of any of them..."

I never paid any mind to the fact that Jermaine called Jennifer, Jen as if he was friends with her. My mind immediately hit overdrive and I wondered if somehow they had already known each other. Then I figured that maybe they met the day he came to the office and somehow connected on more levels than one. I couldn't blame Jen for wanting Jermaine. He was handsome, sexy, and intelligent, with good credentials.

Suddenly pieces of the conversation me and Jen had earlier rushed back...

"How's Jermaine doing?"

"Jermaine?"

"Yeah, your fiancé. At least that's what he told me he was when he came here the other day. Is everything okay between y'all?"

I just thought the fat bitch was being nosey. My arrogance never allowed me to question her motive for asking me such personal questions. Then she masterfully disguised her reasons for asking the questions. I never imagined in my most wildest dreams that they would be interested in one another on a sexual level. I allowed myself a quick smile, I realized all the while I commiserated over how bad I hurt Jermaine and the fact that he had to be destroyed about my infidelity.

The truth was that my boyfriend was getting his fuck on be-hind my back, probably the whole time. I had to smile at the fact that the joke was indeed on me. Jen knew that I'd stay at work and work on David Battle's case and Jermaine had to have told her that I'd left him and hadn't been home in days. They both had means and opportunity to orchestrate a tryst. I wiped the smile off my face as my anger rose. My boss and my man. A scene ready made for the lifetime movie channel. It was time to make my presence known. I walked over to the light switch and flipped it on.

Jermaine and Jen both froze and looked in my direction. Suddenly, Jen pushed upwards and Jermaine's dick fell out of her mouth. She grabbed the sheets and covered her disgusting nakedness Jermaine rolled off the bed and stood on the side clos-est to the back wall. His erect dick instantly losing it's erection.

"Zin...please don't misunderstanding...I...I..." Jen stut-tered.

"You what Jen? Got lost, ended up at my condo, then acci-dentally got naked and sucked my boyfriend's dick?"

"It's...not...what it looks like."

"It's not what it looks like? Jen, I work for you, with you. I just saw you and talked to you this morning. Tonight I come home and find you naked in my fucking bed with your pussy in my man's mouth and his dick in yours. Now, please explain to me what it's not supposed to look like. Because I see my boss and my man...or should I say ex-man in my bed executing the sixty-nine position perfectly. So, if it's not what it looks like to me, then what is it? Y'all were doing research?"

"Zin..." Jen started, but stopped mid-sentence. "I should just go, I'm sorry Zin. Please..."

"Get the fuck out of my condo Jen, before I lose my cool with you. You got..." I looked at my watch. "...three minutes and then..."

Jen got off the bed and dashed past me out into the hallway. I was surprised at her quickness. Minutes later, I heard the door to the condo open and close. Without saying a word, Jermaine walked over to where his boxers were, picked them up, and put them on. The smug look on his face as he leaned on the dresser and faced me made my blood boil.

"What now?" he asked.

"What now? You know what happens now. But let me ask you a question. You're slumming ain't you brother?"

"How so?"

"Didn't know you were into white bitches. Fat, white bitches at that. How long have you had that problem?"

Jermaine shrugged his shoulders, "We fuck who we fuck when the situation presents itself. You, more than anyone have to agree with that."

"Yeah, I do, but this isn't about me, this is about you."

"That's where you're wrong, Zin. If this is about anything, it's about you. You started this shit, you pushed me to do that shit. You cheated on me."

"I don't disagree with any of that, I just thought you have better taste. It's a little insulting to come home and find you in the bed with Jabba the Hut. I didn't know that you were into fat, white bitches, that's all."

"After all these years, there's a lot about me that you don't know, Zin. Just like there's a lot about you, I thought I knew, but I was wrong."

"Nasty, fat white bitches, though, Jermaine?"

A scowl crossed Jermaine's face. "How the fuck you gon stand there and judge me. Look who's talking, ain't you running around with a criminal? A fucking street thug? Didn't know that you were into the gangster element."

That was my cue to leave before things went down hill. "You know what…fuck this. I'm outta here, you can fuck Frosty the Snowman for all I care…"

"That's it, run away. Just like you always do, run from the truth. You ain't up on your soap box no more, huh? Didn't think I knew about your precious gangster? What's his name? Oh yeah…Quran!"

I turned to leave, but stopped in my tracks when Jermaine said Quran's name.

"Quran Bashir, right? The same muthafucka that you called out his name while we were fucking on two occasions. And you had the temerity to look me right in the eyes both times and lie to me about what you said. Now you stand there and tell me, I'm slumming. What do you call an up-worldly mobile licensed defense attorney fucking a low life, scum criminal, gangster, homeboy? Cat got your tongue, Zin, huh? Answer that with your slick talking ass."

Jermaine attacking my character, I could deal with, but his unwarranted attack on Quran made me mad. So, I went for the jugular.

"You're right, Jermaine, I did call out Quran's name while we were fucking. But I hadn't fucked him then. I just fantasized about it every time you touched me. Every time you put your small dick inside me, I was wishing it was him. I wanted his big dick, Jermaine. You're some shit in bed, I stayed with you because I thought at some point, you'd get it together, but you never did. So, I went an fucked and sucked another dick, a bigger…better…"

Jermaine closed the space between us in seconds and smacked the shit outta me. The force of the open palm smack sent me reeling into the wall behind me. I was shocked, outraged. Grabbing my cheek, I rubbed it, to try to soothe the sharp stinging sensation that I felt there. I stood up erect and tears formed in my eyes and fell.

"That was your first and last time ever putting your hands on me. Did that make you feel better? I hope so, because it makes me feel better about leaving you for good. And you were right I was slumming, but it wasn't with Quran. I was slumming when I decided to be with you."

Jermaine stood inches away from me. He raised his hand as if he was gonna strike me again.

"Go ahead and do it." I taunted. "Do it and I guarantee that you will be dead in forty eight hours. Compliments of that low life, scumbag thug that you were just talking about." I looked Jermaine right in his eyes and didn't flinch. "Try me, if you think I'm bullshitting."

Jermaine dropped his hand and his head, then turned and walked over to the bed. He laid down and locked his hands behind his head as if he as deep in thought.

"Punk ass nigga." I muttered as I massaged my face and walked into the walk-in closet. I put a few outfits in a roll out styled carry on bag and added shoes, purses, and accessories. Then from my drawers, I added underwear, panty hose, and socks. I decided to shop for brand new toiletries. "I'll be back in a few days for the rest of my things. I'll make sure to call before I come next time." I left the condo and that was that. A surprising end to another chapter of my life.

Chapter Thirty-Three
Quran

"How do you like your eggs?"

I sat on a barstool in Ki-Ki's kitchen and flipped the page of the book that Ki-Ki had recommended. It was called *'The Ultimate Sacrifice'*. The book was a page turner and I could really identify with the main character. The story was set in D.C. so that made the joint that much more realistic and exciting to me. "This nigga, Khadafi is an animal. I love this, nigga."

"What? I didn't ask you about no Khadafi, boy. I asked you how do you like your eggs?" Ki-Ki repeated.

"Huh?" I said looking up from the book. "Uh my eggs, how do I like my eggs? Scrambled with cheese."

Ki-Ki, went back to cooking. "I knew that you was gonna like that book. As soon as I read it, I thought about you. I know the guy that wrote it, he's a friend of mine. His picture is in the back of the book and he's from D.C. See if you know him."

I flipped to the back pages of the book until I came across a picture of the author and a short bio on him. "Anthony 'Buckey' Fields...Buckey Fields...I definitely heard the name before, but I don't know him personally. I'm digging his writing style, though. What's up with him?"

"He cool, I met his sister at a book signing and she told me that he wanted me to direct his path in getting his book published. I hollered at him and hooked him up with my girl. She's the one who put his book out. Did you get the chance to read the books I gave you? The two that I wrote?"

"No doubt, you're the best female street lit writer in the game, boo." I lied.

"You think so?" Ki-Ki asked smiling from ear to ear.

"Damn right, ain't nobody fuckin' wit' you."

"Thank you, baby. That means a lot to me coming from a real street nigga like you. I try to..."

I tuned Ki-Ki completely as I got back to the book. I was more interested in the crazy ass character in the book. Ten minute later, Ki-Ki placed a plate of cheese eggs, home fried potatoes, and turkey sausage links in front of me. Buttered biscuits and jelly came next.

"What do you wanna drink."

"Orange Juice, if you got it. Where your plate at?"

"I nibble while I was cooking, I'm good. Besides I'm tryna lose a little weight. Do it look like I need to lose some weight, baby?" Ki-Ki asked and slowly spent around.

She had definitely gained a few pounds since we'd last been together, but it wasn't that bad. Noticeable, but not out of control. "Naw, boo, you look good the way you are. As a matter of fact, come here." I stood up, grabbed Ki-Ki and pulled her close. I kissed her soft, pretty lips, and instantly got an erection.

She was wearing only a T-shirt and lace thong. Grabbing both of her ass cheeks in my palms, I squeezed until she begged me to stop.

"What you think my ass is them oranges that they squeezed to make that orange juice in your glass, nigga? You gonna leave a mark."

I kissed Ki-Ki to quiet her.

"Que, stop!" Ki-Ki purred. "Eat your food before you start something you can't finish."

"Is that right, is that a microwave over there in the corner?" I asked as I licked all over Ki-Ki's neck, deep inside, wishing she was Zin.

"Yeah…but…stop it, Que!"

"I can warm my food up after I finish what I just started."

"No…boy. Stop it, Que. All we been doing is fucking, since you been here."

"So what, we gon' fuck until I leave. The last time you was in D.C., you showed me that joystick, joyride. Remember that?"

"Of course, I do."

"You said that's how y'all get down in Virginia Beach."

"And I meant every word."

"Well, it's my turn. In D.C. we got something called Desk Detail. You gotta desk in your den, right?"

"That's where I write, of course."

I used my left hand to go under the T-shirt and rub Ki-Ki's pussy through the material of the thong. "Well, lead the way, then."

Ki-Ki led me through her house until we reached the den.

"This is my private office. All my books start and end in here. That computer right there brings my imagination to life. Let me move some of this stuff…"

"Ain't no need to move nothing. Come on." I walked over to the leather chair that was pushed up to the desk. Pulling it out with enough room to spare, I tugged at the drawstring on my Solbiato sweatpants and let them fall down my legs. I stepped out of the sweats and then removed my boxers and tank top. Sitting down in the chair, I spread my legs apart, and motioned for Ki-Ki to come to me.

"The desk detail, huh?" Ki-Ki asked with her eyes focused on my erect dick.

"Yeah." I answered and pulled Ki-Ki between my legs. "Turn around and face the desk. Take your shirt off, but leave your thong on." After waiting until Ki-Ki had followed my instructions, I told her, "Move the thong to the side and squat down onto this dick."

Ki-Ki did exactly as she was told. "D-d-a-a-m-m-n…Q-q-u-u-e-e! Your…your…dick…is so…!"

"Be quiet." I snapped. "So you can hear me as I tell you what to do. Lean forward and stretch out your arms until they reach the desk top. Yeah…like that, now lift your feet up in the air." I reached down and grabbed both of Ki-Ki's ankles in each of my hands.

"What…the…fuck! Oh…my gawd…Que…this feels so good!"

I worked my thrusts in small six-inch circles and watched my dick go in and out of Ki-Ki. Her pussy was wet as hell and it felt like her cum had ran out and pooled at the base of my dick. She had my dick hard as granite stone because her fat ass jiggled with every bounce and thrust.

"When I let your ankles go, try to keep them in the air, okay."

"O…o…o…kay!"

Letting her ankles go, I lifted Ki-Ki a little and backed up an inch. Then I took the juices pooled at the base of my dick, moistened my fingers, and rubbed it on her ass. I eased my fingers into her back door as I continued fucking her in short thrusts. Ki-Ki went nuts and all I could do was smile. We did desk detail for as long as it took me to finally bust a nut. Afterwards, I was exhausted and drained. I wanted to eat and rest, but Ki-Ki had other plans. Ki-Ki stood up and left the room, a few minutes later she returned. She tossed a small bottle to me.

"What's this?" I asked catching it.

"Read the label and see." Ki-Ki replied with a devilish grin.

"KY liquid lubrication jell with warming sensation. We don't need this, your pussy stay wet."

"Ha…ha…ha…you got jokes. You know that ain't for my pussy. You put your finger in my ass and started something, so now you gotta finish it."

"That's the second time today you done told me I started something. Aren't you tired of me finished shit?" I joked.

"Ask me that question after you fuck this ass." Ki-Ki walked over to the desk and bent over it. "What are you waiting for? You got lube and enough dick to give a bitch hemorrhoids so let's get started. Put some of that lube on me first."

"I got you, boo and don't worry, I ain't gon' give you hemorrhoids."

"Okay, baby and please be gentle with it until I get used to it. After that you can handle it any way you like."

At the sight of Ki-Ki's puckered brown eye winking at me, my dick got rock hard. I eased into Ki-Ki's ass and wore her ass out literally and figuratively.

Later that day, Ki-Ki and I went to the beach and lounged around enjoying the beautiful fall weather. We shopped at Military Circle Mall, then went out to eat. When we finally got back to Ki-Ki's house, I decided to check my phone to see who had called. I was surprised to see that Zin had called me four times. Mike Carter had called, and Jihad had left a text message. I read the text first...

//: I'm burying our brother tomorrow. Even if he dishonored himself, he still deserves a proper burial. An Islamic burial. What can I say bruh, you were right, and I was wrong? Tabu crossed over and that made his blood lawful. But it still hurts, if you decide to come to the funeral, it's being held at Masjid Muhammad at 10 a.m. If not, I understand, I love you, big boy. Call me when you can. Where the hell are you, anyway?

I decided to call Zin once I got back to D.C. Being in Virginia Beach had been fun, but it was time to go home. Mike Carter, having called me was the indicator that the bills had to be paid, so work had to be put in. I wondered who was the newest contestant on the 'Game of Death.' I put off calling everybody back until I got home. After deciding to leave in the morning, I found Ki-Ki in the living room and fucked her right there on the couch. I didn't even give her a chance to take her clothes completely off. I just pulled her pants down to her ankles, put her feet on my shoulders, and made her scream out my name.

"You gon' put me in your next book?" I asked as I put my dick game down.

"If you want me to." Ki-Ki replied under duress.

I worked my dick in and out of her wet pussy in circles, hitting every wall.

"I want you to get at your friend, the dude that wrote the other book I read. Sacrifice, you hear me?"

"Y-y-y-e-e-s-s-s!"

"Do a callabo and put me with that nigga, Khadafi. Let us tear a rack of shit up, you got that."

"I-I-I...got...you...Que! Fuck...me!"

As tired as I was sleep wouldn't find me. As I listened to Ki-Ki's light snores beside me, my mind was back in D.C. with Zin. No matter what I did or who I was with, I couldn't shake the visual images of Zinfandel Carter. My heart was in special need of a surgery that only she could provide the fix. She possessed the antedote that would cure all of my ill symptoms.

I could find no escape from myself imposed prison that had Zin on one side and what I'd done to my brother on the other. Another thought crossed my mind, the one that I had spoke aloud to myself. I had tested Zin's character and her fortitude to see if she was ride or die or crash and burn. I had to know where I stood with her and what she was made of. So, committing a murder in front of her, was my way of testing her. The results had been good so far. As far as I knew, the cops weren't looking for me for murder. So, Zin hadn't snitched, she probably never told a soul and that spoke volumes about her character. She might be wifey material.

Thinking about Zin, brought on thoughts of the man who birthed her. Michael Carter, Michael Carter was like a Soduku puzzle that was impossible to solve. And our bond was even more of an enigma. Our lives had been connected for over nineteen years. Starting with the first murder he told me to commit until now. Now, our lives are connected in another way…through Zin. I knew exactly who Zin was from the beginning and saw no reason not to pursue her.

I knew who her father was and the secrets we held between us. But for some reason I decided to keep another secret. On two fronts, I never told Zin that not only did I know her father, but I also killed people for him as he ordered deaths from his Pennsylvania prison cell. And I never told Mike that I was in love with and fucking his only daughter. There was one other secret that I could never reveal to Zin. This secret was the most important one of all. This secret would destroy her whole world…change her life totally. This secret had to remain just that, a secret, at all cost. The repercussions behind it were catastrophic. That was my last conscious thought before sleep finally found me.

Chapter Thirty-Four
Jihad

"Straighten out the ranks for me, brothers. Shoulder to shoulder, heel to heel. And remember in the funeral prayer 'Janazah', there are four takbirs, two rakahs."

I lined up with the Muslim brothers, while the women prayed behind the men. Although I was born and raised Muslim, I hadn't been on my deen in years. Not since I was a kid, living in a non-Muslim country and being around Christians and heathens all day everyday would throw any good Muslim off balance. The call of the streets reached my heart and pulled me. Ever since then I been answering the call. It felt funny being in the Masjid because I hadn't stepped foot in one in over ten years. The last time being the funeral for my mother.

"Allahu Akbar...Allahu Akbar...Allahu Akbar...Allahu Akbar..."

As I listened to the Iman recite dua, the Fatiha, and then Surahs from the Quran, I wanted to shed a tear. After leaving Quran's condo the night he killed Tabu, I drove to the scene of the crime. Knowing the projects like the back of my hand, it didn't take long to find my brother right where Quran said he was. My heart broke as I saw him hanging there. His face was almost unrecognizable with all the dried blood, and his eye was popped out. I stood in that spot and cried for about thirty minutes.

I wanted to pull him down from there, but I decided not to because that would put DNA on his body. I thought about everything Quran had said to me about his reasons for killing Tabu and as bad as I felt. I had to admit that he was right, Tabu knew the repercussions behind his actions and he decided to become a rat. There are two kinds of men that I detest with a passion and they are baby rapist and rats. They deserve to die a vicious death, but like Quran had said and hit close to home. I had killed rats before and didn't feel a thing, but never had I killed one who was so close to my heart as my brother.

When I could finally not stand seeing anymore, hanging there, I walked outside, got on my cell phone and called an ambulance. Then I drove to Douglas Middle School, sat in the parking lot and watched the ambulance arrive, then the police cars, and finally the coroner van. By the time the local news van showed up, I was long gone. I spent the next couple days in one of our trap houses, coming to grips with my brother's death. Somewhere in there I was able to arrange his funeral.

"O Allah, forgive our people who are still alive and who have passed away. Forgive those who are present here and those who are absent. Forgive our young and our elderly. Forgive our males or females. O Allah, the one whom you wish to keep alive from among us, make him live according to Islam. And anyone whom you wish to die from among us, let him die in belief and faith. O Allah, do not deprive us from your reward and don't put us in Fitna after death...Allahuma Maghfirli Hay-yina wa may-yitina..."

After the prayer, the casket was closed. I scanned the crowd in hopes of seeing Quran, but he was nowhere to be found. I wasn't surprised, though, but there was a face in the crowd that I spotted. I saw her and had mixed feelings towards her. Her eyes found mine and then she walked over to me.

"Jihad, right?" Zin Carter asked.

I nodded my head.

"I'm sorry about your brother, really I am."

"Yeah, me too." I replied with a little venom.

"Hold on...do you blame me for what happened to Khitab?"

"You took the paperwork to Quran, didn't you?"

"Of course I did, but I didn't know what would...didn't think...look Quran paid David's legal fees. I knew their relationship, when my office presented me with the paperwork and Khitab's signature was one it, that broke my heart. I knew how much those papers would hurt Quran. But I had to show them to him. At the very worst, I thought that Quran could talk his brother out of testifying against David Battle and the government. What was I supposed to do? Let Khitab testify against

David and never tell him or Quran? Was I supposed to let my client get blindsided and betrayed by a person that he thought was a friend?"

"I never said that you are the reason why my brother is dead. I never said that your weren't supposed to show those papers to Quran. I understand the position that you were in and it's nobody's fault but Tabu's.

"Your brother was my client and that represented a conflict of interest as well…"

"Listen Zinfandel, is said…"

"Please call me Zin."

"Zin, I am deeply hurt by what my brother did and even more hurt by his passing, but he knew the rules that govern the streets. You did what you had to do. Quran explained everything to me…"

"Everything?" Zin repeated.

"Eeverything. I know that you were there when he killed Tabu. And I know why he wanted you to be there. So, no, I don't wish that you had never given that paperwork to Quran…"

"Wait a minute…"

"Let me finish, all I'm saying is that Quran never told me what he was gonna do because he knew that I loved Tabu too much to just let him kill him. When I said I wish that you wouldn't have given the papers to Quran. I only meant that I wish you could've give it to me. I would've went about things differently, Tabu would be long gone from D.C., but at least he's still be alive. It was nice seeing you and talking to you, Ms. Carter. But I gotta go and bury my brother.

I watched Zin turn to leave and decided it was only fair that I picked one curveball to even the count at one ball, one strike. "And when you talk to your father, tell Mike that Jihad said hello." Before she could respond, I stepped off.

"How do I say goodbye to what we had?
The good times that made us laugh outweighed the bad
I thought we'd get to see forever, but forever's blown away
It's so hard to say goodbye to yesterday

I don't know where this road is going to lead
All I know is where we've been and what we've been through
If it gets me to tomorrow, I hope it's worth all the pain
It's so hard to say goodbye to yesterday..."

I stood at my brother's grave site and stared at the fresh earth that covered his casket. Reminiscent of that scene out of the *'Cooley High'* movie. I sung the words to the *Boyz II Men* version of *'It's so hard'*. I sung it loud and off key, but what the hell, nobody was listening. Everybody was long gone, even the grounds crew that put Tabu in the ground and covered him up.

I stood with a gun in each hand and cried as I sung. I was hurting bad and I wanted to kill somebody bad. I wanted to inflict pain that would equal my emotional distress. My pain was constant, constant and deep. I never imagined a day where my younger brother wouldn't be by my side. I never imagined that he'd die at the hand of his blood...my blood...our blood. I never imagined him dishonoring himself and doing the unthinkable, the inexcusable.

"Why did you do that shit, Tab? Why?" I pointed both of my guns in the air and let them roar. I wanted all of the dead and the living to hear my cries. My guns were extensions of my arms and I felt good releasing them. When both clips were empty, I stooped down, took one gun, my favorite Sig Sauer .45, and buried it in the dirt with Tab. I wiped my eyes, stood up, and said, "That's for your spirit bruh. You gon' need it where you're headed."

I walked down Harmony Cemetery's winding hills and roads in my Acura. I pulled off with pain in my heart and murder on my mind. Howard Road was filled with all of my men who all knew the truth about what had happened to my brother and why. There were no R.I.P shirts, no liquor being poured out in honor of the dead. There would be no blunts sparked, no bottles popped, no more tears. I parked the Acura and silently walked past everybody outside until I reached my building.

I put the key in the apartment door and opened it. I took three steps inside and jumped a little out of surprise. Out of the kitchen stepped Quran. My eyes found my older brother's and held his gaze. He broke the mental embrace and walked over to me. He grabbed me and pulled me into his body...we embraced.

"I love you, baby boy. Until death do us...don't ever forget that." Quran said in my ear. "What happened to Tab had to happen. Let's leave it buried with him. I don't ever wanna argue or beef with you about this again. You feel me?"

"I feel you slim. It's buried with Tab. I love you, too big brother. Til' death do us."

Quran kissed my cheek and then broke our embrace. "That's enough of the sentimental shit, nigga." He said and smiled. "We got work to do."

"That's exactly what I needed to hear, what the business is?"

My brother didn't respond, he pulled out his cellphone and dialed a number. Seconds later, he spoke into the phone. "What's good, big homie? I got my partner right here and he just asked me what the business is. Give us the details, I'ma put you on speaker."

"What's up, Jay." The voice said through the speaker.

"Mike, what's good, old timer?" I replied.

"You, youngin, you good?"

I caught the undertones of what Mike said and asked, "I'm good, fucked up in the head still, but I'm good."

"That's to be expected, but you'll heal. Your ability to adapt is your strength. Now listen closely, the target is a dude named 'Cat Eye Dave'. You hipped to him?"

I wasn't, but Quran was.

"About my age, from Simple City, but hangs out on Alabama Avenue. Light skinned dude with green eyes, getting a little money, I'm hip to him. He's one of them, too huh?"

"Yeah, he's crossed over. There's a dude out Atwater named Lamont 'L.B.' Barnes. Youngin' been in like fifteen or sixteen years. He came in on a body and got thirty-five years. The dude 'Cat Eye Dave' was his partner in the streets. They hustled and put a lot of work in together. The two of them were the only ones that knew where the bodies were buried, and which closet held the skeletons. At some point, in the last year or so, an indictment came down from the whole Simple City and Alabama Avenue.

"The feds snatched up 'Cat Eye Dave'. A couple days later, he's back on the street, while all of his codefendants are still over D.C. jail. Dudes speculated, but nothing concrete was known. Evidently, he must've made some type of an agreement with the feds to tell on cold case murders and shit. Out of nowhere he contacts L.B. and asked to come and visit. L.B. not thinking any harmful intent gets the visit approved. He goes to see L.B. and takes a couple of bitches and some dope.

"The feds must've told Dave to get L.B. to confess to old murders and other crimes because he asked all kinds of crazy questions that L.B. ignored. After about the fourth visit, L.B. figures out that Dave is wired for sound. One day, he goes to see L.B. alone and they haven't been seated ten minutes before the questions start. He asked about a specific murder where three people got killed on Benning Road, one of them a sixteen year old girl.

He says, "L.B., remember that day when we found out Petey, was working with them people. Remember how we went down the Market and you killed him, Spider and that little girl?"

L.B.'s hip to the game by now, so he leans in close to Dave and says "Naw, moe you got it all wrong. You killed them three people down on the market that day."

Cat Eye Dave jumps up and shouts, "Stop lying, slim! I didn't kill nobody! You did…you killed them people!" Then he bolts out of the visiting room.

"To make a long story short, L.B.'s uncle is here with me and he wants to make sure that Cat Eye Dave never gets the chance to do any good men anymore harm. Feel me?"

"I feel you." Quran said.

"I feel that." I concurred.

"Good. The money will be paid through the usual channels. Half now, the rest upon confirmation. And Que?"

"Yeah?"

"That's a rush job, good men got courts dates coming up."

"That's done, I'll get back in a few days. I'm out." Quran said and ended the call. He turned facing me. "You ready to go to work?"

"Ready as I'll ever be."

Chapter Thirty-Five
Quran

I drove all through Simple City projects and couldn't spot Cat Eye Dave nowhere. I checked the Circle, Alabama Avenue, and Benning Park for the nigga. Word on the street was that Dave was still moving major weight despite the fact that all of his circle was behind bars. And the crazy part was that dudes suspected that he was hot, but they still copped drugs for him.

"I'm telling you, baby boy, this shit is crazy. Niggas out here in these streets be knowing that niggas is rats they still deal with 'em. They still cop coke from 'em and they still bust guns with 'em. I ain't gon never understand that shit."

Jihad rolled a blunt of hydro and nodded his head, "I'm already hip. You preachin' to the choir, big boy. That's why I know that, that nigga Rayful is home. He out Maryland or Virginia somewhere hustling and niggas is fuckin' with him."

"Maryland or Virginia? Naw, that nigga right here in the city somewhere."

"You think so?"

"I'm confident that he is. He in his forties now, these young niggas don't know who he is. All the niggas that know him are either dead, locked up, or working every day."

"Naw, bruh, I can't go for that." Jihad said and lit the blunt. "He told on too many real niggas. Colombians and all, if he was out here in D.C., somebody would've seen him and tried to kill him."

"Picture that, these streets are filled with rats and potential rats that just ain't seen the right shit tell on. And everybody else is struggling to survive. Ain't nobody gonna take one for the team like that. Killing that nigga is gonna get a nigga sixty-years, so muthafuckas probably look at it like, 'Man, fuck that nigga'."

"You think Alpo home, too?"

"Been home, he up New York chilling with them Dip Set niggas. Dame Dash, Cam'ron and them nigga love that rat. He probably up there doing mix tapes and shit."

Jihad laughed and coughed at the same time, I laughed too.

"Man fuck them niggas, you think we gon find Cat Eye Dave?"

"Like all rats, he'll step into a sticky rat trap eventually and we'll be there to send his ass to the after-life."

I had just walked through the door of my condo when my cell phone vibrated and I saw that the caller was Zin. I hadn't called her yet like I meant to, but I was glad that she called. A big smile crossed my face as I answered the call.

"Hey."

"I need to talk to you and not over the phone." Zin demanded.

Her tone sounded urgent and serious. I wondered what she could possibly be upset with me about. It had to be about Tabu. "Do you want me to come to you or you come to me?"

"Where are you right now?"

"Where I was the night you gave me the papers on my brother."

"I'm on my way." Zin disconnected the call.

Fifteen minutes later, Zin was at my door. I opened it and she pushed pass me and stormed into my living room.

"I'm trying to understand something. Why didn't you tell me that you know my father? All this time we been fucking around, and you conveniently forgot to mention that to me. Why?"

Did Mike tell her that we knew each other? If not him, how in the hell had Zin found out about me knowing her father? And how much did she know about us? Do I deny knowing Mike Carter or just go with it and see where it leads? I chose the latter.

"I never thought it was that big of a deal. Everybody who grew up in Barry Farms, Park Chester, and Sheridan Terrace knows your father. I assumed that you knew that I knew him. That's why I never mentioned it."

"You assumed that I knew? How could I have known that?" Zin shouted.

"Baby girl, slow your roll, you need to calm down. You coming all up in here ranting and raving 'bout nothing. What the fuck difference does it make if I know your father or not? What does that have to do with us? Did your father tell you something about me?"

Zin stopped pouting, huffing, and puffing long enough to say, "Say something about you? My father has no clue that I even know you."

Deep inside I was relieved, but offended at the same time. I decided to flip the script and put Zin on the defensive. "Hold...hold...hold up. You all bent out of shape because I never told you that I knew your father, but that was inadvertent. But you never told your father about me. Why is that?"

I watched Zin's whole demeanor change. She exhaled as if she had the wind knocked out of her. "Quran, it's not what you think."

"Tell me what I think, Zin."

Zin searched my face for answers that weren't there. Then finally she said, "You think that I'm ashamed of you, don't you?"

"You said it, not me."

"Well, I'm not. I just never mentioned to my father that I wasn't interested in Jermaine anymore. He likes the fact that I have a straight boyfriend. Straight as in 'not in the streets'. My father always told me not to fall in love with a thug and that I'm better than that." Zin looked me straight in the eyes. "But I guess I'm not. Because I still fell for a thug. I could never be ashamed of you, for what? You are the epitome of street with a swagger off the charts.

"Your body needs to be on calendars. Your sex appeal weakens me every time is see you. Your eyes...damn...those eyes. They hypnotize me and bewitch me all at the same time. I love you, Quran and I don't care who knows it. My aunt...that's who I've been staying with by the way, because after I left you that night you...you...you know what I mean. That night I went home to Jermaine and he knew something was up. He interrogated me and accused me of cheating.

"So, I admitted my infidelity and left the condo. I've been at my aunt's house ever since. She's the one that raised me after my father went to prison. Linda…that's my aunt, she knows all about you, Quran. Everybody knows about you, but my father, but I'ma tell him…"

"Naw…naw don't do that." I interjected.

"But why not?" Zin asked puzzled.

"He doesn't need to know, ain't no sense in getting him upset by telling him that you went against his admonitions and fell for a street nigga. I don't plan to live this forever, Zin. And you can delay telling your father until I do make a change. Then, you won't have to tell him that the man you love is in the streets. Does that make sense to you?" I prayed that it did.

Zin nodded her head, "I guess so but…"

"But nothing, when the time is right, the whole world is gonna know about us. That's my word, because I can picture you being Mrs. Quran Bashir."

"Or you can take my last name and become Quran Carter." Zin smiled.

"Where they do that at?" I said as I crossed the room and embraced Zin. I kissed her lips and savored their flavor.

"Quran…stop," Zin protested in between kisses. "Let me tell you what happened at my condo with…"

I smothered Zin with kisses. "Tell me later, right now, all I wanna hear is you calling my name and telling me that you're coming."

Zin was wearing grey pinstriped slacks that hugged her every curve. Her pink button up blouse accentuated her pink and grey open toed Alexander McQueen heels. Her French pedicured toes were pink with white tips. Slowly, I reached down an lifted the back of Zin's thigh. I brought her foot up to my leg and undid the strap on her shoe. Then I slipped it off, her shoe on the other foot came next. In her bare feet, Zin dwarfed me by at least seven inches. She had to rise up on her tip toes to continue our kiss. I bent down to make her comfortable as my fingers now expertly undid her belt and the top button of her pants. I tugged at her pants until I had them down at her ankles. Zin stepped out of the pants, just as I rose up, and started unbuttoning her blouse.

Zin helped me with the buttons, I guess I was taking too long. I removed her blouse, and she unhooked her bra. Suddenly, I was hungry for her breasts like it was feeding time for a baby. I licked, sucked, and nibbled on her nipples, one by one. Zin's fingers started pulling at my Hugo Boss shirt. I let her lift my shirt until it was time for me to lift my arms. I stopped so that she could pull my shirt over my head. Then I pulled off my tank top, Hugo Boss tennis shoes, and unbuckled my belt. Zin pulled my pants down and kissed my dick through the fabric of my Hugo boxers.

"Damn boy, even your dick smell good." Zin said as she pulled at my boxers and put her face in my trimmed pubic hairs.

I felt Zin's tongue all over my nuts and legs. She stopped only to pull my briefs completely off. Then she got on her knees and kissed my legs all the way up to my dick. Again, Zin tongued my nuts and that made my dick stick straight out. Before putting her mouth on me, Zin tongued the base of my dick as she gently stroked it's length. Then she greedily sucked the head into her wet mouth. My toes curled in my socks. Staring down at Zin sucking my dick was heady.

I felt blessed, her resemblance to Melanie Fiona was uncanny. Her jet black, silky hair fell down her shoulders and back. Getting head form a beautiful woman as an indescribable feeling. I stood there in the middle of the floor and used both of my hands to guide more of me into Zin's mouth. She sucked me with a yearning, an insatiable hunger. I let her get her fill on dick. She could eat me until she felt full. I loved every minute of it, I felt Zin's head back up as she pulled me from her mouth and flicked her tongue all over the head and then she tongued the hole.

Zin licked and tasted my precum, I was ready to bust but I held it. But as soon as she put me back in her mouth and took three deep pulls, I couldn't hold back any longer. I gripped Zin's hair and came deep in her throat as she sucked me and swallowed simultaneously. My body shook with convulsions as I came.

I felt like the cum came from the bottom of the sac and slowly traveled upward. "A-ar-r-g-g-ghh!"

Zin kept right on sucking me until I was completely soft. I used that break in the action to give as good as I had gotten. I lifted Zin up off of her knees and led her to the couch. I laid her down, then I climbed on top of her, but went low to suck on her tiny pretty toes. I licked and sucked on each of Zin's toes on both feet. Then I spread her legs, kissed, and licked up her legs until I found my treasure. Her pussy was leaking by the time I put my tongue to it. I lapped at it like a dog getting water.

I was thirsty for the water that her pussy held. Zin moaned and groaned as I licked her pussy from bottom to top and sucked on her clit. I stayed on her clit as if I was a Pitbull locked on it's prey. I used my lips to massage the pussy lips as my tongue darted in and out of her hole. I tried to put as much tongue as possible inside of her. Zin steadily back up to the couch and I had to grab her and pull her back to me. Once she was back where I wanted her I locked onto her pussy lips and tried to put a passion mark on each side. Her musky scent, mixed with fruits of nature turned me on even more.

I lowered my head, pinned her legs back, and ate her forbidden fruit. When I put my tongue in Zin's ass, she tried to wrestle me away, but I overpowered her, and stayed put. I alternated between her ass and pussy, sucking, licking, and kissing while Zin came multiple times.

"Quran...I...can't...take...no more! I...I...came...to...too much already. Please stop!" Zin wailed.

I paid Zin's protests no mind as I kissed and licked up her body until I was face to face with her. Zin's mouth covered mine and our tongues collided. Then without warning, I pushed my dick into her. Zin bit down on my bottom lip as I eased each inch into her tight pussy. The moisture from her pussy made me slip further into her quicker than her pussy was ready to accommodate. Zin put her nails in my back and drew blood as I dipped all the way into her.

Both of her legs ended up locked around my waist. I gripped the cushions on the couch as I pounded into Zin with a ferocity that I hadn't felt ever before. Zin hollered my name as I fucked her. She whimpered and begged me to stop, but I refused to let up. I thought about the fact that I wanted to claim her pussy, to mark my territory. So I reached behind me and found both of Zin's ankles. I grabbed them and pushed her legs back until both feet were almost touching the cushion that her head laid on.

"Quran...don't do it...like that!"

"Be quiet and take this dick!"

I put that hump in my back and went as deep as I possibly could. Our bodies collided with such force that Zin's toes curled and her cries sounded as if she would shed a tear. I felt like a man possessed as I pinned her down and long dicked her. In minutes, I was coming, I busted my nut deep inside Zin and then let her legs go, then I collapsed on top of her.

"Damn, baby...why you do that?" Zin whined. "I might can't walk tomorrow."

"My bad, boo, I lost myself for a minute."

"You just fucked me like you were mad at me. Were you mad at me?"

My flaccid dick slid out of Zin. I was exhausted, my dick was sore from too much fucking. "Naw Zin, I wasn't mad at you. I was just hungry for you. I haven't had no pussy since the last time you gave me some." I lied.

"Well, I gotta make sure I give you pussy more often because I can't have you fucking me like that too much. You gon mess my pussy walls up. Then ain't nobody gon' want me because my pussy too loose."

"I guess that means that you gotta stay with me forever then."

"As long as you act right, I'ma be with you. I love you more in three months, then I did in six years with Jermaine. And speaking of Jermaine, let me tell you what happened the other night."

I listned attentively to Zin as she told me, about catching Jermaine with Jennifer Wentz.

"I already knew about her. That's why she disgusts me so much. All her fat ass do is chase young, black niggas. I know a rack of niggas that have fucked her big, nasty ass." I told Zin.

"I never knew that."

"I never told you because I saw no reason to. I'm sorry to hear that, though."

Zin rolled over onto her stomach and gripped one of the pillows on the couch. "I'm not, it turned out for the best. But I'm still undecided on whether or not I can go back and work with her."

"You haven't been to work at all since that night?"

Zin shook her head, "Haven't even called."

"What about David and your other clients?" I asked curiously.

Shrugging her shoulders, Zin said, "Haven't talked to any of them. It's only been a few days, ain't nobody gone die before I get back to work. I took some time off to clear my mind. I'm going to call Nikki tomorrow and sit down with her and figure out what's the best direction for me to go in."

"Why don't you go into business for yourself?"

"Huh?"

"Open, your own office. You and a secretary, you don't need Jen and Nikki. You are smarter than the both of them, think about it."

"I never even thought about that. I guess I could, I'ma give it some thought. In the meantime," Zin reached for my dick and stroked it. "Let me get some more of him."

"I thought you just said that your pussy was sore and you're gonna walk funny tomorrow?"

"I can always use a new walk anyway. And my soreness will wear off. We haven't been together for almost two weeks, right? Well, let's get it in, fuck me some more, baby."

My dick must've heard Zin because it got instantly hard. I climbed on Zin's back and eased into her. "Be careful what you ask for." I said into her ear.

Chapter Thirty-Six
Zinfandel

Busboys and Poets on 14th in Northeast was one of my favorite places to eat because of the ambiance. I called Nikki Locks and asked her to meet me there for lunch. Since, parking in downtown D.C. was like figuring out a scrambled seven letter word in Scrabble. I decided to avoid the headache and go there by taxi. The Lincoln Town car yellow cab was spacious in the back and that allowed me to recline, rest, and think. My body was sore from all the wild, intense sex, that I had yesterday with Quran. Just thinking about it made my pussy tingle and throb.

I reminisced on the early morning, months ago when I first ran into Quran and played with my pussy thinking about him. I remembered how I used the shampoo bottle and fucked myself with it imagining that it was Quran. I smiled at the thought and then laughed at the fact that Quran's dick was a lot like that shampoo bottle, big, fat, and long. I switched gears and thought about the drastic changes in my life in the last three to six months. I was amazed how different things were. I no longer lived in the condo in Adams Morgan.

I was no longer in love or in a relationship with Jermaine and I was no longer working at the Locks and Wentz offices. In the blink of an eyes, a lot had changed. I witnessed my first murder and now loved the man who did the killing. If my mother was alive, I could imagine me telling her. '*Mama I'm in love with a gangsta.*' She probably would've fainted. I tried always to repress the nostalgic feelings I had for my mother because it always made me sad, depressed, and ruined my day.

I think about the brutal nature of her death and try to imagine what she was thinking as she experienced what she did. I often wondered why that man…Dontay Samuels picked her to rape and murder. What had my mother done to deserve to die so viciously? As a child, not knowing who to blame for my mother's death. I believe it was then that I chose God. I put the blame on the entity that I couldn't see, couldn't hear, couldn't feel. Then when my father went to prison, I shifted my hate and blame to Greg Gamble. There was no single person that I hated as much as him. I thought of the brief in my attache case and the rebuttal motion that I had prepared to fight him. I wanted to beat him in court and bask in the joy of getting my father free. I pulled my Blackberry out of my purse and quickly texted Johnathan Zucker.

//: Have you heard anything new from the courts about my father's case?

I pressed send and then sent another message to another man in my life.

//: Thank you for yesterday, last night, and this morning. I love you! TTYL!

Again I pressed send and wondered what Quran was doing at that exact moment. I had left him asleep in bed at his condo. I left my car parked on his street and called a taxi, all while thinking about something that he told me yesterday...

"Why don't you go into business for yourself?"

"Huh?"

"Open your own office, you and a secretary. You don't need Jen and Nikki. You are smarter than the both of them, think about it."

Quran's idea was one that I had never thought about before. I never had a reason to. I was happy working with Jen and Nikki. And although, Nikki was still cool, there was no way that I could go back to work there and be around Jen Wentz. Lawyers who worked with and for others had to be able to trust each other and respect one another. The trust and respect that used to be there for Jen went out the condo window the night her fat, naked ass laid in my bed with my boyfriend.

So, the thought of working for myself began to sound better and better as hours passed. And that's exactly what I planned to tell Nikki at lunch. As if on cue, the taxi came to a halt and I glanced out the window and saw the familiar Busboy and Poet's sign atop of the restaurant. I paid the cab driver and exited the vehicle.

"Give me the blackened Salmon, wild rice, and asparagus." Nikki told the waiter. "And a Perrier water, thanks."

I sipped on my Kiwi Strawberry Frappuccino and waited until the waiter had left before speaking. "I'm glad you put aside a few things to come and talk to me."

"Zin, baby, why wouldn't I? You are my prized recruit and I need you to put all emotion aside and come back home."

"Home is where the heart is, Nikki and my heart can't be at Locks and Wentz as long as Jen is there. I wouldn't dream of putting you in the position to choose, so I've decided to leave."

"Leave? Zin you've been with me for two and a half years. Listen, Jen told me everything that happened, and she was wrong as shit. She crossed a line that should never have been crossed. I got on her ass about that and she's remorseful. She's broken up over this, Zin. Jen wants you to come back. I want you to come back. Separate profession and emotion, Zin. It's the way of the world, it makes sense."

"To you, Nikki, but not me. Jen is my boss, just like you. There has to be a certain degree of respect and trust present in order for us to work together. You have to be able to trust the lawyer that you're working with…"

Nikki's water arrived, the waiter put it on the table and left.

"Are you saying that you don't trust Jen, professionally? As a fellow lawyer, as a boss, or as a friend?"

"As a lawyer, I have to admit that she's brilliant and we work well together, but asking me to forget that I just caught her butt ass naked in my house, in my bed with my ex is asking a bit much. Me not being able to be in the same room with her, trumps the brilliance. I was born and raised in the hood, Nikki. About fifteen minutes from where we now sit. You can take the girl out of the hood, but you can't take the hood out of the girl. Where I came from, women get killed for fucking other women's men. How can I work with her, when I want to whip her ass? Even though I'm not with Jermaine…"

"And you cheated on him." Nikki nonchalantly added.

"How did you know that?" I asked testily.

"Jen told me, she said that your boyfriend…ex-boyfriend came to the office looking for you. He stayed and questioned Jen and told her that he believed that you were seeing another man. Somehow, him and Jen exchanged numbers. She says that he was so despondent that she was worried about and she wanted to talk him out of doing anything foolish. He called her one night after you came home late and admitted that you were cheating. He told Jen that you'd left. Her gullible ass ended up in his bed…"

"In my bed, Nikki. In my fuckin' bed. Irregardless of what I did or didn't do, she knew who he was. What he was to me. There's no way that my infidelity is relevant to this conversation. She was my boss and my friend. She was never supposed to go there. You said that like it's my fault."

Nikki shook her head and vehemently denied disputed what I said, "I just pointed out one of the factors, that's all. I'm a lawyer, Zin, it's a habit. In no way are you at fault here. But you're not the victim either."

My face reddened and my anger rose. I was ready to go the fuck off. "And who is, Nikki, if it ain't me, who is the victim?"

"Nobody is. That's what I'm trying to get you to see. There is no victim here. Jen and Jermaine are at fault, but you there are no victims here."

"I can't believe that you are really sitting here saying this shit to me."

"Zin calm down, all I'm doing is playing devil's advocate and asking you to be objective and not obtuse in your thinking. I want you to come back and work for me, with me, and let's get this money. Because, baby, at the end of the day that's all that matters. The money, you've made pretty good money working with us. Where else would you go and make what you make now, when you are two years removed from law school? Come on, Zin, think this through. That's why I say don't mix emotion with business. You can hate Jen's guts…hell, you can hate my guts too, but you can continue to work with us. I work every day around people that I can't stomach personally. But I still work, Zin, that's the way life goes. You already know that."

The waiter brought my soup, clam chowder, and salad. He also placed Nikki's food on the table. "Will there be anything else ladies?"

"No thank you." I replied as I stood. I fished in my purse and pulled out some bills. I tossed a one hundred dollar bill onto the table. "I won't be staying for lunch, but both meals are on me, please keep the change."

"Zin, please sit down, stop being childish..."

"Enjoy your lunch, Ms. Locks. I'll send for my things in the office. You take care."

I walked my childish ass out of there and hailed a taxi.

"Where to ma'am?" the foreign cab driver asked.

"1901 D Street, please...1901 D Street Southeast."

"The D.C. jail, ma'am?"

"Yeah, thank you!"

***

After filling out all of the necessary paperwork, I got on the elevator and got off on the third floor.

"The inmate will be down here, shortly ma'am." A tall, handsome correctional officer in the visiting bubble said.

"Thank you." I replied and found an empty room.

I sat my attache case on the table and pulled out the government's motion to admit statements by dead people. I was going over my rebuttal motion, ten minutes later when David Battle walked into the room, I stood up, and shook his hand.

"You must've read my mind." David said as he sat in the chair across the table from me.

"They say that great minds think alike. Did you call me?"

"I called the office, twice and somebody said that you weren't in and they didn't know when you'd return."

"Well, I'm here now. I'll explain all about that later, but right now you need to see this." I handed David a copy of Greg Gamble's motion.

He read the first page silently, then the next. "Can they do this? I never heard of the court's allowing the testimonies of dead muthafuckas."

"That's because the D.C. courts have never done it. Never allowed it, ever. But times have changed and other jurisdictions have been getting away with introducing deceased witnesses testimony at trial, so I believe that the D.C. circuit will probably allow it. I believe that they will grant the U.S. Attorney's motion. You did notice that the motion is signed as being prepared by the U.S. Attorney himself, and not one of the hundreds of assistants U.S. Attorneys? For some reason the big man himself wants you to go to prison for a long, long time."

"I don't know why. I ain't never done nothing to that muthafucka. What's his name, I can't read his handwriting?" David asked grim faced.

"Greg Gamble. He took over when Eric Holder left." I explained.

"Like I said I don't even know that nigga. So, what happens now?"

"That depends."

"Depends on what?"

"On you."

"What are you talking about?"

"Today, I quit working for Locks and Wentz. I'm about to open my own office. And I want to remain your lawyer, but it's up to you. Your case was taken by Jen and Nikki, and given to me, an employee of their firm. If you decide to retain me as an independent lawyer, you have to sign a contract. One that I will provide. Your legal fees are paid, so that won't be a problem. We just have to tell the courts and let them ask you a few questions and that's that. The transition would be smooth. I'll keep fighting for you and we won't miss a beat. Obviously, you'll be my first and only client for the moment and that will work in your favor. Your case will get all of my time. But now, on the flipside of that coin. You could decide to stay with Locks and Wentz and either one of them would take over your case. They are familiar with it and they will do a good job, but not like me. So, the choice is yours."

"Do you mind if I ask you why you quit?" David replied.

"I'd rather you didn't, but you can and I'll answer." I said.

"Fuck it, I don't even wanna know. Them white bitches in that office be trippin' like shit. Whatever they did…you probably needed to quit."

"I need to know what you want to do, so I'll know how to proceed. Because either way, I'll have to alert the clerk of the court. Do we work together or not?"

David got silent and ran his hands over his face. "I hope that I'm not making a mistake…but I'm comfortable with you. I like you, Ms. Carter and you're real. You don't bullshit and I like that. Plus my man Quran speaks highly of you. So, I'ma stay with you, you help me beat this shit and I'll make sure that you have more clients than you can handle. Agreed!"

I smiled my second smile of the day, "Agreed, I've already prepared a rebuttal motion to combat everything that Greg Gamble put in his motion. He used case law that was adopted in other circuits and not recognized her in D.C. Even if this judge allows the testimonies of the deceased, I don't see a jury convicting and there's a sixth amendment hurdle that they won't be able to leap. Under the Confrontation Clause, you have to be able to cross examine the witnesses against you. And…"

"You can't cross examine dead people." David stated.

"You took the words right out of my mouth. They'll fight, but we'll win. I'll put my law degree on that."

"You sound really confident, Ms. Carter."

"I am David, I am. I was made for this."

"Okay, I'm game. Where do I sign and when do I go to court?"

"Give me a minute." I wrote up a one page agreement that gave the Law Office of Zinfandel Carter all legal rights to act as the attorney for David L. Battle. A fee of fifteen thousand dollar already paid in full. I slid the written page across the table to David.

He read the paper, then signed it, and passed it back to me.

I folded the paper and put it in my purse. "I'll type this up and send you a copy. Then I'll go and see the clerk of the court personally and explain the situation. You had a court date for Tuesday, but it'll probably be pushed back a week or two." I wrote my cell phone number down and gave it to David. "Call me tomorrow, and I'll have more info for you. Is there anything else I need to know?"

"Naw, can I keep this motion that the government...this U.S. Attorney filed?"

"Sure, that's your copy and here's your copy of my rebuttal motion." I stood up and reached my hand out. "Call me tomorrow."

David shook my hand, "Don't make me regret this Ms. Carter."

"You won't, David... you won't."

Chapter Thirty-Seven
Quran

Finding and killing Cat Eye Dave was becoming a full time job and I was getting more irritated as the days went by. I kept thinking about what Mike Carter had said…

"That's a rush job. Good men got court dates coming up."

"This nigga is starting to piss me off, baby boy." I said in exasperation to Jihad, who sat in the passenger seat of the GMC Yukon with me.

"I'm hip, I gotta bad ass bitch named Tomeeka Maddox that I'm tryna fuck waiting on my call. We need to crush this nigga soon, so I can get all up in shorty's little coochie."

I laughed at what Jihad said and scanned the area again for my target. He was nowhere to be found. My cellphone vibrated, the caller was Sean Branch. "What's up, slim?"

"I'ma have to get with you in a day or so. I gotta line on that nigga Kenny Sparrow and I'm tryna go holla at him. Feel me?" Sean said.

"I feel you, slim. Holla back when you need me and I'm there."

"A'ight, be safe, Ock. Assalaamu Alaikum."

"Wa Alaikum Assalaam." I ended the call.

"Who was that…Mike?" Jihad asked.

"Naw, that was Sean."

"Sean…what Sean?"

"Branch." I rolled my window down to let the fresh air into the truck. It was starting to smell like weed and perspiration.

"I been meaning to ask you, bruh. Where you know slim from?"

"Who Sean?"

Jihad nodded his head.

"I met Sean before he went to jail. Mike hooked us up, I was about fourteen years old then and Mike was fuckin' with them Spanish niggas Carlos Trinidad and nem. After pop died, Mike kept Sean with him to squash all beefs."

"Squash all beefs translates into the fact that Sean used to kill for Mike too, right?"

I nodded my head. "I went on a few moves with Sean and he liked the way a young nigga put his murder game down. We been friends ever since."

"I can dig it, what's up with him?"

"He's out to settle a rack of old scores, I'ma roll with him."

"Be careful, big boy. You know they say that he kills all of his friends."

I laughed. "Who said that?"

Jihad eyed me with a goofy look. "Who else, the streets said it."

"You can't listen to the streets all the time. Sometimes the streets will say anything."

Leaning back in his seat, Jihad started laughing. "The streets not only watching but they talking now. Got me circling the block before I'm parking now. Don't get it twisted, I ain't bitching. I'm just cautious now, sub under the parks, extra cartridge now. I feel the vibe and I hear the rumors. Fuck it, I'm still alive and I'm still in Jumah. I know astaphallah..."

"Okay then Beanie Siegal, I hear you."

"Aye, big boy, go back down this nigga mother's house and park. Let's see if he comes to momma."

I started the truck up and drove down Texas Avenue. Ten minute later, I pulled onto Falls Terrace, then F Street. Cat Eye Dave's mother's building was the third building of a row of five. The sun had gone down and dusk was settling on the city. It was also getting nippy outside. I rolled my window back up and pulled into the dark parking lot that faced the buildings. With the exception of the parking lot, the buildings were obscured by woods on every side. The perfect place to commit a murder. I wondered how often Cat Eye Dave visited his mother? It was obvious that he didn't live in the building on F Street.

"They say he's pushing a silver Acura truck, right?"

"Yeah." Jihad answered. "Either that or a metallic blue S 550 Mercedes Benz."

"I'ma dawg this niggas ass for making me look for him like this. You ain't the only one with other shit to do and women to see." I closed my eyes.

"Aye, Que." Jihad called out.

"Yeah, baby boy."

"Do you love her?"

"Who, Zin?"

"Yeah, do you love her or are you just fuckin' her."

I didn't have to think about my answer at all. "I love her, slim. I ain't never felt like this or no other bitch. I miss her when she ain't around and I think about her all the time. I'm focused on killing this nigga, but I been thinking about her all day. If that ain't love, I don't know what is. And speaking of Zin, don't think that I don't know what you did." I opened my eyes and looked at Jihad. He played coy, acting like he didn't know what I was talking about.

"What did I do?" he asked.

"You told Zin to tell her father hello."

"Slip of the tongue, bruh."

"The hell it was, I know you like a book, nigga. I raised you, you knew that I never told Zin that we knew Mike. And you knew why I never told her. You also knew that she'd come to me and question me why I never told her that we knew her father. You thought that it would create a problem for me. But I'm too smooth for that lil' kid shit. You was mad at me about Tab and threw that out there to create a little tension. I'm hip to you, it's all good though. I forgive you, for all your sins."

"Nigga, fuck you." Jihad replied. "Think you know everything."

"I do know everything, and nigga don't fuck me, fuck with me." I smiled and closed my eyes again.

"Que, wake up, big boy! I think that's him." Jihad exclaimed.

I opened my eyes and tried to focus on the dimly lit parking lot. I saw a blue Mercedes Benz that had twenty four inch rims on it and tinted windows, pulling into a parking space in front of 3110. Dave's mother's building.

"I think you right, baby boy. You ready?" I said.

"I'm geekin' to kill this nigga."

We watched Cat Eye Dave get out of the car and walk around to the passenger side back door. Then we both exited the truck, as I walked up the parking lot with Jihad by my side. I could see Cat Eye Dave lift a small child from the back seat and carry it. The child looked to be about three or four. I pulled my mask down and Jihad followed suit.

"Baby boy, I'ma go right at him. You go round the black car right there and come out on the other side of him. That way he can't run."

"Got your bruh." Jihad said and broke off from me.

I walked in between two cars and came out on the sidewalk. He never heard my footsteps until it was too late.

"Who the fuck...?" Cat Eye Dave uttered fearful.

I pulled my gun and told him, "Put the kid down, Dave."

Cat Eye Dave looked to his right and saw Jihad appear out of the shadows.

"What's this all about?"

"Don't make me kill the kid, too, because I will."

"Don't kill my son! Please don't kill my son!" Dave begged.

"Put him down and I won't. If you hold him, he dies with you. You got two seconds to decide. One..."

"Okay...okay!"

Cat Eye Dave's shoulders slumped as he accepted his fate. He walked over to the metal fencing that lined the building where his mother lived. After gently kissing the little boy and saying, "Daddy loves you," he sat the kid down in the grass.

The little boy, now wide awake, and staring between his father and us, never made a sound. Tears rolled down Dave's cheeks as he turned to face me. I eyed Jihad and just like always, we opened fire. My first bullets struck Dave in the chest and knocked him back. Jihad went for the head. His shots pushed him forward. When Dave's body finally fell, we unloaded our clips into his hot ass, case closed.

***

Later, I pulled my Lexus in front of a house on Tecumseh Drive. I got on my cell phone and dialed Zin's number. "Hey…I'm outside."

"Good, park your car and come in." Zin replied and ended the call.

I parked and walked up to the front door of the house. The door opened as I approached and in the doorway stood the most beautiful person I'd seen all day. We embraced for what seemed like an eternity. Finally, I broke the embrace.

"You smell good as shit."

"You ain't the only one around here that can smell good."

Just then I noticed something was different about Zin. Her hair, her usual long, straight back, silky do had been replaced with bangs, side-swept, and cut into layers with blond streaks. The blond streaks and highlights accentuated Zin's eyes and I'd never seen her look more beautiful.

"You changed your hair, huh?"

Zin stood on her tippy toes and kissed my lips sensually. "I'm glad that you noticed. I read in a Cosmo magazine a few months ago that if a woman gets her hair done and her man doesn't notice, that means he's really not into her."

"Well, the article doesn't apply to me."

"I know and I'm glad that it doesn't. I try not to pay attention to a lot of that shit, but sometimes those articles be on point. Along with the Steve Harvey show."

"Fuck, Steve Harvey unfunny ass. Him and hating ass Shirley Strawberry. Talkin' 'bout she ain't had no dick in ten years. She faking like shit."

"Maybe…maybe not…anyway, my new hairdo represents my new lease on life. Does it show?"

"Uh…I guess so. What's new in your life beside your hair-style?"

"You, and for the first time in my life, I'm extremely happy in my relationship. Despite what you do for a living, you are perfect for me. I got a song that I want you to listen to called 'One Day, Jasmine Sullivan, it's lyrics were made for our life. But that's something for later. I got a new design on my fingers...see?" Zin put up both of her hands. "I usually do the French manicure, but today I went for the new, more in style look. I channeled my inner Beyonce and Rihanna, and my toes are all different colors."

I looked down at Zin's pretty feet and instantly got turned on. Everything about her was perfect and beautiful.

"I did all that to celebrate my new found liberation. My release from the consummate ball and chain. Today, I took your advice...hold on, why are we still standing in the doorway? Come in, I want you to meet my aunt Linda."

Zin grabbed my hand and led me through what seemed like a labyrinth before we finally reached the kitchen. At the table sat a woman who resembled Zin, but was older with sprinkles of grey in her long silky hair that fell down her back. She was caramel complexioned, about an inch taller than Zin, and dressed in loose fitting stylish pajamas.

When she looked up from the magazine she was sifting through, she stood, walked around the table, and hugged me. "You must be Quran."

Linda Carter let me go, stepped back, and gave me the once over. "Zin, I like...I like. Eye candy all day, chile. Keep this exquisite specimen of a man." To me she said, "Damn you are fine, Mr. Quran. Like a tall cup of hazelnut coffee on a rainy Monday morning. And them eyes...good grief. You better pull him away from me before I..."

"Auntie, you are so crazy. Quran, this is my aunt Linda, and auntie this is Quran Bashir."

Linda Carter, looked at me again and her facial expression changed. "Bashir? Oh my gawd, I should've know by them damn grey eyes. Ain't that many black folks walking around out here with no grey eyes. Your father had those same eyes."

At that moment, it dawned on me that Linda was Mike Carter's sister and had to have known my father.

"You knew Quran's father auntie?" Zin asked.

"I did, but not only me." Linda Carter said, her eyes in a reflective state. "The whole Southeast, D.C. knew his father. Ameen Bashir was the end all and be all on the streets back in the day. Me and all my girlfriends were in love with him. I used to talk to him on the phone and hang onto his every word until Mike found out and put a stop to it."

"Why did he put a stop to it?"

"Because he said that Ameen wasn't for me. He was a street dude and your father never wanted his life, the street life for me. Besides, he and Ameen were best friends, and Mike didn't want Ameen with his sister. I was mad at Mike for a long time afterwards, but then one day, he came to me, and explained to me what Ameen Bashir did in the streets."

"And what was that?" Zin questioned.

"He killed people for Mike an for anybody that needed a person killed. So, I got over my infatuation real fast. You didn't know Quran's father was your father's best friend back in the day?"

Zin directly at me with a scowl on her face, "Nope, never got that memo. Did you know that, Quran?"

I lied to Zin for the second time in three days, "Naw, nobody ever told me that."

"Then later I heard that he married the little Muslim chick that lived on Talbert Street."

"That would be my mother, he married my mother Khadijah." I told Linda Carter.

"Small world, damn you do look just like your father. We were all saddened when he died."

"When he got killed you mean? I know, it's been twenty one years and I'm still not completely over it."

"Well," Linda said, "It was nice meeting you, baby and I have to tell you one thing. Please don't ever put your hands on my niece. That, I will not tolerate. And if you ain't gonna love her the way she deserves to be loved, then leave her alone. Do I make myself clear?"

"Crystal."

"Good now, I'ma leave you two alone. Zin, I'm going to bed, I'll see you in the a.m. before you leave, okay?"

"Okay auntie, goodnight."

"Goodnight y'all." Linda Carter disappeared around a corner.

"It seems like your life and mine is connected in more ways than one, huh?" Zin said.

"It looks that way, I miss you. I love you, I need you right now." I replied and my arms found Zin and hugged her. I kissed her all over her neck and face.

"Quran, stop it, boy. I gotta finish what I was doing." Zin protested.

"What were you doing?"

"Let me show you, and give you my other good news." Zin took me to the living room where her laptop was setup. "I had lunch with Nikki and this bitch started tripping on me like it was my fault that Jen and Jermaine got caught fucking around. Told me not to play the victim and all that other bullshit. So, I took your advice and quit. Now, I'm starting my own practice. I left Nikki at the restaurant and went to D.C. jail."

"You went over the jail?"

"Yes, I went to see David Battle. I wanted to see if he wanted to remain my client as I transition into running my own firm." Zin said and sat down in front of the lap top.

"And what did he say?" I asked.

"He said yes, so that law office of Zinfandel Carter, has it's first client. Take a look." Zin turned the laptop screen around to face me.

On the screen was a website setup that showed a picture of Zin at her desk at work and the new name of her company.

"Nice, huh?" Zin asked.

"Yeah, I didn't know that you freelanced as a web designer. I like it."

"The way technology is today, I can do anything and be anyone that I want to be."

"That's great and all, but I kinda had a long day and I need some loving. I need you to be a porn star, right now. Ms. I can be anybody I wanna be."

"Later, baby, I promise you that it'll be worth the wait. I was able to create the website using software that I purchased from Staples today. All I had to do was register a domain name and set it up. While I was there, I got stationary, letterheads, and business cards made with the name of the company on them. I opened a business account at Bank of America using the name of the company, too. Since I haven't found any office space yet, I secured a P.O. Box, so that I can get mail."

"You had a full day today, didn't you?"

"Pretty much, I just hope that everything works out. This is a big step, stepping out on my own on a wish and a prayer."

"It's more than a wish and a prayer. And I got plenty of money to invest in you. I can be like a silent partner, and investigator or something."

"Whatever, I cannot be associating with thugs. I'll lose my business."

"So, we're back to that 'associating with thugs' crap, again huh?" I said smiling. "All I'm good for is my bedroom techniques, huh?"

"Would you please stop ending every sentence with huh, please? And as for your bedroom techniques, you are pretty good sir, but I gotta few myself. Come on let me show you one or two of them." Zin said, rising to her feet, powering down her laptop.

"Here." I asked.

"Yes, here. Why not? My bedroom is on this floor. My aunt's upstairs, she won't hear us, trust me I know."

I smacked Zin on her ass, "Yeah, I bet you do."

"Stop it, boy. Didn't you hear my aunt say not to put your hands on me? Well, respect that, then. Tonight, you don't use your hands at all. Only I get to use mine, but only once or twice mister. I gotta get up early tomorrow and go to court on David's behalf. Then I gotta go to the SBA office and register my company and get a business license, tax ID's, the words. Now c'mon."

Zin led me to her bedroom and did things to me that should be mandatory in every bedroom in America.

Chapter Thirty-Eight
Zinfandel

In the complex world of truths and falsehood, there are great liars and bad liars. A good attorney is trained to spot a liar and to put them in either or categories. Either you're lying or you're not and either you're good at it or you're not. Quran was a liar and a bad one at that. I laid in my bed with Quran sleeping next to me and thought about the two lies that I was sure he had told. And for some reason, both of those had something to do with my father.

There was something up and I saw it, but I couldn't figure out what it was. Why would Quran's demeanor change whenever my father's name came up? Was there a common thread between them that bonded them together? My father has to know Quran, and yet he's never mentioned him. But then again, why would he? The chances of me hooking up with his best friend's son was probably a longshot. Or so he probably thought. As I tossed and turned different theories swarmed around in my head. But no matter what conclusion I arrived at, I still ended up dismissing it. I couldn't get Quran's lies out of my head…

"I'm trying to understand something. Why didn't you tell me that you knew my father? All this time we been fucking around, and you conveniently forgot to mention that to me. Why?"

"I never thought it was a big deal. Everybody who grew up in Barry Farms, Park Chester, and Sheridan Terrace, knows your father. I assumed that you knew that I knew him. That's why I never mentioned it."

I knew that Quran was lying then, but I let it go. I can't let it go twice…

"You didn't know that your father and Quran's father were best friends back in the day?"

"Nope, never got that memo. Did you know that, Quran?"

"Naw, nobody never told me that."

That was the second lie and I need to know the truth about my father, Quran and a lot of other stuff.

"I was mad at Mike for a long time afterwards, but then one day, he came to me and explained to me what Ameen Bashir did in the streets."

"And what was that?"

"He killed people for Mike..."

Quran told me once that his father got killed in nineteen ninety-one. He was eleven years old then, I quickly did the math in my head. Today in two thousand twelve, Quran is thirty-two years old. I was six years old in ninety-one. My father was twenty-seven. He went to prison for years later in nineteen ninety-five and by then Quran was fifteen years old. Ameen Bashir was my father's best friend then and Quran was his son. His fifteen-year-old son who'd been killing people since he was thirteen years old.

"I kill people for a living, I been doing it since I was thirteen years old."

My aunt's words came back at that moment...

"He killed people for Mike or anybody that needed a person killed..."

The picture was starting to get clearer to me. I wasn't sure if I was right, but I was willing to wager that after Ameen Bashir was killed, his son took over for his father. And that meant that my father had Quran killing people for him, too. A slight head-ache formed around in my temples as I realized that Quran Bashir and my father were not only known to each other, they were a lot closer than I had ever known...then Quran had said.

Although, I had pieced together enough fabric to form a blanketed assumption in my mind, there was still one question that I couldn't answer. Quran had admitted to me that he killed people for a living, so why hide the fact that he knew my father and the fact that he killed people for him after his father got killed. I tried a few likely scenarios in my head, but still came up drawing a blank. I massaged my aching head for a while, then closed my eyes. It was time to go back to U.S.P Canaan. It was time to pay my father a visit. But that would come later, I had other fish to fry first.

***

One Week Later...

"Your honor, Gregory Gamble, standing in for Susan Rosenthal, on behalf of the government."

"And for the defense, your honor, Zinfandel Carter, on behalf of David Battle who is not present."

"Good morning to both counselors." Judge Gary Kalfani said as he shifted papers around. "We are here today for a pretrial matter. I ordered that the defendant be left out of this hearing for reasons known to both counselors. But for the record, I will say that there are grave security concerns in this matter. Apparently, all of the government witnesses have been murdered prior to trial and the government seeks to have these deceased witness's testimonies admitted into evidence and presented at trial. Mr. Gamble, does the government still wish to proceed with a trial in this matter of the U.S. versus David Battle?"

I watched the United States Attorney stand and clear his throat and I hated his guts more and more.

"We do, your honor. The government's position is that the wheels of justice should not be curtailed. We never give in to tyranny and oppression or terrorism, be it foreign or domestic…"

"Mr. Gamble, please save the melodramatic oratories for the news media. In this courtroom, when I ask you a simple question, I want a simple answer. There will be no grandstanding and speeches from soap boxes. Do we understand each other?"

"Yes, your honor, my apologies to the court."

I allowed myself the first smile of the day. The public rebuking of suck a grandiose public figure didn't happen every day. I loved it!

"And Ms. Carter, I understand that you have recently started your own practice and reentered your appearance as counsel for the defendant, correct?"

I stood up, "That's correct your honor. I am no longer with Locks and Wentz. The defendant is aware of that and wishes to continue to retain me as his defense counsel."

"Okay, then with all that asked and answered, let's get down to business. Ms. Carter, I will allow you to go first. I have your rebuttal motion in front of me."

The acid in my stomach killed all the butterflies that were there moments ago. I was dressed to impress and armed with a new attitude. I reminded myself that I was one of the best defense attorney's in D.C., stood up, and gave my spiel. "Your honor, the government in this case has submitted a motion asking this court to admit the testimonies of three deceases witnesses. For the record, your honor, I would like to remind this court, that the defendant has not been accused or charged with any malfeasance in regard t the dead witnesses..."

"We're not here for that, counselor." The judge interjected.

"The government's motion relies on case law from nineteen seventy-six, your honor. In the U.S. versus Suarez. To succeed with this motion, the government must identify and exception to the rule against hearsay, as well as hurdle the Confrontation Clause of the Constitution. The government relies on three subsections of the Federal Rules of Evidence, 804 B, one, three, and five. First, 804B one allows testimony given as a witness at another hearing of the same or different proceeding...if the party against whom the testimony is now offered had an opportunity and similar motive to develop the testimony by direct, cross or redirect testimony.

Second rule 804 B, three admits statements which when made were so far contrary to the declarants pecuniary or proprietary interest, or so far tended to subject the declarant to civil or criminal liability. Rules 804 B one and three are of no assistance to the government. What remains is subsection 804 B five, which contains a catch all provision designed to ensure the admission of inherently trustworthy statements not covered by another exception. For this section to apply, this court must determine that the hearsay statements have 'equivalent circumstantial guarantees of trustworthiness, that is offered to prove and materialize fact and is more probative of that fact than any other evidence...

In cases Ohio versus Robinson, US versus Zannino, and Idaho versus Wright, the Supreme Court, had determined that when a hearsay declarant is not present for cross examination at trial, the Confrontation Clause normally requires a showing that he or she is unavailable. Even then, his or her statement is admissible only if it bears adequate 'indicia of reliability'. Reliability can be inferred..."

As soon as I stepped out of the courtroom, I exhaled. My spirits were good, but my body felt like I had just fought in a championship fight. "I gotta slow down on the marathon sex with Quran." I fished my Blackberry out of my purse and checked my messages. I had an email from my father via Corrlinks, one from his lawyer telling me to give him a call, two from Nikki Locks, one from Jermaine, a call marked 'private', and two texts...well, sex messages from Quran.

Thinking about Quran always made me smile. Suddenly, my cell phone chirped, the caller was Nikki Locks. I wanted to ignore the call, but decided to answer to see what she wanted.

"Zinfandel Carter, how may I help you?"

"Zin, can you cut the theatrics, you know it's me. I come in peace."

"Is that right?" I replied.

"That's right, contrary to what you may believe, Zin. I am not your enemy and vice versa. I apologies for my uncaring and insensitive remarks that I made to you a week ago. That wasn't my intention, my intentions was to sincerely convince you to come back to work. But that was my time of the month and things didn't go as I expected them to.

"In any event I received your resignation papers, the notice of removal that you filed with the clerk of the court, the signed contract for David Battle entering you as his new attorney, and the news of the opening of your own office. And I can appreciate that heads up you gave us. Thank you, Zin, I wish you the best and again I apologize for what Jen did to you and for the way I acted at lunch. If there is anything I can do to aid you or give you any advice about anything, please feel free to call me."

"Nikki thank you. I respect you and I appreciate the call. Communication is the key to healthy relationships. Personal and professional, if I need anything I'll be sure to call you. And thank you for dropping my stuff off at the condo, but I don't live there anymore. Jermain left me a message telling me that you came by."

"Don't mention it. It was the least I could do. I like to believe that in a few years when you blow up and be the best female defense lawyer in the city that I had a hand in that in some kind of way. Even if it was negative."

"Never that, Nikki. You gave me the push I needed when I needed it. I wasn't going to stay with Locks and Wentz forever. A few more years maybe, but all you did was stop me from prolonging the inevitable. So, I need to be thanking you."

"Girl power is the key to us taking over the world. Did you have the hearing to rebut Greg Gamble's motion yet?"

"Actually, it was today. I just left out of the courtroom a few minutes ago."

"How did it go? Well at least, how do you think it went?"

"I think both sides made some good points. I hammered home the sixth amendment and the Confrontation Clause violation. But he also hammered home the Rule 804 B so, it's either sides ball game right now. I think this judge will side with the U.S. Attorney because he's former government attorney. He came out of that office and cronyism still rules the day. But we'll see, the judge said he'll rule in a few days."

"Well, keep me posted and don't forget what I said, call me anytime."

"I'll do that, Nikki, you take care and be safe. And if you run into any conflicts of interest, I can always use a few new clients."

"You got that Zin, just breathe in deeply, stay grounded, and do your thing. You'll knock 'em dead. Give them hell, kid."

"Thanks, Nikki, talk to you later."

I ended the call and was about to dial Quran when somebody tapped my shoulder. I turned around and came face to face with the devil. I can't deny the fact that he was a handsome older man and he had a smile that could disarm a bandit. But he was the man that I hated most in the world.

"Ms. Carter, I need to have a word with you." Greg Gamble said.

"Well, speak." I replied snidely.

"I was thinking maybe a sit down in the café…"

"Here, we can talk here, what's on your mind?"

"Okay, let's do this here. Do you really want to go toe to toe with me?"

"Toe to toe? Excuse me, but are we professional officers of the court or are we boxers?" *'Who the hell does this muthafucka think he is?'*

"I thought that we could civilly come to some type of agreement here, but I see that you want to play hard ball, so let's play."

"Are you a closet sports buff?" He was starting to piss me off. "Because all of your sports clichés are a little asinine."

"Your client thought that he was doing himself a favor by having all of the witnesses against him killed. He thought that, that would free him, but he was wrong. Just like your father was wrong."

If looks could kill, Greg Gamble would've been dead and I'd have been in prison for murder. His mentioning my father threw me for a loop and it took me a moment to untangle myself.

"What did you just say?" I snapped.

Greg Gamble smiled his killer smile and hissed, "You heard me. You didn't think that I knew who you were? I didn't get to the top seat in the U.S. Attorney's office because of my good looks. I do my homework. I'm a research buff and I have the capacity to memorize everything that I've ever heard or saw. When I first heard your name, I knew it sounded familiar. But I didn't figure it out right away. When I saw you for the first time on T.V. after the Sean Branch acquittal, it came to me.

"The resemblance is uncanny. It's been sixteen years, but every case I've ever prosecuted is still in my head. I went back and checked my files and sure enough, Zinfandel Carter, and Michael Carter are related. The day he got found guilty in court, he screamed out, *'I love you, Zin!'* I never forgot that. A condemned man's love for his only daughter. One that sat through his trial and eventually cried for her guilty father.

"Did daddy's little girl come off the porch and become a lawyer to wrestle around in the yard with the big dogs? Then again, don't answer that, but let me tell you that behind the scenes your father had certain people from the Trinidad Organization try and intimidate witnesses. A few were even killed, but in any fight where there's good versus evil, the good will always prevail.

I found a way then, to produce other witnesses and secure a conviction against your father. And I will repeat history in this same courtroom by find a way to convict your client. David Battle will never see the light of day again, not as long as I am alive and breathing. And you know why? Because of you, because you decided to fuck with my office. You should've stayed away from Sean Branch and you should've stayed away from this case. But since you didn't, I have to put you humble back in your place. And that my dear is in the kitchen, or a hip hop video somewhere. It's personal to me now, and even though you've left the office you worked in. I won't rest until you, Jen Wentz, and Nikki Locks is handling mail in the Post Office. So, prepare yourself for the fight of a lifetime."

Before I could utter a word, Greg Gamble turned and left. I felt like a ten-year-old child again. I felt I had been slapped, I was mad as shit.

Chapter Thirty-Nine
Quran

Seeing Zin, upset at someone other than me was amusing, but I couldn't laugh at her out on the open. So, I held it in, as I leaned out the dishwasher in my kitchen and listened to Zin rant about the U.S. Attorney and what he'd said to her. I silently admired her curvaceous hips and thick thighs stuffed into a black Michael Kors skirt that I had bought her. Her fuscia colored blouse was out of her skirt and hanging. The shirt was unbuttoned to the middle of her chest, giving me a peak at the fuscia colored bra that struggled to hold her pretty breasts inside of it. For the first time ever I noticed a gold link chain that held a locket on it as a charm. I'd never seen it before, Zin's panty hose were black, but sheer enough for her skin to be seen. I openly ogled her gorgeous stockinged feet and tried to make out the small enameled letter Q's that Zin had painted onto both of her big toes.

"Right now, I put Q's on my fingers and toes and next comes the tattoo. But that's something for a later date." She'd said after leaving the nail salon. I watched Zin go in and out of my refrigerator and cabinets, while ranting, still trying to gather food to cook.

"And this muthafucka gon tell me that he figured out who I was after he saw me on T.V. with Sean Branch. He did his research and found out that Michael Carter had a daughter named Zinfandel." Zin stopped momentarily and faced me. "He even remembered me as a kid, the day my father got found guilty, I heard him say, *'I love you, Zin!'* Greg Gamble remembered that too. He said something about my father having some of his witnesses killed, too. Did you ever hear that my father was connected to the dude Carlos Trinidad? He asked me did I come off the porch to roll around in the yard with the dogs or some crazy ass shit like that. That muthafucka is lunching good as shit, boo. He called him good and me evil. Good versus evil, can you believe that shit? He's fighting the good fight and I guess I ain't. *'Good always prevails'*, he said." Zin went back to mixing vegetables in a big salad bowl and talked to herself and answered herself a few times.

I was starting to think that she was becoming unraveled. Zin slammed down the salad bowl as fresh vegetables flew out of the bowl and landed onto the floor and counter. Then she faced me again.

"He threatened me, Quran. Can he do that…can he threatened a lawyer and get away with it? Well, I guess he could. Because nobody would believe me if I reported him. You know what, fuck him! Fuck that arrogant, Denzel Washington looking ass nigga. I can't stand his ass, he probably gay. Gay ass, faggot ass punk. Talking about David will never see the light of day. Not as long as he's alive and breathing. Because of me, because I fucked with his office. Can you believe that shit? Talking about he gon' put me back in my place. How the fuck he gon' do that? He can't touch me, fuck him!" Then suddenly Zin started laughing. A loud manical laugh.

"What the hell are you laughing at?" I asked.

Zin bent over in laughter. After a minute or two, she stood up erect. Tears were in her eyes, she wiped them away. "I just thought of something else that faggot said to me and it tickled the shit out of me just now. I conjured up the expression on his face as he said it and everything. When he said it to me, it wasn't funny, I wanted to fight his ass, but it's funny now."

"What did he say?" I asked, reached down to pick up Romain lettuce off the floor.

"He told me that he was gonna put me back in my place and that's a hip hop video somewhere." Zin started laughing again.

I didn't find humor in the sexist rebuke that the U.S. Attorney gave my woman, but I smiled anyway.

"Then said that's he's not going to rest until me, Jen, and Nikki is out of our jobs and working for the post office. That's when he threatened me. Told me to prepare for the biggest fight of my lifetime." As suddenly as she started laughing, she stopped, Zin got mad all over again. "Fuck that punk!"

***

"Oowww…owww…Quran…it hurts, baby! B…a…b…by! It's hurting so bad! Quran…owww…you're hurting me…oowww!"

Zin was on all fours on my bed, with her skirt up around her waist. Her panties, and panty hose were huddled at her ankles that hung off he bed. I stood behind her dressed in only my boxers, my pants at my ankles, and shirt on the floor. My hands were both on top of Zin's ass cheeks as I used them to navigate her deeper onto my dick that was halfway in her ass. Her sour mood turned me on and she wanted to be fucked real good. Her anger called out for pain she said, and she asked me to be rough with her as I fucked her. Then after she'd cum once, she begged to her virgin ass.

"You told me, that night at the Embassy Suites that you wanted my ass because nobody ever had it. Well, it's yours, get something to lubricate me, and take it. I want you to have y ass Quran. Fuck me in my ass baby. I wanna give my whole self to you."

Who was I to deny Zin her wishes? I grabbed some baby oil gel off the dresser and squirted a generous amount on my dick, then on Zin's ass.

"Do you want me to stop, Zin? I don't wanna hurt you." I told her.

"Ooww…oww…no…don't stop! It hurt, but it feels good, too. Don't stop…baby…fuck me! Quran…fuck me in my ass!"

I eased myself deeper into Zin, inch by inch she relaxed enough to take all of me in her ass. I grabbed a hold of her waist and pounded into her with a touch of gentleness and a little force. Easy, hard, easy, hard. I listened to Zin whimper and moan and didn't know if I should stop or keep going. Zin's cries were muffled by the blanket on the bed that she'd grabbed and bit into. I couldn't believe that she was actually giving me her ass.

"Zin…are you okay?" I asked concerned.

"Fuck me…Quran! Fuck me, baby and don't stop until you cum in my ass!"

And I did just that about ten minutes later.

***

"Quran, are you awake?"

I laid in my bed spooning with Zin as I dozed off. Showers always made me sleepy after sex. "Naw I'm up, what's up baby?"

"Did it feel good to you?" Zin asked.

"What, did what feel good?"

"Fucking me in my ass, did it feel good?"

"Yeah, baby it felt good as shit."

"Did you feel like you were in control of me?"

"Control of you, Zin what the hell are you saying, boo?"

"Just answer the question. Did you feel like you were in control of me?"

My nose was inches away from Zin's hair. I could smell her shampoo and lotion. Her ass was backed into my dick. "I guess I did, boo. Doggy style is designed for the man to be in control."

Zin got quiet and I wondered why she's asked me those questions.

"Now you've had all of me. That's what I wanted you to have. And as you fucked me, I felt helpless. I felt vulnerable, I felt defenseless as you stood behind me and fucked me in my ass. And you know what? That's the same way I felt today outside of the courtroom when Greg Gamble threatened me."

I didn't know exactly what to say to that so I remained silent. Zin got silent again and just when I thought she's fallen asleep, she spoke.

"If I asked you to, would you kill Greg Gamble?"

"Would I kill the United States Attorney?" I repeated.

"Yeah, would you do it, if I asked you to?"

I closed my eyes and hugged Zin tight. I inhaled her aroma again, then I said, "In a heartbeat, baby, in a heartbeat."

The next thing I heard was Zin's light snores.

Groggily, I walked into the bathroom to answer the call of nature. In the bathroom mirror stood Zin, fixing her hair, and brushing her teeth. I whipped out my dick and aimed at the toilet. Pissing felt so good that my eyes closed. I heard a slight 'ahem' and opened my eyes to see Zin, staring at me. Her eyes fell to my dick and bright urine beelining into the toilet. "What?"

Zin giggled, "I ain't never saw a man use the bathroom before, that's all. How can your dick be hard and you still piss?"

I shrugged my shoulders. "I don't have a clue, all I know is that, that's the way it be in the morning. You mean to tell me that you lived with dude..."

"Jermaine."

"Yeah, him, you lived with him for five years and never saw him take a piss?"

Zin shook her head.

"A shit?"

"U-ggh boy, never."

"That's crazy, you ain't never seen that man shit or piss and y'all lived together for years."

Zin went back to fixing her hair. "He never let me in there when he was in there. I didn't think nothing of it. A lot of people are like that, I guess. He never came in the bathroom when I was in there, either though."

"If he had tried to come in, would you have let him?"

"Probably not, I don't know."

I shook my dick and put it back in my boxers. "So, you wouldn't let me come in here if you were taking a shit?"

Zin looked at me and rolled her eyes, "I might as well, because you know exactly what my ass smells like now that you done had your dick all in my ass. So, ain't nothing left to hide from you. Would you shit in front of me?"

"In a heartbeat."

"In a heartbeat, huh?" Zin repeated, staring into the mirror.

"Yeah, in a heartbeat. I don't give a fuck. Why? You don't believe me?"

"Nothing like that. I just repeated what you said because that's the last thing that you said to me last night. You said, in a heartbeat, baby…in a heartbeat."

"I remember what I said and I meant every word of it." I walked over to the sink and stood behind Zin. I encircled her waist with my arms and kissed her neck.

"Ugh Quran, you touching me and you ain't even wash your hands."

"Wash my hands? All I did was touch my dick and it's clean. You touched my dick before you got up, did you wash your hands?"

Zin started giggling, "That's different though."

"No it ain't…speaking of my dick, give him a good morning kiss."

"Didn't you just piss? There might be leftover piss still on it."

"So what, kiss him, Zin." I playfully demanded.

"Okay, okay, but all he get is a kiss and I ain't playing." Zin said, the put down her wire brush and dropped to her knees. She grabbed my dick, smelled it, and then kissed it. She kissed it again and then put her tongue on it. The next thing I knew I was in her mouth. Zin sucked my dick until I came in her mouth. She swallowed my seeds, kissed my dick again, and got up. "Damn your dick taste good."

***

Outside on the street, I leaned onto the driver's door of Zin's Infiniti. "So, what's on your agenda for today?"

Zin leaned back in her seat after putting on her seatbelt. "Um…let me see…I have to go over the jail to see David and a few other new clients. I have to go to the bank to withdraw money that I need to put down before I sign the lease for the office space. And I have to go and see my father's lawyer. He wants to see, so I hope it's good news. It better be, since he couldn't say it over the phone. I might do a little shopping to find me something to wear for the weekend."

"The weekend? Where are you going this weekend?"

"I gotta date, but other than that. I'll be working hard, what about you?"

"I gotta date, too."

"Anybody I know?" Zin asked.

I shook my head and said, "Naw."

"Well, whoever she is, just make sure that she leave with a sore ass, too. I shouldn't be the only one with a tender butt." Zin reached out the window and grabbed my shirt. She pulled me down to her face and kissed my lips. "Quran don't make me hurt your ass, okay. I love you, baby. Let me go before I'm really late, be safe."

I kissed Zin slowly and wanted to take her back upstairs, but I couldn't.

She pushed me away, "Call me later. I love you."

Then I stood there and watched Zin's Infiniti disappear around a corner. I jogged across the parking lot to the Yukon and hopped in.

Anthony Fields

Chapter Forty
Quran

"Young boy Que, what's up?" Sean Branch shouted in the phone.

"Why are you shouting, slim?" I asked.

"It's jive loud in this spot where I'm at. Where you at?"

I looked around for a second, "I'm on Stanton Road about to turn onto Suitland Parkway."

"Cool, don't go to my house. I want you to come here, I'm at the Carolina Kitchen joint on Shopper's Way. Out in Largo, by the Boulevard."

"I know the place, I'll be there in fifteen minutes."

Ending the call, I couldn't help but smile as I thought back to the day that I first met Sean…

It was my fourteenth birthday and I had already killed four people in my young life. After avenging the death of my father, I just kept killing. For no other reason, other than I could. Mike Carter came to my house and picked me up in his brand new seven series BMW. I rode through the streets of Southeast with him and felt majestic. Everywhere we went, people stared. The fear, respect, and power that having money gave. I yearned to taste it, I wanted it all. And I vowed to myself to never be broke. I was already a man-child, even at fourteen. I was five feet nine inches tall and over one hundred eight pounds of ripped muscles that I had honed to perfection in my mother's basement every night. The scenery changed after we'd been riding a while and I thought I was in Maryland, the state that borders D.C…

"We're out in Maryland, huh?" I asked Mike.

He laughed at my ignorance, "Naw, Quran, we still in D.C. this is just the good looking part of the city. This neighborhood we're in is called Langdon Park. It's surrounded by Michigan Road, South Dakota Park, Rigg's Park and Fort Totten. When you're old enough to drive, I'ma cop you something nice and you can explore the city on your own. You gotta get out. You can't just limit yourself to Southeast D.C., it's small, but at the same time it's big. You gotta hit Southwest, Northwest, and Northeast. This is Northeast we're in now and it's filled with private homes, driveways, and two or three car garages. It's clean as shit, ain't it? I know, but don't let the smooth taste fool you and get it twisted. These clean streets and pretty houses have produced the richest niggas, D.C. had ever seen, but it's also birthed some of the most heartless, vicious killers, ever. I brought you here with me to meet one of them."

The car stopped in front of a three story, red brick house, with a manicured lawn, and automated sprinkler system. Mike picked up his car phone and dialed a number. "I'm outside."

Seconds later, the door to the house opened and out stepped a spanish dude, short, and thin, with dark curly hair. He was dressed in an all black Polo Sports sweat hoody, black jeans, and black Timberland boots.

I turned to Mike and said, "What is he, a Mexican or something?"

Mike bust out laughing again, "Naw, youngin' he's black, he just looks like that."

The curly haired dude walked up to the BMW and got into the backseat.

"Who this? The youngsta you been telling me about?" the dude asked as he closed the car door.

"Yeah, that's him." Mike pulled away from the house.

"Youngin' what's up?" Curly hair asked from the backseat.

"Ain't shit." I replied and reached my hand over my shoulder and over the headrest. I felt a palm smack my palm.

The car fell silent as we rode through the city to an unknown destination. That destination turned out to be a small sportswear store on Benning Road called 'All Dayz 24/7'. We all got out of the BMW and walked up the steps to the stairs front door. Before going inside, Mike stopped and said, "Que, are you strapped?"

I nodded my head, then we went inside. In the gallery of the store were three men present and behind the counter was one stocky dude.

One dude in the gallery sat on a stool with a remote, flipping channels on a T.V. mounted to the wall. The other two dude, one tall, and one short leaned on the glass display case at the counter. All three were dressed in 'All Dayz' sportswear.

"Rick, what's up?" Mike said to the man behind the counter.

The stocky, brown-skinned dude poked out his bottom lip, scowled, and replied, "What do you want to be up, Mike?"

I watched the three men in the gallery and they all seemed to be focused on the curly haired dude, like they knew him.

"Where's Curtbone at?"

"He's not here, I told you that before."

"Did you Curt what I said?"

The stocky dude nodded, "I did, he said that he talked to Carlos Trinidad himself..."

"Wrong answer, Rick." Mike said and turned to face the curly haired dude.

The curly haired dude pulled twin handguns from under his sweat hoody, and with a gun in each hand, he shot the two dudes that leaned on the counter first. Then he stepped in front of the third dude, who was about to run and shot him. I stood riveted to my spot as the curly haired dude stepped up to each man and put the finishing bullets in each man's head.

Mike turned to me and said, "Que this tough ass nigga right here is Rick Love. He hot as shit, but he's tough. What did I tell you about rats?"

"A rat anywhere is a threat to good men everywhere." I replied.

"Kill his ass for me."

I pulled my Beretta and shot the stocky dude named Rick Love in the chest. He threw up his arms to ward off the bullets, but they found their mark anyway. When his body finally dropped, I hopped up onto the counter, and finished him off, with all bullets to the head. Curly hair and Mike leaped the counter and walked to the back of the store. I followed them, in an office in the back, a man was found. He was on his knees, hiding under the desk

"Curt, I thought you wasn't here?" Mike mocked him.

"Don't do this, Mike, I got money, joe. You know I can pay."
Curt said.

"Bring your fat scared ass from under the desk, Curtbone."

"Don't kill me! Please don't kill me, I can pay y'all!"

"Can't spare you, Curt. Trinidad says you're a piece of shit
informant. So, you know what happens to rats Curts. Say your
prayers." Mike looked over at me. "Kill him."

Like a trained attack dog, I leapt into action. I stooped down
and lit a fire in Curtbone's ass. I emptied my clip in his ass.

About thirty minutes later, at the greasy spoon carryout
called 'French's' on Benning Road, me and the curly haired
dude stood out front, while Mike ordered food.

"Here you go, youngin'." Curly hair said and passed me a
wad of money. "That's courtesy of Curtbone's hot ass. I like
your style, you remind me of me when I was your age. What are
you about, fifteen...sixteen years old?"

"Naw, I'm fourteen, today's my birthday."

"Okay, then, happy birthday, young nigga. What's your
name again?"

"Quran, like the Holy book Muslim's read."

"Nice to meet you Quran, I'm Sean Branch."

I pulled into a parking space in front of Carolina Kitchen and
called Sean's cellphone. He picked up quickly.

"Where you at, Que?"

"I'm parked outside in a Yukon."

"Well, get out and come in there's something I want you to
see."

Inside the Carolina Kitchen business was booming. Lunch
time patrons over populated the small restaurant. I spotted Sean
sitting in a booth by himself. His eyes were on the T.V. screen
mounted to the table.

"You're just in time. This is what I been waiting for, check
it out."

My eyes followed Sean's to the thirteen-inch T.V. screen
where the news was coming on...

"D.C. police were called to the rear of Emery Elementary School, near Lincoln Road in Northeast, where the bodies of two men were discovered by children who were playing nearby. Authorities believe that both bodies have been on the school playground since last night. Sources close to the scene have identified the bodies as brothers Tracy and Eric Kay. The Kay brothers were known confidential informants for the F.B.I. The local branch of the F.B.I. are investigating the deaths...

In other news today, D.C. police have identified three men killed over the weekend and believe that their deaths are linked together. A South Carolina man who was in town visiting family members was slain outside of a barbershop on Bay Street in Northeast. That man was identified as forty-three old Leon Clea. D.C. police believe Leon Clea was killed due to his testimony against prominent gang members that were tried and convicted in the early nineties. Leon Clea provided testimony against the notorious R Street Crew. The other victims of one of the most-deadly weekends ever in the city, since D.C. was the Murder Capital, were identified as well. Although killed in different places and hours apart, the victims were identified as Rick Bailey and Frank Bailey. Both men were brothers... In other news Mayor Vincent Gray's office is again besieged by scandal...

I looked over at Sean, whose face bore the same wicked smile I'd witnessed on his face eighteen years ago in the 'All Dayz' store. Suddenly, he stood and said, "C'mon, let's bounce."

Outside, Sean motioned for me to get into a black on black Dodge Journey Caravan. "I need your help with something."

I hopped into the passenger seat of the caravan and immediately smelled a funny smell. I believed I knew what it was, but kept quiet. Sean, a man of few words hit a button on the dashboard and rap music filled the air...

'I would never violate the codes of the streets
I would never make a promise that I knew I couldn't keep
I would never testify or cop out to a plea or surrender information on my boys to the police

It could never be said that I went out like a ho
Never punked, never let it slide, never let it go
It's never in question, for my manhood, I'll get down
I'll never switch, never snitch, never sit down
I'll never hesitate to squeeze off six rounds
I'll never squat to take a piss
Who's the bitch now...'

The caravan turned off of Minnesota Avenue and onto Ely Place. Another sharp right took us behind an equestrian park and horse stables. The woods adjacent to the Dupont Ice Skating Rink were thick.

"I had to come back in the day time so that I could see what I was doing. Help me grab this nigga out the back." Sean said and then exited the caravan. We met at the back door of the Dodge Journey. Inside on the floor, was a body. It had just started to smell.

I grabbed the legs and Sean hoisted the upper part of the body onto his shoulders and we set off into the woods.

"Where are we taking him." I asked.

"You'll see in a minute." Sean replied and got quiet again.

The thick foliage opened up to an area that looked to have been used as a picnic area before. On the ground, but propped up on two different trees were two different bodies. The smell was stronger than the one in the van. It was the smell of rotting flesh.

"Man, what the fuck?" I said as I dropped the legs of the body we was carrying. "Who the fuck..." the faces were all un-known to me.

Sean smiled his killer smile and said, "These niggas," he pointed at the bodies up against the trees. "They been here a few days. They stink like shit, huh? Well fuck 'em."

"Who are they?"

"Rats. They told on me and some of my men. The nigga over there to your left is Stephon Hartwell. He told on my man Mack from R Street. Faggie ass nigga. Him over there to your right is Maurice Brooks. Bitch nigga grew up with us and everything and he still told. I'm thinking about killing his mother. And this rat right here." Sean pointed at the man at our feet. "Is Frank, he thought that a nigga wasn't gonna come for his ass. Just like all the rest of them muthafuckas thought. But now look at 'em."

"So, what's next? You gon' leave 'em all out here?" I asked.

"I wish, I can't leave 'em to be found. All them niggas the news just named, I killed them all. In my rage, I left too many clues. It won't be long before the cops connect me to something. If these niggas turn up dead, they gon' know I'm doing the killing. So, we gotta bury 'em, slim. That's why I needed your help. I'ma go back to the van and get the shovels. I'll be right back."

***

By the time Sean and I finished digging a hole big enough for three bodies, putting the bodies in it, and shoveling dirt back into to hole, hours had passed. I was dirty, sweaty, clothes were ruined, and I was irritated like shit. And Sean read my mood perfectly.

"I know you fucked up at me, slim. I couldn't tell you what was up because I didn't want you to turn me down. I needed you."

"It's all good, slim. I just feel like this is a scene off that Goodfellas movie. We out here burying muthafuckas in the desert and shit."

Sean laughed at me, "They should've killed that rat nigga Henry Hill."

"He just died in real life, I saw it on the news."

"That's good for his hot ass. Listen, you go home and shower and shit. Then I'm coming back to get you. I got one more rat to trap and he's the biggest one of all."

"And who might that be?"

"Kenneth Sparrow."

Chapter Forty-One
Zinfandel

Johnathan Zucker's office was on 30th and M Street in Georgetown and right next door was a coffee shop. In a daze, I walked inside and ordered a Brazilian Hazelnut café latte. The coffee shop had Wi-Fi, so I pulled out my iPad three and logged onto Corrlinks. I typed my father a short message letting him know that I was coming up this weekend to visit and that I had good news. My heart was a flutter with feelings that I hadn't felt since I was a little girl. The news that I had gotten from my father's lawyer wouldn't leave my mind. I remembered Johnathan Zucker's every word…

"I asked you to come by my office due to the sensitive nature of what I am about to tell you. You have to keep this information between us until I can decide how best to maximize on it. Last week, I received a call from Gary Kolman, and as you well know, Gary Kolman was your father's trial attorney in nineteen ninety-six. His office received by certified mail, an envelope addressed to him. He opened the envelope, read its contents, and then immediately called me. I went to his office and picked up a three-page, handwritten affidavit that alleges that the prosecutor in your father's trial paid a witness to lie in trial.

"The affidavit was prepared by a Mrs. Maryann Settles, witnessed by her husband Christopher Settles and notorized by a notary. Mrs. Settles, was one of the two eyewitnesses that testified against your father. For reasons known only to Mrs. Settles, she's come forward sixteen years later and now wants to recant that testimony and tell the truth about what lead her to implicate Michael Carter in the Samuels murder.

"Mrs. Settles alleges that she was bribed, coerced, and instructed to lie on your father by none other than AUSA Greg Gamble. In the three page affidavit she asserts that she was arrested on January seventeen, nineteen, ninety-six on Talbert Street with a half gram of Heroin. While awaiting arrangement she was approached by a white female who identified herself as

Susan Rosenthal. Susan Rosenthal took Mrs. Settles to see a man that she later learned was Greg Gamble.

"Maryann Settles explains in detail that because of her home address being directly at the murder scene of Dontay Samuels, she was offered a deal. And that deal consisted of her drug charge being dismissed and financial compensation in exchange for perjured testimony against a man that she knew from the neighborhood as Mike Carter. Scared of going to prison for her 3rd consecutive drug offense, she agreed to lie on your father. She never saw Mike Carter shoot and kill Dontay Samuels.

"She was in fact ten miles away at a family outing when the shooting took place. Maryann Settles alleges that she was paid secretly through a 3rd party, cash, payments, from January nineteen ninety-six, until January nineteen ninety-seven. She swears under the penalties of perjury and says that she can make herself available to tell her story in open court.

"I did my own investigation and found that a Maryann Settles was arrested on January seventeenth nineteen ninety-six, but found no record of what happened to her case. Apparently, Zin, this is the real deal and what we have is corruption, bribery, and misconduct on the part of the now U.S. Attorney. This affidavit and Maryann Settles testimony will knock the roof off of the U.S. Attorney's office building. I want to get your advice on how you best feel that we should go about proceeding with this. Because, obviously this would free your father..."

And that was all I had really heard. The thought of my father as a free man shook me to the core. The inflammatory accusations against Greg Gamble were like icing on the cake. I don't even remember what I said to Johnathan Zucker or what he said to me. I barely remembered leaving the office. Sitting in the coffee shop, I emailed Quran's phone and sent him a text message since he wasn't answering his phone. After drinking my coffee, I paid my bill, packed up my things, and left.

Now that I had good news, the visit with my father seemed all the more bittersweet. Instead of going shopping, I decided to just go to the condo and pick up the rest of my clothes. I could fit as much as I could into my car and the trunk, the rest I'd come back for. It took me ten minutes to drive from Georgetown to Adams Morgan. In the parking garage, I looked for Jermaine's Jaguar and didn't see it. I breathed a sigh of relief and exited the Infiniti. A few minutes later, I was turning the door knob and entering the condo.

To my surprise, there were boxes everywhere that lined the living room and bedroom. Apparently, Jermaine was moving out as well. I noticed then that several boxes were marked Zin in black magic marker. Those boxes totaled seven, on box was my stuff from the office that Nikki Locks had dropped off. There was one box in particular that got my attention. This box was different from all the others and I recognized it instantly.

This was the box that had been in storage with some other stuff that had belonged to my mother. I had been contacted by the storage company a few years ago and told to come and get the contents of storage room nine because the storage spaces lease was up and no one had come forward to renew. I drove to the storage company to retrieve the items. The furniture and clothes I took to my aunts house and put them in the basement.

The lone box I took to the condo to go through at a later date, but that date never came and I never got the chance to go in it. After a while, I simply forgot that it was in the closet at the condo. Until now!

I pulled pieces of clothing out of the box and fingered the fabric, remembering Patricia Mitchell-Carter. My mother was radiant, elegant, and beautiful. Her posture and demeanor made it hard to believe that she was born and raised in D.C.'s harshest ghettos in Southeast. She talked as if she'd attended the finest academies the nation had to offer. But she hadn't even graduated from high school. I fingered the locket around my neck that held my mother's picture and felt myself getting nostalgic and emotional. Each box contained a separate piece of my mother. Her expensive shoes were a perfect size seven. Just like my own, I pulled a pair of suede Gucci heels out and sat them down. I tried to remember my mother wearing them, but I couldn't.

I undid the clasps on my Michael Kors opened toe pumps and pulled them off one by one. Then I slipped my feet into my mother's shoes. A perfect fit, I stood and walked around the condo in my mother's shoes and suddenly I felt closer to her. I went back to the boxes and pulled out a gown. It was a white beaded and lace Chanel dress that I guessed had to have been my mother's wedding dress. Tears came to my eyes as I fingered the dress and imagined my mother wearing it. Inside that same box was a jewelry box and a small shoe box filled with papers. I opened the jewelry box and smelled it. The chain smelled of metal, I walked over to dresser and put the chain around my neck. It fell loosely around my neck.

'Why had I never checked the boxes before?" I asked myself.

I went back to the box and pulled out a small box of papers. I rifled through the papers and found my mother's license, social security car, a voter registration card, and several credit cards. The cards were for stores that were no longer in business like Montgomery Ward, Woodward & Lothrop, and Hecht's. There were plenty of photos of me as a baby, me as a kid up until my mother's death, and several pictures of her and my father together. They looked to be happy in each photo. And they made a beautiful couple. I smiled to myself as I remembered how much they seemed to love each other.

There was a small manila envelope amongst the paper. One that I had never seen before. I turned it over in my hand and noticed that it was sealed. The envelope bore no markings. I shook it and held it up to the light to see if I could see inside of it. I couldn't, how long had it been in the box? And where did it come from? I used one of the keys on my key ring to tip the envelope and then tear it along the flap. Inside the envelope were several pieces of yellow paper.

The type of paper that was sold as a legal pad. I pulled the papers out of the envelope and unfolded them. There was writing on most of the pages, front, back. I recognized my mother's handwriting immediately. Her cursive was fluent and legible, unmistakable. The pages totaled four altogether. I started from the first page and read. The words were my mother's words that obviously she had written to someone or herself, I couldn't be sure…

'Things grow progressively worse each day now. Our relationship has changed drastically in the last year or so. The way that he looks at me, touches me, it's all so foreign to me. It's as if I am living with a stranger. Gone is the loving way that he'd touch me. Sex is beastial and degrading. I feel as if I am his whore instead of his wife. I believe that he knows, he has to. That is the only explanation for the cold look in his eyes and the distance between us. I feel like a prisoner in my own home at times. And my husband as my jailer. The way he watches me…it's spooky. When he's home, it's as if he's far away, and when he's far away, it's as if he's here…staring at me, accusing me. Is it possible that he can see the stain of betrayal in my eyes, in my heart? Is love that powerful? I cry myself to sleep at night and pray that our daughter doesn't hear me. My sweet, precious daughter. I love her so and so does her, without her, I'd go crazy. Cooking, cleaning, and caring for Zin is my perpetual nirvana. Her smile, her voice, her laugh, it comforts me.

I paused to wipe the tears from my eyes. It was as if I could hear my mother speaking to me from the grave.

'It's been four years since Ameen's death and I still feel his absence, his loss. I knew that having an affair with my husband's best friend was dangerous and wrong, but the man was like forbidden fruit that I had to taste. His body, his demeanor, his sex appeal, his light grey eyes, they were too much for me to resist. I believe that my husband knows of my infidelity. He knows and he's mentally punishing me. The last night of my lover's life, as we made love in my bed while my husband was away, I heard a noise in the house, but dismissed it that night as one of the things that go bump in the night. I was too caught up in that act of my betrayal to think clearly and investigate the sounds that I heard. But as sure as I sit here and write this down on paper, I know what I heard.

I now believe that my husband was here that night. He was here and he saw us. I may be delusional or may just be paranoid, I don't know. But I believe that my husband saw us and that he killed my lover. His best friend, these are words that I can never speak to a soul, so I must write them down to get them out of my head, my heart and my soul. As sure as I write this today, I believe that Mike killed Ameen. And I also believe that one day soon he's going to kill me. I can feel it, people say that before you die, your whole life flashes before your eyes. I took that to mean that if flashed before your eyes at the moment of your death, but now I know different. Your life flashes before your eyes in stages and you can feel that death is near, I feel that now.

My husband had taken to disrespecting me publicly. He brings the reminder of my betrayal to our house from time to time and every time that I see Ameen's son Quran, I think of his father and our infidelity. Quran has a friend named Dontay and they ride with Mike everywhere. They kill people for Mike, that I know for sure and for some reason, I believe that they will kill me. It's in their young eyes, both are teenagers. Teenaged killers. When I die and I believe that I will die soon, my husband and his boys assassins will be my executioners. I won't miss my life, but I will miss my daughter. Zin is the only thing good and pure in my life, and I love her with all my heart...'

My heart stopped momentarily as I recorded my mother's words. My tears fell by the twos and threes with each drop. My soul was devastated, my mind was befogged. All I could do was shake my head as I dropped the papers. It can't be, what my mother wrote couldn't be true...could it? I picked up the papers and reread them again. I stopped at the part about Quran. Not only had Quran known my father, he also knew my mother. He'd met her, and he neglected to tell me that as well. The next line made my hands shake...

'Quran has a friend named Dontay and they ride with Mike everywhere...they kill people for Mike. That I know for sure and for some reason, I believe they will kill me...'

My cries, turned into ear piercing screams as I realized that my mother had predicted her own death. And she had even predicted who her killers would be, and she was right. I dropped to my knees and buried my face in my hands. I had been lied to, tricked, and deceived. By my father, and by the man that I loved. My father was behind my mother's murder…her rape…her beating…killed for an act of betrayal. Killed by Dontay Samuels and Quran Bashir. The two men that I loved the most in my life. I slowly rose to my feet and wiped my nose and eyes.

I wanted justice for my mother…I wanted revenge!

To Be Continued…
If You Cross Me Once 2
Coming Soon

Submission Guideline

Submit the first three chapters of your completed manuscript to ldpsubmissions@gmail.com, subject line: Your book's title. The manuscript must be in a .doc file and sent as an attachment. Document should be in Times New Roman, double spaced and in size 12 font. Also, provide your synopsis and full contact information. If sending multiple submissions, they must each be in a separate email.

Have a story but no way to send it electronically? You can still submit to LDP/Ca$h Presents. Send in the first three chapters, written or typed, of your completed manuscript to:

LDP: Submissions Dept
Po Box 944
Stockbridge, Ga 30281

DO NOT send original manuscript. Must be a duplicate.

Provide your synopsis and a cover letter containing your full contact information.

Thanks for considering LDP and Ca$h Presents.

BOW DOWN TO MY GANGSTA
By **Ca$h**
TORN BETWEEN TWO
By **Coffee**
THE STREETS STAINED MY SOUL **II**
By **Marcellus Allen**
BLOOD OF A BOSS **VI**
SHADOWS OF THE GAME II
By **Askari**
LOYAL TO THE GAME **IV**
By **T.J. & Jelissa**
A DOPEBOY'S PRAYER **II**
By **Eddie "Wolf" Lee**
IF LOVING YOU IS WRONG… **III**
By **Jelissa**
TRUE SAVAGE **VII**
MIDNIGHT CARTEL III
DOPE BOY MAGIC IV
By **Chris Green**
BLAST FOR ME **III**
A SAVAGE DOPEBOY III
CUTTHROAT MAFIA II
By **Ghost**
A HUSTLER'S DECEIT III
KILL ZONE **II**
BAE BELONGS TO ME III
A DOPE BOY'S QUEEN II
By **Aryanna**

CHAINED TO THE STREETS III

By **J-Blunt**

COKE KINGS V

KING OF THE TRAP II

By **T.J. Edwards**

GORILLAZ IN THE BAY V

TEARS OF A GANGSTA II

De'Kari

THE STREETS ARE CALLING II

Duquie Wilson

KINGPIN KILLAZ IV

STREET KINGS III

PAID IN BLOOD III

CARTEL KILLAZ IV

DOPE GODS II

Hood Rich

SINS OF A HUSTLA II

ASAD

TRIGGADALE III

Elijah R. Freeman

KINGZ OF THE GAME V

Playa Ray

SLAUGHTER GANG IV

RUTHLESS HEART IV

By **Willie Slaughter**

THE HEART OF A SAVAGE III

By **Jibril Williams**

FUK SHYT II

By **Blakk Diamond**

THE REALEST KILLAS

If You Cross Me Once

By Tranay Adams
TRAP GOD II
By Troublesome
YAYO III
A SHOOTER'S AMBITION III
By S. Allen
GHOST MOB
Stilloan Robinson
KINGPIN DREAMS II
By Paper Boi Rari
CREAM
By Yolanda Moore
SON OF A DOPE FIEND II
By Renta
FOREVER GANGSTA II
GLOCKS ON SATIN SHEETS II
By Adrian Dulan
LOYALTY AIN'T PROMISED II
By Keith Williams
THE PRICE YOU PAY FOR LOVE II
DOPE GIRL MAGIC III
By Destiny Skai
CONFESSIONS OF A GANGSTA II
By Nicholas Lock
I'M NOTHING WITHOUT HIS LOVE II
By Monet Dragun
CAUGHT UP IN THE LIFE III
By Robert Baptiste
NEW TO THE GAME III
By **Malik D. Rice**

LIFE OF A SAVAGE III
By **Romell Tukes**
QUIET MONEY II
By **Trai'Quan**
THE STREETS MADE ME II
By **Larry D. Wright**
THE ULTIMATE SACRIFICE VI
IF YOU CROSSM ME ONCE II
By **Anthony Fields**
THE LIFE OF A HOOD STAR
By Ca$h & Rashia Wilson

Available Now

RESTRAINING ORDER **I & II**
By **CA$H & Coffee**
LOVE KNOWS NO BOUNDARIES **I II & III**
By **Coffee**
RAISED AS A GOON I, II, III & IV
BRED BY THE SLUMS I, II, III
BLAST FOR ME I & II
ROTTEN TO THE CORE I II III
A BRONX TALE I, II, III
DUFFEL BAG CARTEL I II III IV
HEARTLESS GOON I II III IV
A SAVAGE DOPEBOY I II
HEARTLESS GOON I II III
DRUG LORDS I II III

CUTTHROAT MAFIA

By **Ghost**

LAY IT DOWN **I & II**

LAST OF A DYING BREED

BLOOD STAINS OF A SHOTTA I & II III

By **Jamaica**

LOYAL TO THE GAME I II III

LIFE OF SIN I, II III

By **TJ & Jelissa**

BLOODY COMMAS I & II

SKI MASK CARTEL I II & III

KING OF NEW YORK I II,III IV V

RISE TO POWER I II III

COKE KINGS I II III IV

BORN HEARTLESS I II III IV

KING OF THE TRAP

By **T.J. Edwards**

IF LOVING HIM IS WRONG…I & II

LOVE ME EVEN WHEN IT HURTS I II III

By **Jelissa**

WHEN THE STREETS CLAP BACK I & II III

THE HEART OF A SAVAGE I II

By **Jibril Williams**

A DISTINGUISHED THUG STOLE MY HEART I II & III

LOVE SHOULDN'T HURT I II III IV

RENEGADE BOYS I II III IV

PAID IN KARMA I II III

By **Meesha**

A GANGSTER'S CODE I &, II III

A GANGSTER'S SYN I II III

THE SAVAGE LIFE I II III

CHAINED TO THE STREETS I II

By J-Blunt

PUSH IT TO THE LIMIT

By **Bre' Hayes**

BLOOD OF A BOSS **I, II, III, IV, V**

SHADOWS OF THE GAME

By **Askari**

THE STREETS BLEED MURDER **I, II & III**

THE HEART OF A GANGSTA I II& III

By **Jerry Jackson**

CUM FOR ME I II III IV V

An **LDP Erotica Collaboration**

BRIDE OF A HUSTLA **I II & II**

THE FETTI GIRLS **I, II& III**

CORRUPTED BY A GANGSTA I, II III, IV

BLINDED BY HIS LOVE

THE PRICE YOU PAY FOR LOVE

DOPE GIRL MAGIC I II

By **Destiny Skai**

WHEN A GOOD GIRL GOES BAD

By **Adrienne**

THE COST OF LOYALTY I II III

By Kweli

A GANGSTER'S REVENGE **I II III & IV**

THE BOSS MAN'S DAUGHTERS I II III IV V

A SAVAGE LOVE **I & II**

BAE BELONGS TO ME I II

A HUSTLER'S DECEIT I, II, III

WHAT BAD BITCHES DO I, II, III

SOUL OF A MONSTER I II III
KILL ZONE
A DOPE BOY'S QUEEN
By **Aryanna**
A KINGPIN'S AMBITON
A KINGPIN'S AMBITION **II**
I MURDER FOR THE DOUGH
By **Ambitious**
TRUE SAVAGE I II III IV V VI
DOPE BOY MAGIC I, II, III
MIDNIGHT CARTEL I II
By **Chris Green**
A DOPEBOY'S PRAYER
By **Eddie "Wolf" Lee**
THE KING CARTEL **I, II & III**
By **Frank Gresham**
THESE NIGGAS AIN'T LOYAL **I, II & III**
By **Nikki Tee**
GANGSTA SHYT **I II &III**
By **CATO**
THE ULTIMATE BETRAYAL
By **Phoenix**
BOSS'N UP **I , II & III**
By **Royal Nicole**
I LOVE YOU TO DEATH
By Destiny J
I RIDE FOR MY HITTA
I STILL RIDE FOR MY HITTA
By **Misty Holt**
LOVE & CHASIN' PAPER

277

Anthony Fields

Renta
GORILLAZ IN THE BAY **I II III IV**
TEARS OF A GANGSTA
DE'KARI
TRIGGADALE I II
Elijah R. Freeman
GOD BLESS THE TRAPPERS I, II, III
THESE SCANDALOUS STREETS I, II, III
FEAR MY GANGSTA I, II, III
THESE STREETS DON'T LOVE NOBODY I, II
BURY ME A G I, II, III, IV, V
A GANGSTA'S EMPIRE I, II, III, IV
THE DOPEMAN'S BODYGAURD I II
Tranay Adams
THE STREETS ARE CALLING
Duquie Wilson
MARRIED TO A BOSS... I II III
By Destiny Skai & Chris Green
KINGZ OF THE GAME I II III IV
Playa Ray
SLAUGHTER GANG I II III
RUTHLESS HEART I II III
By Willie Slaughter
FUK SHYT
By Blakk Diamond
DON'T F#CK WITH MY HEART I II
By Linnea
ADDICTED TO THE DRAMA I II III
By Jamila
YAYO I II

A SHOOTER'S AMBITION I II

By S. Allen

TRAP GOD

By Troublesome

FOREVER GANGSTA

GLOCKS ON SATIN SHEETS

By Adrian Dulan

TOE TAGZ I II III

By Ah'Million

KINGPIN DREAMS

By Paper Boi Rari

CONFESSIONS OF A GANGSTA

By Nicholas Lock

I'M NOTHING WITHOUT HIS LOVE

By Monet Dragun

CAUGHT UP IN THE LIFE I II

By Robert Baptiste

NEW TO THE GAME I II

By **Malik D. Rice**

Life of a Savage I II

By **Romell Tukes**

LOYALTY AIN'T PROMISED

By Keith Williams

Quiet Money

By **Trai'Quan**

THE STREETS MADE ME

By **Larry D. Wright**

THE ULTIMATE SACRIFICE I, II, III, IV, V

KHADIFI

IF YOU CROSS ME ONCE

By **Anthony Fields**

THE LIFE OF A HOOD STAR

By Ca$h & Rashia Wilson

BOOKS BY LDP'S CEO, CA$H

TRUST IN NO MAN

TRUST IN NO MAN 2

TRUST IN NO MAN 3

BONDED BY BLOOD

SHORTY GOT A THUG

THUGS CRY

THUGS CRY 2

THUGS CRY 3

TRUST NO BITCH

TRUST NO BITCH 2

TRUST NO BITCH 3

TIL MY CASKET DROPS

RESTRAINING ORDER

RESTRAINING ORDER 2

IN LOVE WITH A CONVICT

LIFE OF A HOOD STAR

Coming Soon

BONDED BY BLOOD 2

BOW DOWN TO MY GANGSTA

If You Cross Me Once

283